A MATTER OF TIME

A MATTER OF TIME

Shashi Deshpande

Afterword by Ritu Menon

The Feminist Press at The City University of New York
New York

Published by The Feminist Press at The City University of New York
City College, Wingate Hall, Convent Avenue at 138th Street, New York, NY 10031

First U.S. edition, 1999

First published in 1996 by Penguin Books India, New Delhi, India

Library of Congress Cataloging-in-Publication Data

Deshpande, Shashi.
    A matter of time / by Shashi Deshpande ; afterword by Ritu Menon. – 1st U.S. ed.
        p   cm.
    1-55861-214-9 (alk. paper)
    I. Title.
    PR9499.3.D474M38   1999
    823—dc21   98-52896
                                                                         CIP

The Feminist Press is grateful to the Ford Foundation for their generous support
of our work. This publication is made possible, in part, by public funds from the
National Endowment for the Arts and the New York State Council on the Arts. The
Feminist Press would also like to thank Elizabeth Janeway, Joanne Markell,
Caroline Urvater, and Genevieve Vaughan for their generosity in supporting this
publication.

Printed on acid-free paper by RR Donnelley & Sons.
Manufactured in the United States of America

05 04 03 02 01 00 99   5 4 3 2

ACKNOWLEDGEMENTS

The lines quoted on p. 112 are from A.K. Ramanujan's translation of early classical Tamil poetry in *Poems of Love and War* and reproduced here by the kind permission of Oxford University Press.

The verses from the Upanishads on pages (1), (91) and (181) are Dr. S. Radhakrishnan's translations, taken from *The Principal Upanishads* and used here by kind permission of HarperCollins Publishers India Pvt. Ltd.

The lines on p. 186 are from Robert Ernest Hume's *The Thirteen Principal Upanishads*.

THE HOUSE

❧

'Maitreyi,' said Yajnavalkya, 'verily I
am about to go forth from this
state (of householder).'

—*Brhad-aranyaka Upanishad* (II.4.1)

THE HOUSE IS called Vishwas, named, not as one would imagine for the abstract quality of trust, but after an ancestor, the man who came down South with the Peshwa's invading army and established the family there. The name, etched into a stone tablet set in the wall, seems to be fading into itself, the process of erosion having made it almost undecipherable. And yet the house proclaims the meaning of its name by its very presence, its solidity. It is obvious that it was built by a man not just for himself, but for his sons and his son's sons. Built to endure—as it has. Perhaps the simplicity of the design helps; apart from the two delicately fluted columns that hold up the porch, there is none of the ornamentation that was so common in the time it was built. Just a bare square facade that offers no room for dilapidation; there are no edges to be frayed, no frills to hang untidily. Signs of wear and neglect lie elsewhere: in the wide gaps in the stonework of the compound wall, the large gate that looks as if it would fall to pieces if touched, the smaller one that sags on a single hinge.

The front yard is bare. Nothing, it seems, has ever grown or will grow on the hard unyielding ground. A star-shaped sunken pond is now only a pit harbouring all the trash blown in by the wind. A festoon of cobwebs, hanging in a canopy over the huge front door, speaks of its being rarely used. The family entrance is obviously at the side of the house, where stone steps, eroded with use, lead through a wooden wicket-gate to a veranda. The house is the Big House to its inhabitants, getting its name from the comparison to an outhouse built for the live-in help of a cook. Renovated since then and rented out to a family, the outhouse now looks as if it has been placed there to show off the size and grandeur of the Big House. The doll's house effect is carried over into its miniature garden, which, with its tiny stone-paved path, dainty tulsi brindavan and dwarf bushes, forms a startling, almost comical contrast to the garden behind the Big House. The coconut palms here tower beyond neck-straining vision, the drumstick trees branch out in exuberant generosity and the usually dainty curry-leaf tree has a trunk that rivals that of the neem tree.

The fourth side of the house shows yet another face. Everything grows wild here, nothing is scaled down to a cultivated prettiness. The bougainvillaea has become a monster parasite clinging passionately to its neighbour, the akash mallige, cutting deep grooves in its trunk, as if intent on strangulating it. But high above, the two flower together amicably, as if the cruelty below is an event of the past, wholly forgotten. The champak seems to have no relation to the graceful tree that grows in other people's yards. Grown to an enormous height, its flowers can neither be plucked nor seen, but the fragrance comes down each year like a message that it is flowering time again. The branches of the three mango trees are so tangled together it is as if they have closed ranks to protect the walls of the house, which remain damp, months after the rains. And during the monsoon, dark, woolly, itchy insects cling to them in colonies, covering them in a thick, horrifying, moving mass. The scabrous bark of the mango trees is, however, given over to more innocuous creatures, large black gangly ants that move, not in an orderly line, but in a wild, frantic scurrying, and yet, miraculously, never losing their hold on this hazardous, uneven terrain. Strangely enough, no birds nest in these trees; in the daytime, there is absolute silence, though at night there are ominous rustlings, sounds of unknown creatures of the night.

Inside, the house seems to echo the schizophrenic character of its exterior. A long passage running along the length of the house bisects it with an almost mathematical accuracy, marking out clearly the two parts of its divided personality. The rooms on the left, uninhabited for years, are dark, brooding and cavernous. The rooms on the right, where the family lives, though too large to be cosy, have a lived-in look, with the constant disorder of living. An L-shaped veranda running from the back of the house is a workplace where it encloses the kitchen, storeroom and bathroom. The smaller arm, outside the dining room and bedrooms, is not only the family entrance, it is also their sitting room, a built-in stone seat being the centre of it.

The small hall into which the front door opens is no-man's land, belonging to neither zone. It has the look of a set for a period movie, with its antique hat-and-umbrella stand, portraits on the wall, and a staircase that curves gracefully up into an unseen landing. The staircase raises expectations of an entire floor above, but there is in fact only one room, obviously added on later. Looked at from the outside, it looks like an excrescence perched on top of the house, detracting from its main quality of integrity.

The house attracts a great number of stares from passers-by, and not just because of its size and age. There is, to the fanciful at least, a sense of expectancy about the house, as if it were holding its breath, waiting for something.

Kalyani, whose father built the house, is enormously proud of it.

'People used to come just to look at it,' she says. 'There was no house like it in the city,' she adds.

However exaggerated the statement, it has now taken

on the colour of truth, for now the house is, in a sense, unique. It is the only one of its kind, of its size and period, left in the neighbourhood. The sharks who have devoured all the rest are eyeing it greedily, but the curious history of the house and of its two occupants has kept them at bay. Until now.

౭

SHE IS LYING full length on the sofa, watching a movie on TV, her eyes fixed unblinking on the screen as if she has never seen these things before: a circus. A clown in the centre of the arena, singing and dancing. And the spectators, in the manner of the spectators in any movie, gazing ahead in complete unison. Perhaps, in a sense, it is true that she has not really seen this before. She had never been to the circus as a child; children don't go, they are taken. And who could have taken them, Premi and her? In fact, the first (and the last) time she saw a circus was when Gopal and she had taken their daughters to one. The girls, four and five then, has been enthralled and Gopal's enjoyment had been almost as childlike as theirs.

But she had been appalled. She had hated all of it—the dust, the noise, the smell of the animals and their fears, almost as malodorous as the stench of their dung. It had made her sick. Even the acrobats had made her uneasy. She had sensed an enormous despair behind the bravado of their feats, a fear under the star-spangled gaiety of their costumes. Skilful, yes, but desperate. Like a statement—'we have to do these things in order to live, yet ....'

It was only the music that had made it bearable for her. There was something about it, rousing her expectations to a pitch so that her heart seemed to expand in her chest, throbbing like a powerful drum. The music created an illusion of magnificence, of drama to come, an expectation that was never fulfilled. Everything that came after, every act, seemed slightly tawdry, like tinsel crowns seen in the daylight, after the play is over.

Now she is watching the circus at a safe distance. Diminished by the size of the screen, yes, but with the dirt, the smells, the fear and despair left out. Sanitized. Bacteria-free. And the clown, prancing and skipping in the centre of the ring, allowed a dignity a clown in a real circus never has. And instead of the heart-throbbing music, this melodious song ....

Gopal comes in. Thinking that he will join her, she draws up her feet, making room for him on the sofa. But he goes to a chair opposite her, from where, she knows, he cannot see the TV. She gestures to him to turn it round. When he does nothing, scarcely, in fact, notices her gesture, she begins reluctantly to get up to do it herself. This time he stops her with a word—'don't!' And only then, for the first time, she turns her eyes away from the screen and gives him her whole attention. Something unusual about him that has nothing to do with the fact that he has not changed into his pyjamas ... She can't pinpoint anything specific, just this odd feeling that he seems—disjointed? Uncoordinated?

And then, suddenly she has a feeling as if someone has nudged her, telling her that something unpleasant is approaching, that she should get up and walk away. Later, she will wonder if she could have escaped, if, in fact, the moment of speaking would have passed for Gopal if she had walked away. But that is not how it is to be. 'I want to talk to you,' he says and abruptly begins. And she sits and listens in silence to what he has to say to her.

The TV goes on through his talk, neither of them thinks of turning it off, or turning down the sound either, so that his words come to her against the background of the clown's song: *Jeena yahan, mama yahan, iske siwa jana kahan.*

The telling of what he has come to say takes him so little time that when he has done, the song is still going on. He looks at her for a reaction, but she is gazing at him just as expectantly, waiting for him to go on. The realization that there is nothing more to be said—by either of them—comes to them almost simultaneously and he goes out as quietly as he had come in.

She continues to watch the movie until the end, when the clown, tragic, doomed victim, dies. She goes to bed with the song still going on in her head, the slightly off-key voice of Mukesh singing *'jeena yahan, mama yahan,'* the nimble feet of the clown dancing to its tune. And as if this is all there is at present to trouble her, her mind puzzles over the meaning of the words: what do they mean? That this world is all we have and therefore there is nowhere else for us to go? That we have to live here and die here? Or does it mean: *this* is what we have, *this* area of action is enough for us, we live here and die here, we need no more?

Her mind slides from one interpretation to another, over and over again, until in sheer exhaustion she falls asleep. And gets up abruptly at three in the morning, a panicked waking as if someone has prodded her awake. She finds herself alone in bed, the pillow by her side cold and smooth, the other half of the bed unrumpled, the blanket still folded. So it is true what he told her, he meant it, he's already done it.

Having reached this conclusion, she lies still, waiting for the dawn. There is none of the tangle of the internal colloquy of last night in her now. Her mind is crystal clear, she knows what has happened, she sees the picture with a detachment that will not be hers, not for a very long while. With infinite patience she waits until the early morning light dispels the shadows and makes every object in the room clearly visible. Only then does she get out of bed, wash, make tea for all of them and go into her daughters' room to tell them what has happened. And now the thought comes to her—he could have spared me this, he could have spoken to them himself. But she does not draw back from what she has to do; she tells them about it, almost exactly repeating Gopal's words, leaving out nothing.

And so it is that Aru, a few days before her seventeenth

birthday, wakes up to the knowledge that her father has walked out on them.

Once, years back, when Aru was only a child (but she was born an adult, Gopal used to think, when he remembered this incident), she had been separated from Gopal in a crowd. Gopal, frantically searching for her, had found her at exactly the same spot where she had realized he was no longer with her.

'*I* was not lost,' she had said to him after their initial hysteria had subsided. 'It was *you* who got lost.'

Now, it is as if the same thing has happened all over again. But this time, though it is her father who has gone away, Aru knows the panic, the disorientation of being lost. It will be very long before she will realize that something ended for her, for all of them, that morning. Perhaps it is Sumi's behaviour that makes it so difficult for them to understand the enormity of what has happened. She answers all their questions with infinite patience, she listens to their repeated exclamations with what looks like composure; there are no signs of irritation or annoyance. Aru is adult enough to be conscious of the curtain beyond which her parents lived their life together as man and woman. Yet Sumi seems to give the impression that the room did not exist, that whatever life they lived together was with their daughters. And she has revealed all of it to them.

To the astonishment of her daughters, Sumi's routine that day is as usual. They are baffled, but as if she has set the tone for them, they go through the motions of their normal routine as well. Sumi's calmness, her normality, make it possible for them to think—'it was only a quarrel'; it makes it possible for them to hope—'he will come back'. When she returns home in the evening, Aru looks around quickly, eagerly, for some sign that he has returned; but nothing has changed since the morning.

In the next few days the girls can almost imagine that there is, indeed, nothing wrong, that their father has gone out for a few days and will soon return, but for the fact that Sumi, despite her facade of normality, has a quality about her—a kind of blankness—that makes them uneasy. The two older girls feel that they should do something, but they do not know what it is they can do. They are waiting for a lead from their mother, but she gives them none. In fact, after that first morning when she spoke to them about it, she has not mentioned Gopal's name; nor, when they speak of him, does she show either distress or anger.

And then their grandfather arrives. The sight of him in their house is so rare that it is loaded with significance. There is no doubt that he knows, that he has come for a definite purpose. It is Sumi who tells them that he has come to take them to the Big House.

'For how long?'

Sumi does not know; in fact, she makes it clear she does not care about it either way. She seems, in a strange way, relieved at having the burden of decision taken off her. The girls cannot argue with such indifference; they cannot speak with their grandfather, either. His authority has been too long established for them to think of questioning it.

Yet, Aru lingers. 'You go on,' she says. 'I'll follow you later on my moped.'

What had she hoped to achieve by staying on? There is nothing in the house to hold her there. The momentary desire to rebel, to be by herself, not to follow her grandfather meekly at his beckoning, leaves her. It seems pointless. She has to be with her mother and sisters. And there is her grandmother, Kalyani.

But Kalyani does not know what has happened, she has not been told that they are coming. Her surprise at seeing them, her open-mouthed stupefaction when she realizes they are staying, speak of her ignorance.

'But what's the matter?'

'We'll speak of it tomorrow. Right now, we need to sleep.'

Suddenly abandoning her questions, Kalyani throws herself with a frenzy into making arrangements for them to sleep. She pulls out sheets, old saris, pillows, cushions, and flings them about, speaking ceaselessly all the while.

'Sumi, you take my bed, I'll sleep here on the floor. Aru, this is for you ....'

And then Seema tells her. Throwing off the blanket Kalyani has covered her with, she sits up and announces the fact. Bluntly, matter-of-factly. And bursts into tears. The exaggerated, purposeful tears of a child, who, seeing her mother, dredges up her sorrow over an old hurt. Kalyani looks at Sumi's face for confirmation and finds it there.

Kalyani's reaction astounds her granddaughters. 'No,' she cries out, 'no, my God, not again.' She begins to cry, sounding so much like an animal in pain that Aru covers her ears against the sound. Suddenly, the dam that Sumi had built with her silence gives way and they are submerged in the awareness of loss. Aru is overcome by a sense of unreality; she finds herself unable to connect herself to her surroundings, to these people around her and their distress. My God, what's happening to us and what am I doing, lying here on the floor like a refugee?

'We're staying the night,' Sumi had said, but it is obviously going to be a much longer stay. The girls who have brought nothing with them but a nightdress and a toothbrush apiece have to keep moving up and down between the two houses, getting the things they need for each day, living, not out of suitcases, but out of plastic bags. Aru, with her innate sense of order has to work hard at not becoming part of the house, putting things in a kind of temporary order, so that the mattresses, rolled up each morning, are left on the floor and the clothes, folded as soon as they are dry, are not put away but piled on the table. The room is like a guest's, who, having to catch a train in the evening, is almost packed and ready to leave. Kalyani enters the game, too; the extra cups, plates and glasses go back into storage after every meal, from where they have to be retrieved each time they are needed.

'How long do we go on like this?'

Aru has just returned from her third trip of the day, getting some books, and her face is hollow with exhaustion. 'Do you think, Charu, he's dead?'

'Don't you think Sumi would have known if he was? No, I don't think he's dead.'

'But then what? My God, we've got to do something.'

'What do we do? Put an ad in the paper saying—"Come home, Papa, Sumi ill, all forgiven". Or do we stick him among the missing persons on TV?'

My father a missing person? Do we put him among the juvenile delinquents, the retarded children and adults? And what do we say? Missing, a man of—forty-six? No, forty-seven. And—but how tall is he? He's thin—so thin you can count his ribs. So we say 'of slender build'. And a wheat complexion—that's how it's put, isn't it? He has a scar over his left eyebrow. Wears glasses. Speaks English, Kannada, some Marathi, and a kind of Hindi we all laugh at. Fingers like mine—knobbly, large-knuckled, tapering at the tips. Feet like Seema's—long and narrow. When he's pleased with you, he says 'Shabaash' and when he speaks English, he begins almost every third sentence with a 'You see', pausing after that. And I said to him once, 'But what is it we have to see, Papa?' and he laughed.

Suddenly, Aru stops. But I don't know him, I don't know him at all, she thinks despairingly. All these things mean nothing, they don't add up to anything, certainly not to a reason for walking out on us. Even Sumi says she doesn't know why he did it and I have to believe her, she doesn't lie, but ....

'You see,' Charu says in reply to Aru's long silence, 'there is really nothing we can do.'

Aru is soon to realize something else: they are trapped into inactivity by that greatest fear of all—the fear of losing face. Gopal's desertion is not just a tragedy, it is both a shame and a disgrace. There was a time when a man could have walked out of his home and the seamless whole of the joint family would have enclosed his wife and children, covered his absence. Now the rent in the fabric, gaping wide, is there for all to see. Nevertheless it has to be concealed, an attempt made to turn people's eyes away from it. Aru realizes that none of the family have visited them, not Goda, sharer of all Kalyani's joys and sorrows, or her daughter Devaki, Sumi's special ally, or even Ramesh, so close to Gopal, and such a constant visitor to their house. Their staying away is deliberate; they know, but they don't want to come to us with the knowledge. Only Nagi, after ten years of working with Kalyani, has no such scruples. She knows—has Kalyani told her? Or is she guessing?—and makes this clear to them by her repeated 'poor things', her clucks of sympathy.

'Stop staring, Nagi,' Aru exclaims angrily. 'Have I suddenly grown an extra nose?'

'What's the use of getting angry with me? It's all our luck, it's written here, we can't escape it. Look at my poor Lakshmi, we thought he was such a good man and he left her for that other woman ....'

'Oh God!'

'What's wrong with your sister?' Nagi asks Charu when Aru stalks out.

'Nothing, you know how she is. And for God's sake, Nagi,' Charu tries to change the subject, 'what is that you're wiping the floor with?'

'It's Amma's petticoat. What can I do? I don't want to ask Amma to get me a mopping cloth, not at such a time, I know she has troubles, and you—don't you waste your time talking to me, you go on with your reading. Yes, you study and get a job soon so that you can help your poor mother.'

Aru hears her and thinks—maybe Nagi's way of saying it straight out is better, after all. Anything is better than this deviousness, this circling round the truth.

But the truth is that there is no moment when tragedy is certain. Each moment they are balanced on the edge of hope; every time the gate creaks, it could be Gopal, each time the phone rings there is the possibility that they will hear Gopal's voice saying 'Gopal here'. Even Sumi, despite her apparent stoicism, is not immune from this hope. Aru realizes it the day she comes home with Gopal's scooter and Sumi, alerted by the sound, rushes out. Aru, getting off the scooter, sees the eagerness on her mother's face, watches the hope dying out. For a moment they stare at each other wordlessly. Then Sumi goes back in and Aru thinks, I've got to do something.

That same night she rings up Premi.

Premi's arrival is like the acknowledgement of a crisis. For the first time something is spelled out that none of them has admitted so far. Perhaps it is this that makes Sumi say abruptly to her sister, 'Why have you come?'

She recovers and corrects herself almost immediately. 'That's a stupid question to ask. Who told you?'

'I did.'

The way Aru stands next to her aunt, confronting her mother, is like a challenge. But Sumi ignores it. She reverts to a normal tone, speaks of the usual things—how is Nikhil? And Anil?

To Premi this conversation conveys a message—not so much 'we're not going to talk about it now' as 'I'm not going to talk to *you* about it.' She finds it impossible after this to say the things she had wanted to say, to ask the questions that have been thronging her mind since Aru spoke to her.

The questions come only after Sumi has gone to bed. Sumi has moved out of the room she shared with her daughters into a bedroom in the other wing. With the large hall between them, it is almost impossible for her to hear them; nevertheless they speak in low tones. The conversation centres around: where is he? Has no one any idea? Only when they have exhausted all the possibilities of this do they go on to the 'why'.

And now Premi, practical and matter-of-fact as she had decided she would be, brings out the list she has ready.

Quarrels? Money? Is it because of what happened in the Department? His resignation was a hint that Gopal was not in a very normal frame of mind. No man gives up a University teaching job just like that! Perhaps the attack on him by his students threw him—here Premi hesitates, for these are Gopal's daughters—off balance?

But the girls have nothing to offer her, no answers to any of these questions, only an acceptance of the fact of his having gone away as opposed to her disbelief.

Premi ventures on her next question with even more hesitation, and this time not because she is speaking to Gopal's daughters but because she is talking of Gopal and Sumi. (And this is the thought that has been beating in her mind since last night—Gopal walking out on Sumi? I can't, I never will believe it.) Is there any other woman? she asks.

She is astonished that there is a pause, a kind of jerk before a reply. The two sisters give an impression of having spoken about this, of having argued about it.

'There was an anonymous letter to Sumi a year back.'

'Don't be silly, Charu. Nobody believed that. Sumi laughed, you know that. Kantamani and Papa! She was such a—so pathetic! And anyway, Premi-mavshi, she isn't here any more, she's gone abroad.'

'What does Sumi say?'

'Nothing.'

Premi shouldn't be surprised, not if she remembers Sumi's response to Gopal's resigning. 'For Heaven's sake, does it matter why he's doing it! He doesn't want to go on and that's that!'

'But, Sumi, what about money? I mean, how will you live?'

'He'll get a job—he told me someone has already approached him, they want him to write some articles, maybe even work for them. Oh, I'm not worried!'

But, for God's sake, this is her husband and her marriage of twenty years, Premi thinks ....

Their talk becomes rambling and inconsequential after this. They keep pulling things out of the past, each memory like a grappling hook bringing up a question—was it because of this? At times the talk gets snagged on the unsaid things that lie between them: *They must have quarrelled, I heard them once, late at night....*

Perhaps it's because of me, the things I said to Papa when he decided to resign ....

Sumi took Gopal and her marriage too casually, she never cared as much as she should have ....

'Fate.'

The word, thrown into their midst by Kalyani, startles them. Premi had been both anxious and apprehensive about her mother's reaction. How has she taken it? Will she create a scene? But Kalyani has been surprisingly silent, especially this last hour, and entirely still, except for the ceaseless movement of her hands stroking her tiny feet as if they hurt her. She has made her presence felt only by her loud yawns at regular intervals. And now suddenly she says 'Fate'. And just as abruptly walks out, leaving the word lingering among them. None of them is inclined to pick it up. In fact, no more is said.

Lying in bed, listening to the easy breathing of her two nieces on the floor, Premi is thinking of how they are always on the same side of the invisible dotted lines that mark out alliances and divides in families. The relationship between them arouses a sense of deprivation in her. Sumi and I, we were never like this. She was ahead of me and I was forever trailing behind, never able to catch up with her. And it makes no difference that I am now a successful professional, mother of a seven-year-old son, wife of a prosperous lawyer. The moment I come home, all this dwindles into nothing and I can feel myself sliding back into adolescence, getting once again under the skin of that frightened child Premi who's always waiting here for me.

'Why are you here?'

At the question, all Premi's sense of being needed, of

being able to offer solace and help, had seeped away from her, leaving her again the child who, heart thudding in fear, had climbed up the forbidden stairs, opened the door and met the blank stare, the question: Why are you here?

'My father never spoke to me until I was ten,' she had told Anil after their marriage and he had not believed her. Just as she wouldn't have believed, if she had not seen it herself, that there could be families like Anil's. At first it had been like watching a movie—it was pleasing, interesting, pretty, but it could not possibly be true. People did not really talk to each other so easily, they did not hug and touch and use words of endearment so casually. No, it was a false picture. The truth was a father who stayed in his room, who never came out, never spoke to you, a mother who put her hand on your mouth so that you did not cry out ....

'My father did not speak to me until I was ten.'

But that's not true. 'Why are you here?'—those four words he had said then had meant nothing. He had scarcely looked at her when he spoke. The first time he really talked to her was when she had completed her medical finals; he had called her up to his room then, summoned her actually, to tell her she would be marrying Anil.

Since then, going to his room has been a formality she has scrupulously observed on every visit home. And he speaks to her—no, not as if she is his daughter, she has seen Gopal with his daughters and she knows that this is not how fathers speak to their daughters—but as if she is an acquaintance. But even this is an ordeal for her; the early years have so marked their relationship that she finds it difficult to speak to him. She is stiff, uneasy, often, like a stupid child, repeating his words as if bereft of her own. It will be the same this time too, she thinks, climbing the stairs slowly, reluctantly, as if there is still the possibility of being dragged down, of her fingers being prised away from the railings.

And it is—exactly the same. He asks her about Nikhil,

speaks of Anil and of Anil's father, who had been his colleague at one time. Nothing is said about Gopal and Sumi.

Of course, he cannot speak of Gopal. To mention Gopal, to speak of what he has done, is to let down the drawbridge into his own past. Nothing has changed, nothing ever changes here. I was a fool to imagine I could do something, that I could be of any use.

'I think I'd better go,' she tells Aru apologetically. 'I'd stay if I thought I could help, but there's nothing I can do. If we knew where Gopal was, perhaps, but ... You'll call me, Aru, won't you, when you find out where he is?'

'That may never happen.'

'Don't be silly. Any time you need me, for anything, even if it's not important, just ring me up and I'll come right away.'

જ

PREMI'S VISIT, IF nothing else, has opened a door through which the family enters, converging on Sumi and her daughters to perform its role. They congregate like mourners after a death in the family—but a death in a distant land, a death without a body. There is a blank space where the body should have been. None of the stock phrases, none of the comforting formulas, fit. Even to speak of what has happened as a tragedy is to make it one, for it is like affirming that Gopal will never return. There is an awkwardness about the whole thing, and discomfort and uneasiness pervade more than grief and anger.

Sumi, the person they come to comfort, is an enigma. She accepts Goda's dumb sympathy, Devaki's fierce loyalty and Ramesh's stupefied bewilderment, as if they are all the same to her. Unable to find the right way of dealing with her apparent stoicism, they are reduced to treating her as an invalid, bringing her fruits, magazines and books.

'You didn't have to bring this, Ramesh.'

Kalyani makes a formal protest when Ramesh comes with a large pack of ice-cream.

'I was just passing by,' he murmurs.

'He's trying to cheer us up, Amma.'

Ramesh gives Sumi an embarrassed, almost agonised look that silences her.

It is when she is serving the ice-cream that Aru suddenly asks Ramesh, as if she has been pondering on this all the while, 'Don't you have any idea where he could be? You must be having some clue, maybe there are people we don't know about ....'

'I've tried all the places I could think of, Aru. And I've been trying to get in touch with anyone who had some contact with Guru. But it's so hard to explain, I don't know what to say to them ....'

'Say it, Ramesh, say he's missing, say he's walked out on his wife and children. It's got to come out some time, how long are we going to hide it from the world? And do you think people don't know? I'm sure they do and frankly I don't care.'

'You don't care?' Aru's reaction to her mother's words is violent and sharp. 'That's wonderful. You don't care about his having gone, you don't care where he is, you don't care what people think—but I care, yes, I do, I care about Papa having left us, I care about not having our own house. I don't want to live like this, as if we're sitting on a railway platform, I want my home back, I want my father back ....'

After a moment's stunned silence, they move towards the sobbing girl, all of them except Sumi, who walks out.

When Ramesh comes out in search of her, he sees her standing still, her face lifted to the sky, a reflective look on it, as if she is weighing something. A lover watching her would be intrigued; but for Ramesh, it only means a moment of respite he welcomes. When he joins her she has resumed her pacing. They walk together in silence for a while, Sumi scarcely aware, he thinks, that he is with her. She speaks only when they reach the gate.

'I never thought Aru would take this so hard. I was more anxious about Seema, but ....'

Sumi has suddenly stopped. The strong odour of the plant which Kalyani swears keeps snakes away, assails them and they move on.

'Once when Aru was little we'd gone somewhere, I don't remember where, now. At night, I can remember this, she wouldn't go to bed. I want my own bed, she kept crying.'

'I never thought Guru would do such a thing, I never imagined he's this kind of a man ....'

'What kind of a man is he, Ramesh?'

Ramesh looks at her in surprise. But no, she isn't being sarcastic, she's entirely serious, she wants the answer to her question.

'Yes, tell me, Ramesh, what kind of a man do you think he is? Sometimes I think you know him better than any one of us does. Sudha was more like a mother than a sister to him, you're a kind of brother, not a nephew. He was closer to you than anyone else I know.'

'Guru? I was eight when he left home. I don't know why he left, nobody ever told me. When you're a kid, you accept these things, you never ask why. But I can remember that my mother was very upset, that she used to cry a lot. And I can vaguely remember us, my parents and I, sitting in a train and my mother crying. I think that was the time we left him in Shivpur. Something happened to him then, my mother told me that later. He suddenly decided he didn't want to live with us in Bombay, he decided he'd join a college in Shivpur ....'

'Gopal himself never spoke of this to you?'

'No, never. He did come home during vacations, not every vacation though. It was only when he got a job and stayed here in your house—I visited him, remember?—it was only then that we became friends. I went back home so full of "Gopal this" and "Gopal that" that my father began to call him "your Guru". And that's how he became Guru—Sumi, do you think he's had some kind of a breakdown? I can't help thinking it has to be something like that.'

'No, I don't think that's what's happened. He was very clear and very calm when he spoke to me, he was ...' Suddenly she shivers. 'I'm feeling cold.'

'Shall I get you a shawl?'

'No, let's go in.'

'What are you going to do, Sumi?'

'I don't know, I don't know anything, not as yet. Premi

wanted me to go to Bombay with her, but I can't think of anything, not as yet. I need time, Ramesh, give me some time.'

Lying in the semi-darkness, listening to the patter of raindrops on the mango leaves, each sound distinct, framed in the surrounding silence, Sumi is tantalized by a sense of *deja vu*. I have been in this room before, I have woken up here, just this way, watching the morning light slowly fill the room, relieved to see the menacing shadow in the corner become a cupboard. It's a child's fear that comes back to me. Did I ever sleep in this room as a child? This is my grandfather's room, the room where he lived and died. Perhaps that's why Kalyani didn't want me to move in here. But she didn't say that.

'Why do you want to be alone?' she had asked.

Not to lose sight of my loneliness, not to let the empty sound of it be muffled by the voices of other humans during the day, by the sounds of their breathing and rustlings in the night. It takes time to get used to sharing your life with another person, now I have to get used to being alone.

Of course, Sumi had not said any of this to her mother. She has to smile at the thought of it. And the truth is that it is not loneliness that is her enemy right now, it is a sense of alienation. The sight of Premi flanked by her daughters, the hostility on Aru's face as she said 'I rang her up', had made Sumi feel suddenly vulnerable.

The three of them ranged against me. Am I the enemy? Do my daughters blame me for what Gopal has done? Do they think it is my fault? Why can't I talk to them, tell them what I feel, how it was? Why can't I open my heart to them?

Sa-hriday—Gopal and she had argued about the meaning of the word once. Smiling at her attempt to find an English equivalent, Gopal had said, 'There's no word in English that can fit the concept. English is a practical language, it has no words for the impossible. *Sa-hriday* in the sense of oneness is an impossible concept.'

Then, abruptly, he had pulled her close to himself and said, 'Listen, can you hear? It's two hearts beating. They can never beat in such unison that there's only one sound. Hear that?'

It was these unexpected quirks in Gopal that had at first fascinated Sumi. Not for long, though; she had soon ceased to find them amusing or interesting. Nevertheless, she knows now that they were hints, telling her that it was always there in Gopal, the potential to walk out on her and their children.

Unlike her daughters, Sumi has no fears of his death; on the contrary, there is a certainty of his being alive, of his steadily pursuing his own purposes. While the others are trying to find reasons for what he has done, she knows that the reason lies inside him, the reason *is him.*

Sumi remembers, now, the night she had gone to his room, knowing that only this way could she break out of her father's authority. But Gopal, to her consternation, had closed himself against her. 'Go back, Sumi,' he had said, almost coldly. Only her stubbornness and the thought that she could not possibly return to the room she shared with Premi, had kept her there, alone in the room, that whole long night, while Gopal sat out in the tiny, open veranda. Until morning, when he had come in and put his arms about her, as if folding her into himself, into his life. And she had heard his heart beating.

Two hearts, two sounds. Gopal is right. *Sa-hriday*—there is no such thing, there can be no such thing.

'Is he all right with you?' Sudha had asked anxiously when they had gone to visit her and P.K. after their marriage.

'All right? Do you mean, does he scold me and beat me? No, he doesn't.'

I was only eighteen then, I could joke about it. But Gopal's sister did not laugh. She knew him, yes, she did, much better than I did. Or still do.

'Destiny is just us.'

Gopal's words come back to Sumi when, clearing up the large cupboard to make room for her things, she comes across the photographs. Deep inside, as if someone has thrust them as far back as possible. Two photographs in an envelope brittle with age. The photographs too, brown with the years, the edges frayed, the corners splitting, the backs slightly gummy to her fingers as if they had been stuck into an album some time earlier.

There are two girls in one picture: Kalyani and Goda, of course, she recognizes them, Kalyani's arm protectively around Goda's shoulder. Kalyani, about fourteen or fifteen perhaps, is already wearing a sari, the sari on her child's body having the effect of a masquerade. A child wearing her mother's sari for fun. But Kalyani's face is anxious, the slight suggestion of a squint accentuated, as it always is, by her distress or anxiety.

Goda provides a contrast both in looks and expression. (It's so hard to remember that Kalyani and Goda are not sisters but the children of a brother and sister, that the lack of resemblance between them invariably comes as a surprise.) Goda, pleasingly plump, is smiling at the camera, obedient perhaps, to the photographer's command. She is wearing a 'half-sari', as the diaphanous veil on her shoulders shows. This, along with her large eyes, her chubby face and the flowers in her hair, gives her the look of a heroine of a South Indian movie of the fifties. She seems docile and agreeable, and though only a child, already good wife-material. It is clear from the picture that she will make some man a good wife, whereas Kalyani ....

It is the other picture that startles Sumi. A classic post-wedding picture, bride and groom formally posed against a dark background, the bride sitting in a chair, the groom by her, a tall table with paper flowers in a vase placed on the other side for symmetry. The bride is wearing a heavy silk, the sari much too heavy for her scrawny girlishness. Her left arm, exposed by the sari's being held up by a brooch, is childishly thin and the weight of the heavy chain and necklaces she is wearing seems to make her neck droop. She is looking not at the camera, but at someone standing by the photographer, the uncertain look of a child seeking approval—am I doing it right? The man on the other hand is stern, his eyes hooded, arms folded across his chest in the usual 'manly pose' demanded by the photographers for such pictures. But the sternness here is not a pose, it is real. And the way he is standing, he gives the impression of being by himself, wholly unaware of the girl sitting by him. His wife.

Husband and wife. Bride and groom. Kalyani and Shripati, my parents. To see them together, even in a picture, gives me an odd, uneasy feeling. It seems wrong somehow, unnatural, even slightly obscene.

'Destiny is just us.'

Yes, their future is here, it can be seen in this picture, clearly, what is to happen to them, to their marriage. We don't always need astrologers, palmists or horoscopes to give us a glimpse of our future lives. They lie within us.

Sumi, who has heard Kalyani say 'fate' or 'destiny' for everything, from the milk boiling over to a sudden death, has never been able to take the word seriously. It was something innocuous, a domestic pet, a cat that lay snoozing in your home. Harmless, though there was always the chance that you could trip over it, fall and hurt yourself. But Gopal's use of the word 'destiny' gives it a different colour. A deeper tinge.

'Destiny is just us, and therefore inescapable, because we can never escape ourselves. Certain actions are inevitable because we are what we are. In a sense, we walk on chalked lines drawn by our own selves.'

Chalked lines? What a strange way of talking about what the living of life is all about, she had thought then. For her, it was a magician's bag, full of odds and ends. Put your hand in and you never know what you might get hold of: a rabbit, a bird, a string of silk scarves, a chain of ten-rupee notes. Chance, yes, haphazard, yes, that too, but nothing predetermined.

But, she thinks now, I forgot one thing. A magician is an

entertainer, and therefore he can't take the chance of ugly, frightening things coming out of his bag. He has to guard against that hazard. So perhaps Gopal's theory fits better after all. Destiny is just us.

And yet, if Gopal's life is shaped by his being what he is, what about us, the girls and me? We are here because of his actions: how does this fit in?

But I have no desire really to pursue these thoughts. Unlike Aru, I know that getting answers to questions will not provide me with any solution. The 'why' that all of them are pursuing leaves me cold. I know that they find it impossible to believe that I have not asked him anything. The truth is, I could not have spoken to him that night— no, it was impossible. But even if it had been possible, if I had asked him 'why', would I have got an answer I could have made sense of?

'I could no longer stand in a position of authority before my students.'

This was his explanation for resigning his job! Just like Gopal, I had thought, both irritated and annoyed, to give such an impossibly metaphysical reason for resigning a job. If I'd asked him, 'why are you leaving me?', I'd have got just such an answer and what would I do with that?

And yet, she thinks, if I meet Gopal I will ask him one question, just one, the question no one has thought of. What is it, Gopal, I will ask him, that makes a man in this age of acquisition and possession walk out on his family and all that he owns? Because, and I remember this so clearly, it was you who said that we are shaped by the age we live in, by the society we are part of. How then can you, in this age, a part of this society, turn your back on everything in your life? Will you be able to give me an answer to this?

It is now over a month since Gopal left home and Sumi knows one decision has to be taken, and immediately.

'Vacàte the house? You must be joking!'

Aru is incredulous. As long as the house is theirs, they still have a home and the hope that Gopal will return, that they will be able to resume their lives. To give up the house, as Sumi is saying they have to do, is to pronounce the death sentence of that hope. Aru wants to say something that will stop her mother from taking the step, but she has no arguments that can contend against the reality of money; she knows herself that they cannot afford to pay the rent for that house any longer.

But Sumi's hurry to have done with this has more to it than these financial considerations. With Gopal's going, it was as if the swift-flowing stream of her being had grown thick and viscous—her movements, her thoughts, her very pulse and heartbeats seemed to have slowed down. It had worried her family, but it has been a necessary physical reaction to her emotional state, as if this slowing down was essential for her survival. Now, like a stunned bird coming back to life, there is a frenzy of movement, a tremendous flurry of activity, a frenetic shaking of feathers. Sumi cannot be still.

On the day they are to move, she is impatient to be gone, to set to work. She frets while Kalyani delays them for breakfast, she paces up and down waiting for Seema to make up her mind about accompanying them, so restless that Kalyani says, 'you go on, if Seema wants to go, I'll ask Hrishi or Devi to take her.'

The house, even in this short time of being unoccupied, smells musty. There is a thick film of dust on the floor, on which their footprints show clear and distinct at first. For a moment, as they stand and take it in, what they have to do seems impossible, their silence becomes a cry of despair: we can't do it. But Sumi allows them no time for melancholy or nostalgia, she sets to work almost immediately and the girls follow. With remarkable swiftness they begin to sort out things, so that when Devaki and Hrishi come to offer their help, old newspapers, bottles and tins have already been set out in the yard.

Watching Sumi and her daughters united in the camaraderie of wordless, rhythmic work, they realize their help is not needed. Hrishi, after some mumbled words to his mother goes away, but Devaki stands about like a visitor in a hospital, watching the doctors and nurses working with both skill and efficiency, knowing she can do nothing, yet unable to go away. She finds the silence in which they work, chilling. No questions are asked, nor is there any sharing of memories; baby clothes and old nursery books are disposed of in the same way as an old wick stove or a pan with its base worn out. Only once there is a slight hiatus when Charu, looking at their old chess-board, hesitantly asks, 'Shall we take this with us?'

Sumi has been ruthless; anything that is of no possible use is discarded. But now, seeing her daughter's face, she says, 'Why not?' And Charu smiles, as if Sumi's response, as well as retaining the chess-board, has lifted some of the oppression off her.

Devaki gets them lunch a little later, from the restaurant round the corner.

'Why are you eating this, Devi?' Sumi asks, as if noticing her for the first time. 'Cold idlis and watery chutney—this isn't for you. And what about your work? You go on, we'll manage.'

By evening, most of it is done. It has been a swift dismemberment. The furniture stands, stark and skeletal in the empty rooms, while bundles, trunks and cartons have been stacked in the front hall, ready to be carried out in the morning. When the door of the steel almirah is banged shut, the clang resounds with a hollow boom through the house and Aru's heart throbs in a panic-filled response, as if she has received an ominous message: it's over, it's over.

The girls fall asleep on the bare mattresses on the floor, exhausted, but Sumi has reached the stage of extreme fatigue in which it seems impossible that she can ever sleep. She feels charged with a kind of energy that makes her think she could go on working all night; her hands itch to pull the mattresses from under the girls, to roll them up and pile them on the stuff in the hall. If the truck was here, she thinks, I would have carried out everything and loaded it myself. But there is nothing left for her to do, and lying down on the sagging sofa, eyes closed, she tries to sleep.

For the first time, the thought comes to her: this is my last night in our house, Gopal's and mine. Sumi has never had the passionate attachment to her home that she has seen in other women, in Devaki and Premi. But now, in the silence of the night, listening to the infinitely pathetic crying of the new-born next door, the house rushes forward to claim her with memories. She has a strange sense of seeing all of them, even her own self, moving about the house, as if they have come together for one last time, re-enacting scenes from the past for her benefit.

Gopal, coming out of the bathroom, vigorously towelling his head, shaking the water out of his hair, singing '*Do naina*' ....

Aru, pinning down a cockroach with a piece of paper, and then, with an agonised face, stamping wildly on it. And Charu, looking on, screaming with laughter.

Gopal saying 'Shaabash' to Seema and Seema's pleased smile ... Aru and Charu playing chess, and Charu's comically astonished look as Aru triumphantly knocks Charu's King off the board.

Though it is nearly dawn before she falls asleep, she is up before the girls. Seeing her mother's face, hollow-eyed, hair dishevelled, Aru feels a pang; this is how she will look when she is old. But when Sumi comes out of the bathroom after her bath, smoothing down the pleats of her sari, she looks so reassuringly normal that Aru has a sudden lift of spirits. Perhaps things will work out, maybe we will be able to go on, even if we can't go back.

When Shripati comes with Seema, Aru's light-heartedness reaches out to her sisters and the three of them flit about the house calling out to one another, to their mother, exclaiming over things, laughing. The brief flare of gaiety evaporates with the arrival of the truck and in a moment the house is full of the loaders' footsteps and their voices. A few neighbours come out to watch the operation. The grandmother next door balances the child she is carrying on the wall and stares at the proceedings with unblinking interest. Her curiosity finally makes her get hold of Sumi, and Aru, seeing them together, wonders what Sumi is telling her. The truth, she thinks, knowing Sumi as she does.

As for Aru herself, she avoids people's eyes. To see their belongings in the open hurts her, they look so pathetic and vulnerable; the stares of the neighbours seem like a violation. Aru's uneasiness extends to the landlord who joins them now. Surely there's an air of familiarity about him that wasn't there before? And why does he look at Sumi that way? Her hackles rise and she doggedly follows them while Sumi, cool and matter-of-fact, takes him round the house on an inventory.

'Oh good,' Sumi says when Devaki and Chitra join them. 'That's two cars, which means we can take everything away at once. And is Hrishi coming?'

'Not much for a family of five, is it?' she asks no one in particular when the truck is finally loaded. 'It's a good thing neither Gopal nor I were acquirers.'

Finally, the house is empty and everyone stands about awkwardly, unable to break away, as if waiting for something. And again it is Sumi who, businesslike, says, 'Let's go. What are we waiting for?'

It is like a caravan when they set off, Hrishi leading the truck on his motorbike, the two cars following and Aru on her moped trailing behind them. When she gets home, Aru does something that astonishes all of them, something that Charu is never to forget. One moment she is stepping over the threshold, parcels in hand, and the next moment she keels over. For an instant no one realizes what has happened, they imagine she has stumbled and fallen. When she continues to lie there in a heap, they rush to her.

'Aru, what's happened?'

'Get some water.'

'Aru, Aru ....'

'I think she's coming out of it.'

Aru sits up, water streaming down her face, her dazed look turning to shame as she realizes what has happened.

'She hasn't had any breakfast, I'm sure that's it.'

'And nothing last night, either.'

'Sumi, how could you?'

'Oh, God, don't fuss, everyone. I'm all right, I'm perfectly all right.'

'Kalyani-mavshi, get her some coffee—with lots of sugar.'

But Kalyani, standing in the doorway, looks petrified, she doesn't move, she scarcely hears Devaki. It is Charu who gets the coffee, Devaki who sets out the breakfast for everyone, while Kalyani, silent and still, watches them eat.

'She's all right, Amma.' Sumi sees her mother's still trembling hand. 'Don't be so scared.'

But it isn't Aru's fainting that has got Kalyani into this state, it's something else none of them has noticed: her rush towards Aru when she fell, her realization, an almost instinctive one, that she was next to Shripati, his abrupt walking away from her. Now she sits unusually silent, frozen into an immobility, unable to shake off the paralysis of fear. She takes no part in the unloading, and it is left to Sumi to instruct the men to distribute her things about the house.

All the extra furniture, except the girls' beds, goes into the small room next to Sumi's bedroom. This room becomes a place of refuge to the girls, a kind of re-creation of their home. Seema, when she is in one of her moods, lies long hours on the large bed, which is the repository of all the extra mattresses, oblivious to everyone, uncaring of anyone calling out for her.

The boxes and trunks are pushed into the storeroom where they settle down as if they belong, soon knitted into their new place by the cobwebs, sealed into it by the dust that settles down on them. Books and clothes find their way to their owners, but the rest of the things lie about for them to stumble on, until, in the mysterious way of all articles, they are absorbed by the house and become part of it.

The girls, too, no longer have the air of visitors living out of suitcases. Their clothes now flutter on the lines till evening, the underclothes stay on ('in purdah', as Charu says, since Kalyani conceals them by hanging towels on the next line) until they are pulled off before their baths the next day. The girls give the impression of having taken up the threads of their life. They are no longer living on the edge of crisis, they have found a routine in which grief and fear have a minor place. Once, however, Sumi sees her two older daughters coming together, holding each other for an infinitesimal moment, giving the impression that it is for mutual comfort, and then parting.

Sumi is the one who has the air of being lost, of having no place in her childhood home. She shows no outward sign of distress, but the girls notice a new habit in her, of touching them, holding their hands, smoothing their hair, as if this physical contact is a manifestation of some intense emotion within her. The first time Aru comes home and finds her mother in the kitchen, she feels as if a weight has been lifted off her. She's all right, she thinks, she'll be all right now. But there is a kind of purposeless extravagance about her movements, an exaggeration that is different from her normal vivacity and quickness. When evening comes, she paces up and down in the front yard, the way she had done the day Ramesh had found her there, from the porch to the gate and then back, pivoting on her heel to make each turn in a stylized manner.

And then one day, she decides to learn to ride the scooter. She begins all by herself, until Prasad, the outhouse tenant, comes to help her. Aru is there to aid her the next day, but it is not long before she dispenses with all help and rides it herself, going in circles round the pond, slowly, ready to put her foot down the moment she feels unsure of her balance. Shyam and Shweta, Prasad and Ratna's children, watch her in fascination, Seema sits dreamily on the steps staring at her mother and Kalyani goes in and out with a nervousness she cannot conceal. The spasmodic sputter of the scooter becomes part of the normal tapestry of sounds and the watchers go back to their usual occupations, except Kalyani who cannot keep away. The next day, Sumi suddenly gathers speed and in a burst of confidence, goes out of the gate.

'She shouldn't have done that, she shouldn't have gone out on the road.'

'Amma, she isn't learning to ride the scooter to whiz around in your front yard!'

Nevertheless, Aru is anxious too; she wanders to the gate and waits there until Sumi returns and runs back in after her. Sumi stops and holds both her arms above her head in a triumphant gesture. The scooter rocks, she clutches at the handlebars and Aru, rushing to her, holds her in a hug that steadies her. Kalyani comes out attracted by their voices, their laughter, unware that above, Shripati is watching the mother and daughter, too, the expression on his face almost identical to Kalyani's.

Three sisters—the very stuff fairy tales are spun out of. Aru must have made the connection even as a child, for there is a story, not apocryphal as family stories often are, of her asking the question: why is the youngest sister always the good and beautiful one? Why can't the eldest be that?

Aru doesn't wholly believe the story herself, she is embarrassed by it (secretly pleased, too, as we all are by tales of our childhood exploits). The story has had a footnote added to it later, Charu's comment: So Aru and I don't get Prince Charming? And then, a typical Charu retort: Who wants him, anyway! Seema can have him.

But to imagine Seema as Cinderella is impossible. Her hair, her clothes, her very shoes have the gloss of much care and rule out the possibility of any association with rags and cinders. She's always 'tip top', as Kalyani says approvingly. And as for Seema slaving away while her sisters go out dancing—this is an even more impossible thought; it is actually the other way round.

'Why do you make Seema's bed, why do you iron her clothes? You're spoiling her,' Charu charges her sister. Aru offers excuses that sound lame even to herself. The truth is that she cannot give up the habit of babying Seema which began when Sumi had been ill and unable to look after the new-born baby. The sense of responsibility that began then, when Aru was only six years old, and Gopal brought the baby back from Kalyani who had looked after her until then, seems never to have left her. She is still that girl, her small face anxious and puckered, trying to soothe the baby who never seemed to stop crying.

Even Charu's protests aginst this coddling of Seema are rare; she, like the rest of the family, accepts the fact that Seema is special, isolated not only by the five-year gap between them but by something else that none of them can spell out. They don't try to, either; the awareness of this is cloaked in silence.

In any case, the three sisters could never qualify for a Cinderella story, for there are no ugly sisters here. Actually, there is not much resemblance between the sisters; they are not even, as siblings often are, variations on a theme. And they emphasize this dissimilarity by the way they dress, by the length and styling of their hair. Yet they are alike in this, that all three of them just escape beauty. Aru, who has no vanity at all about her looks, thinks of herself as the ugly one in the family. My nose is too big, she thinks, my lips too thin, my forehead too bony. She does not realize that she is at her worst when she is looking into the mirror; her unsmiling face looks severe, her jaw more angular than it really is, her cheekbones prominent. It is when she is relaxed and smiling that her face softens, that it is touched by beauty. But this is the face she never sees. Her sternness, like Charu's plumpness and Seema's curious blankness, is the one flaw that mars the picture.

It was Sumi who, after seeing Satyajit Ray's *Charulata*,

chose the name for her second daughter; but sometimes, watching Aru in one of her rare skittish moods, she feels that Aru is the one who is more like Ray's heroine, moving suddenly, unexpectedly, from a sombre gravity to a childlike playfulness. Now, these moods are a thing of the past and Aru is wholly steeped in earnestness. She has taken on a great many of the chores at home. It makes sense, in a way, that she leaves Charu free for her studies in this crucial second year of her college. But there is more to it. She wants to be the man of the family, Sumi thinks, when Aru insists on accompanying her mother to the dentist. She wants to take Gopal's place, she wants to fill the blank Gopal has left in our lives. But Gopal never went to the dentist with me, he didn't do so many of these things Aru is now doing. And yet his absence has left such a vast emptiness that I can't find my bearings, there are no markers any more to show me which way I should go.

Perhaps what Aru is trying is to steer her mother and sisters through the stormy passage of change. In this, however, she comes up against Kalyani.

Kalyani's pattern of housekeeping, a routine carefully built on a foundation of pain, has been disrupted. She finds herself incapable of absorbing four people into her order of things, yet is reluctant to accept help. The result is that the larger issues of treachery and desertion, of grief and anger recede, making way for the minor irritants of food, meal-times and the sharing of chores. Aru finds this heartburning over trivial issues undignified, a kind of comedown. And after Sumi's housekeeping that allowed them to pitch into anything they wanted to do, she finds Kalyani's restrictions hard to bear.

Sumi, caught in the practicalities of moving house, has so far stayed aloof from the problem. But listening to Aru's increasingly irritable responses to Kalyani's questions one morning, she decides to interfere.

'Aru should be studying, Sumi, she should be having fun, she shouldn't be involved with this—this mustard seed of domestic life.'

'And at your age, you shouldn't be burdened with us, either. God knows none of us wants it, but there it is, we're stuck in this situation. So let's make the best of it.'

'But, Sumi, I don't like the idea of a child like Aru slogging.'

'Aru's not a child. And listen, Amma, if we're going to stay here, and who knows how long it's going to be, you'll have to learn to take everyone's help. If you can't, it's going to be hard on all of us.'

It's not a threat, but it seems to frighten Kalyani. Her capitulation is absolute and she endures the occasional forays of the girls into her kitchen in stoic silence. But when Aru comes down with a heavy cold, she can't help sounding triumphant.

'I knew it, I knew you were doing too much, look at you now.'

'It's only a cold, Amma.'

By evening, Aru has fever, mounting so rapidly that she is lying in a kind of stupor, breathing heavily through her open mouth, her lips cracked and dry. Sumi, sitting by her, can feel the heat emanating from her body.

'You should have removed her tonsils, I always said it. My father had it done for both Goda and me and ....'

'She'll be all right, Amma.' Sumi replies, not to Kalyani's reproach, but to the fear in Kalyani's voice, the fear in her own self. At night however, when Aru seems delirious, she succumbs and rings up Ramesh.

After he has gone—'it's only a virus, she'll be okay by morning'—Sumi settles down in a chair by Aru, overruling Kalyani and Charu who want to sit up with her. 'It's not necessary for all of us to lose sleep. I'll call you if there's any need.'

Aru, moving in a strange, shifting, chaotic world, is unaware of everything. The jumble of voices, the constant movement about her bed, seems miles away. She wakes up sometime during the night with parched lips and a burning in her throat.

'Water,' she mumbles, 'water.'

There's someone by her bed, a glass is held to her lips, she can feel a hand supporting her head. Gratefully, she swallows the water and goes off to sleep again. When she wakes up in the morning, clear-headed, her body light and hollow, there is a sense of peace and quiet in the room. The shifting shadows, the confused voices of the night seem to belong to another world.

'Oh God, Aru, I'm sorry I dropped off to sleep.' Sumi is apologetic when she wakes up. 'Don't tell Amma and Charu I slept through the night.'

'But you didn't! You woke up to give me water.'

'I? No, I didn't.'

'Then who did?'

It must have been her grandfather, Aru says, remembering the tall shadow on the wall, the feel of his hand against her head.

'It can't be.' Sumi dismisses the idea. 'Baba never comes down here,' you know that.'

Yes, I know; nevertheless I know it was not a dream, I know it was him. And why is it, it suddenly occurs to her, that he never comes down here?

In a day or two, Aru is up and about, and Ramesh coming to visit them in the evening exclaims in satisfaction at the sight of her sitting up with the rest. Chitra and the twins have come with him and later, Goda and her husband, Satya, join them. The house is full of noise. For the first time since Sumi's return, there is no sense of participating in a wake. Instead, there is a release of spirits, as if they have just escaped some danger and have to celebrate. Part of the liveliness is because of the twins, Jai and Deep. It is a constant source of wonder to everyone who knows them, that parents as quiet and subdued as Ramesh and Chitra can have children like the twins. Even Seema emerges from her self-absorption when they are around. She is both puzzled and fascinated by their enormous energy and high spirits and they, in turn, seem to need her as an audience. Hrishi and Charu come in from their class a little later and the babble of sound enlarges to include Hrishi's loud voice, Charu's laughter.

Kalyani and Goda try to persuade Aru to go to bed, but Aru resists, not so much because she wants to be with them, but more out of a lassitude, a reluctance to face the thought of the coming night. She feels herself encased in a bubble, her connection to the world, to all these people, a tenuous one that can snap at any moment.

And then the thunder of Bhimsen Joshi's voice, regally unrolling the Raag Mian ki Malhar which has formed a background to all this noise, suddenly ceases. None of them notice it—except Kalyani, who stops suddenly in the middle of a sentence, a word, really. It is something she is scarcely aware of, almost a knee-jerk response. Her body becomes tense, her head is slightly raised as if she is listening to the silence upstairs.

Aru comes out of the bubble, her mind razor-sharp and clear, she sees a situation she has taken for granted for years. Why doesn't Baba ever come down? Why doesn't he have his meals here with the rest of us? Why doesn't he ever speak to Kalyani? She is his wife, isn't she? And why is she so frightened of him? He rings the bell and she responds, he controls her from a distance. What has Amma done to make him behave this way towards her?

Poor Amma, Sumi says, poor Amma. But why?

In her confusion, Aru's mind spirals towards Gopal, and his desertion no longer seems a bizarre independent occurence, but connected somehow to the curious story of her grandparents, a story, she realizes only now, she has very little knowledge of.

๛

GOPAL, WHO HAS had no intention of making a mystery of his whereabouts, is living scarcely a few miles away from Sumi and his daughters in the house of an old student of his. This is in an old part of the town, where tiny lanes criss-cross one another and homes, small shops and restaurants jostle together in a jumble of noisy existence. Gopal's room, above the printing press that belongs to his student, is an odd place for a man to 'retreat' to—the thought will occur to all those who visit him. But like the truck drivers, who, after a night of frenetic driving, go to sleep in the womb-like interiors of their driving cabins, wholly insulated from the outside world, Gopal is unaware of the jangle of noises in which he is living his life.

Now the interlude of peace suddenly ends for him. Shankar, still the student, unwilling to sit down in Gopal's presence, is there to tell him that Ramesh had rung up.

'And you told him I was here? It's all right, I never wanted to hide the fact from anyone.'

So Ramesh has traced me here. I should have guessed he would be the first; he has his mother's doggedness, his father's sense of duty. And so, he will be the first to ask me the question, 'Why did you do such a thing, Guru?'

I had prepared myself for this question, I had rehearsed my answers before I spoke to Sumi, I had been ready to counter her arguments. Now I have to be ready to face Ramesh, I have to brush up my reasons, for Ramesh will not let me off easily. What do I say? What were the lines I had prepared?

I heard a voice ....

No, I can't say that, it sounds utterly phoney. Even Joan of Arc didn't get away with that one.

It's a kind of illness, a virus, perhaps, which makes me incapable of functioning as a full human being, as a husband and father ....

This is the right answer to give a doctor and Premi may accept it, but will Ramesh? No, he won't leave it at that, he will ask me for my symptoms, he will try to connect them and ultimately, yes, I'm sure of this, make an appointment for me with a psychiatrist. No, best leave this alone.

I thought of Purandaradasa's line, 'Listen, the hour strikes' and I was terrified, I knew I was running out of time.

Sumi is the one person who may understand this, she will know what I mean. But this is not enough; I have to be more honest with her, more explicit.

What then? What do I say?

I stopped believing in the life I was leading, suddenly it seemed unreal to me and I knew I could not go on.

Is this the truth? Is this why I left my home, my wife and children? Could I have said this to Sumi?

In the event, there was nothing for me to say to Sumi, for she asked me nothing. I am thankful I never had to suffer the mortification of wading through this slush of embarrassing half-truths. I have not been fair to Sumi, I know that now. I should have spoken to her earlier, given her some hint of what was happening to me. But how do you interrupt the commonplace with melodrama? There is never the right time in daily life for these things. The knock on the door, the peal of the bell bringing news of disaster, they can only come from the outside.

Since coming here, I have been dreaming of my father. How do I know that the man I see in my dreams is my father? I was only eight when he died and nothing of him has remained with me, neither his face, nor his voice, nor his manners, nor any memory linking the two of us together. Just a blank. It is odd, yes, when I think of it now, I realize how curious it is. Can one erase a parent, even a dead parent, so completely? To some extent, of course, Sudha was responsible for this. She put away everything that was our parents', even their pictures, immediately after their death. I accepted it then, but now, thinking of it, I can imagine that she must have worked in a frenzy, sweeping the house bare of their presence. And I know this too now, that she did it for me. It was this, and her almost immediate marriage to P.K., that helped the quick transformation of a house of mourning into a normal home in which a family lived. Man, woman and child. P.K., Sudha and I. And so I forgot, how quickly I forgot the faces of my parents. No memories at all. Except that, sometimes, when Sudha laughed, it seemed like something I had heard once.

And yet, I am certain that the man who visits me in my dreams is my father. The knowledge belongs not to me, the man that I am now, but to the I-figure in my dreams, that disembodied self who is always a boy. This father of my dreams smiles at me, we walk the streets together, he waits for me when I lag behind, he holds my hand when I'm tired, he looks at me affectionately ....

I know, of course, what it is I'm doing: I am recreating my father in my dreams as I had done in my waking hours, all those years ago, as a boy. Inventing him. Knowing nothing about him then, except that he had married his brother's widow who became my mother; the possibilities had been innumerable and my adolescent mind had drawn various selves out of the protean being of the father I had imagined. So many of them:

A man who sinned against his brother by loving his wife. The brother dying of grief and the' wife and the man marrying immediately after.

A kind man moved by pity to marry his brother's widow, to make that brother's daughter his own.

A Lakshman-like younger brother, keeping a promise made to his dying elder brother to look after his young widow and child.

(No, this never worked. Lakshman, who never looked at

Sita's face, not once, so that the only bits of her jewellery he could identify after her abduction were her anklets—this devoted brother had to be discarded.)

It was when I read *Hamlet*, fortunately much later, that the most terrible version of my parents' story entered my mind. Just that once, though, for I slammed the door on it immediately. In this story my father became a man succumbing to his passion for his brother's wife, the woman compliant, a pregnancy and a child to come and then, after the husband's convenient death (no, I couldn't, I just couldn't make my father poison his brother) a marriage of convenience.

The facts, of course, few as they are, spell out a different story: Sudha's father died of typhoid and I was born two years after my parents were married.

But that was how it was for me—my father was never a father to me—not after I knew their story. He was my mother's guilty partner, he was Sudha's uncle, her stepfather, he was my mother's husband ....

And now I dream of this kindly man, as if we have, through the years, achieved a kind of peace in our relationship, as if, like any son with a living father, we have finally, after a long struggle, achieved a harmonious relationship.

These are peaceful dreams that don't trouble me—unlike the ugly dreams that tormented me in the last few months before I came here, exhausting dreams that seemed to go on all night, punctuated by the need to empty my bladder. So exhausting that once, waking up, I had been astonished to see that it was only fifteen minutes since I last woke up; those fifteen minutes had seemed a weary lifetime.

All a thing of the past. Now there is only this room in which nothing is mine. For a few days after I came here, I heard Shankar and his wife trying to hush the children and servants; but the noise and bustle in the courtyard do not disturb me, they have nothing to do with me. Like the rain-trees on the road outside, so very mysteriously, wonderfully flourishing in this human jungle, which seem to have raised themselves above all the futile activity on the road below, I am untouched by all that is happening under my window.

Yet sometimes, when I wake up in the morning and see the branches of the rain-trees filling up my window, I feel I am back in that tree-enclosed room of the outhouse behind Kalyani's house. I hear Shankar's wife call out to her children and it is Kalyani's voice calling out, 'Sumi, Premi'.

Yes, I was at peace then too, like I am now. Sudha, absorbed by her young children had freed me from the tug of her concern, I had moved away from Shivpur, from Girija and a relationship that had been threatening to complicate my life. In the outhouse I was left alone, set apart from the Big House by much more than the physical distance between us. It was as if the mist that sometimes came down in the mornings, never lifted, so that the figures I saw seemed always hazy, the voices muted and muffled, coming to me from some great distance. I watched them, after a while it became a pastime, but there never was a sense of involvement. There was the man whom I rarely saw after my first meeting with him, coming out onto the terrace, standing there, gazing at nothing. My landlady, whose tense, small figure advanced towards me in a burst of cordiality, then retreated just as abruptly. The younger girl, sitting on the side steps, silent as a wraith, her knees drawn up to her chest, squeezing herself into the smallest space possible. And the older girl ....

Years later, when we went to Abu, I saw the richly draped idol of Parvati, glowing with colours among the cold, white, marble figures of the Tirthankaras in the Dilwara temple. Sumi was like that, drawing all the colour and movement in that house into herself. She filled me with the same astonishment and delight that the idol of Parvati in the temple had.

I can still remember the day my detachment ended. I woke out of a heavy drugged sleep in the afternoon—it must have been a Sunday—to the sound of girls' voices. I

went out to the tap to wash my face and saw them, Sumi
and a friend, on the stone seat under the neem tree. I went
back to my room, picked up my book and tried to go back
to reading, and the voices and laughter came to me still,
like a distant melody, filling me with ecstasy. I ceased to be
an observer then and, like the king who stood watching
Shakuntala and her two friends, I became part of the
enchantment, I could see the bee hovering, I could hear
its buzzing ....

'We are searching for the truth; you, O bee, have found it.'

Found it? Yes, for a while it was that way. After years of
blundering I had found the truth in my feelings for Sumi,
my love for my children. But now I know I had only lost
myself in that beautiful, dense green foliage.

Can I say this to Ramesh? No, he will never understand
me. Ramesh is the son of P.K., a man whose sense of duty
and responsibility was absolute. And yet, after his death,
when the crows would not come for the *pindas*, the priests
said, 'He must have left something undone.'

'Men don't die easily, Guru,' Ramesh had sobbed out to
me when, as an intern, he had lost his first patient. 'Men
don't die easily.'

Is there to be no end to it even after death? Was a man
to be tied to his duties forever? Could he never be free? It
astonished me that Ramesh so tamely made a promise to
his dead father, as they told him to do, to complete
whatever was undone. He squared his shoulders and
accepted his father's burdens. He will do the same now. He
will not despise or hate me, the bond between us is too
strong for that. Instead, he will make up his mind to take
on the responsibility of my family on himself. And then,
only then, he will tell Sumi where I am.

It is not Sumi, however, but Kalyani who is the first to come
to Gopal. 'There's a lady come to see you, sir,' the press
boys tell him and he thinks it is Sumi. But it isn't, it's

Kalyani. For an instant, perhaps because he has so rarely seen her outside her own home, he does not recognize her. She looks a different person in these alien surroundings. Was she always so tiny, so frail-looking? Charu is with her, Charu who makes it absolutely clear that she is here only as her grandmother's escort. Scarcely looking at her father, she helps Kalyani up the stairs and saying, 'I'll be waiting downstairs for you, Amma,' prepares to leave.

'Don't go, Charu, stay here.'

'Let her go, Gopala. Go, child, I won't take much time.'

'Come out here then.'

He shows her out through the narrow door, into the small terrace behind the room and then hesitates; it's too sunny here, there is no shade at all. But Charu, her back to him, goes and stands near the railing, ignoring him.

The moment he comes back into the room, Kalyani bursts into words.

'What have you done to my daughter, Gopala, don't do this, don't let it happen to my daughter, what happened to me.'

And then she stops, abruptly, a hand to her forehead, as if rebuking herself. This is not what she had intended to say! She begins again, this time saying the things she has come prepared with. She calls him Gopala, dragging out the last vowel, loading the name with affection and tenderness. He is amazed that she speaks without hostility.

'When Sumi married you, she was too young; but I was not anxious for her, you were older, you were sensible and you cared for her, yes, you did. I can still remember how you scolded me for being angry with her when she refused to nurse Seema. She can't help it, Amma, you said to me, she isn't depriving the baby of milk on purpose. How can you change so much, Gopala?'

She goes on, moving from surmise to surmise. Has anyone poisoned his mind against Sumi? Has she done something wrong? Can't he forgive her? She knows—and she says this placatingly, so humbly that it hurts—he is a generous man. And Sumi too—he shouldn't think that her friendliness with others means anything.

'Amma, it's not that, I know Sumi ....'

But she doesn't let him speak. I know she was careless, she says, I know she didn't bother too much about her home, 'But, Gopala,' and now she hesitates, 'how could she have known what being a good wife means when she never saw her mother being one? I taught her nothing, it's all my fault, Gopala, forgive me and don't punish her for it.'

Once again he tries to tell her that he has nothing against Sumi, he tries to convince her that he never expected her to create for him the world he wanted, that he did not make her responsible for giving him all that he wanted in life, but Kalyani hurries on.

'Is it money, Gopala? If it is, you know that Sumi and you will have everything of mine. Premi is comfortable, I am not worried about her. Even my jewellery—most of it is for Sumi ....'

This time he does not have to speak. She looks at his face and stops. And begins to cry. He watches her distress helplessly.

'Look at me, Gopala,' she says when she can speak. 'My father died worrying about me, my mother couldn't die in peace, she held on to life though she was suffering—she suffered terribly—because of me, she didn't want to leave me and go.'

She is crying uncontrollably now, she can't speak. And so he does. He tells her that this has nothing to do with the relationship between Sumi and him, it has nothing to do with Sumi, she has done nothing wrong, she has done him no wrong, on the contrary, it is he ....

Listening to him, she begins to understand that nothing she says can affect him. He can see the anger rising in her, anger she tries to conceal, afraid, perhaps, that she will alienate him by that. Once again, this hurts.

'What about your daughters? Have you thought of

them?' Look at that girl standing out there—she didn't want to come, she came here for my sake. Have you thought of what you have done to them?'

'I thought of everything before I took this step. Do you think, Amma, I haven't?'

There is a long silence after that. Then Kalyani stands up.

'Charu,' she calls out.

Charu stands at the door, blinking, trying to adjust her eyes to the dimness after the strong light outside. She gives Kalyani a quick look, taking in the fact that she has been crying, but she says nothing.

'Let's go, Charu.'

'I'll get an auto, you wait here, Amma.'

'No, don't, Charu. Let's start walking, I'm sure we'll get one on the road. We will, won't we?'

Before leaving, she looks about the room for the first time since she had come in, taking it all in—the thin mattress rolled into a dingy striped carpet, the rough wooden planks of the bed, the bare table, the string on the wall on which he has hung a towel and a shirt ....

'You live here?' she asks him.

'Yes.'

'And who's this Shankar?'

'A student of mine.'

'Oh!'

She is no longer able to sustain interest in anything. The purpose that had upheld her when she came has receded from her. She goes down the stairs like a woman much older than her years, putting both her feet on a step before going to the next one. Charu follows, her dupatta trailing on the floor behind her as usual. Gopal has an urge to pick it up, to put it back on her shoulder, but as if she has guessed his thoughts and wants to forestall him, she picks it up and adjusts it herself. Watching his daughter move away from him, he has a sense of loss so acute, it is like a physical pain. Unable to follow them, he goes back to the room and sits down, listening to their steps recede.

This is part of it, I have to go through all this, I cannot escape. What had I expected, that I could inflict pain and feel none in return?

If Kalyani came as a supplicant, Aru is an adversary, holding her hostility before her like a weapon. A sword, scrubbed to a beautiful silvery sheen, sharp-edged, ready for war. She is determined to behave like an adult, or rather, as she imagines an adult should be—cool and reasonable. She asks the polite questions of a visiting acquaintance, about this room, about Shankar, his press and what work does he do there? He imagines that this is the way a prisoner would feel with a visitor—uneasy, longing for it to be over. He can see the effort she is making, he wants to tell her to stop, he would rather see her grief and anger pour out of her; but she holds him at bay, she won't let him do anything but reply to her questions—until her questions finally peter out and they are left in silence.

'Papa,' she begins, then stops as if this is not how she wants to address him. But the word has opened a valve and now it gushes out. The confusion in her mind is reflected in her language—she skips from Kannada to English and back again, her sentences incomplete, leaving out words that she can't get hold of. Her voice rises, trails away, suddenly becomes gruff and guttural as if something is choking her.

And then she can't go on any longer; she breaks down and begins to sob. But there is no relief in this outpouring, either; she fights against it, her body shaken by the effort to control herself. He gets her a glass of water, tries to make her drink it, but like a petulant child she pushes his hand away. The water slops over, spills, drenching her skirt, his trousers, yet he continues to hold the glass before her until she hiccups herself into silence, wipes her eyes and drinks the water.

But it is not over. She begins again. And this time, like a surgeon who has opened up a patient, she begins to probe, knowing it is there, the tumour, knowing it has to be found and removed for the patient to survive.

Is it because of something Sumi did, something she said? Is it because of us, because of me? Is it because I was rude to you, because I always argued with you? Is it because of what I said to you when you decided to resign? Is it money?

He can see that his silence, his negatives, drive her to desperation and she goes on to memories: 'Do you remember, Papa?' This time the appellation comes easily, she is unconscious of it.

'What can I say to you, Aru?'

'Say it, whatever it is, tell me, I am not a child.'

But it's no use, he cannot give her what she wants, what she has come here for. When she gets up to go, they have both of them the same sense of failure, they are equally exhausted.

Nothing can touch me, I had thought, I'm wearing a bulletproof vest. But what do you do when your opponent comes with a knife, gets under your skin and begins to twist it between your ribs? Aru, in her anger, reminds me of Sumi. But Sumi's anger is sharp: one clean cut and it's over, Sumi is wiping the blade and putting it away. Aru, on the other hand, is hitting out with a blunt weapon, uncaring of where the blow falls, even hurting herself in the process. Her questions are like the Yaksha's questions; a wrong answer will cost me my life. At one moment I almost blurted out what is perhaps the only thing I can say to her: I was frightened, Aru, frightened of the emptiness within me, I was frightened of what I could do to us, to all of you, with that emptiness inside me. That is the real reason why I walked away from Sumi, from you and your sisters.

Frightened—yes, it seems to be the truth, the right

answer beside which all the reasons, all the answers I so carefully framed in the right words become so much trash, crumble into dust. It seems to me, now that I have brought it out into the open, that the fear was always there in me, submerged for a time in my absorption with Sumi and my children.

We bury our fears deep, we stamp hard on the earth, we build our lives on this solid, hard foundation, but suddenly the fears come to life, and the earth shakes with their struggle to surface. It was Sudha, the sight of her when she came to us after her illness, that brought my fear back, so close that the sound of its flapping wings filled my ears to the exclusion of everything else.

Sudha had been a vigorous, healthy, confident girl. And cheerful, yes, even after our parents died she was still that. (Or was that a facade she carefully preserved for my sake?) With marriage and motherhood she blossomed, she became an attractive woman. After P.K.'s sudden death, she looked empty, as if it was all over for her. And then she underwent surgery for her tumour. She came to us to convalesce after that, and this was yet another woman—a peevish, self-centred invalid, constantly complaining of her pains. But I, who knew her so well, realized what she was doing: she was diverting us, cleverly drawing our attention away from her real pain. It was not her illness, not the depletion of her physical self with surgery and post-radiation sickness, not even P.K.'s sudden death or the fact that he died first, when she had, with the knowledge of her cancer, expected to go before him—no, I knew it was something more than all these things that made her the way she was. She had retreated from us; none of us, not her own children, nor I, her brother, nor my children whom she so dearly loved, could reach her. And she was frightened of this world of loneliness she suddenly found herself in.

When she said she wanted to go back home, I did not try to make her change her mind. I rang up her children, and Ramesh and Veena came to take her back. We went to see her off and I knew I would never see her again. She knew it, too, but she turned her face away from us, weary, it seemed, of everything and it was left to Veena and Sumi to say the usual things. And I thought: if it can happen to Sudha, the most generous and loving of women, Sudha who invested all of herself in relationships, if this crutch of family and ties failed her when she needed it most, what hope is there for any of us? Must we reach the terrible point Sudha did before realizing the truth?

Emptiness, I realized then, is always waiting for us. The nightmare we most dread, of waking up among total strangers, is one we can never escape. And so it's a lie, it means nothing, it's just deceiving ourselves when we say we are not alone. It is the desperation of a drowning person that makes us cling to other humans. All human ties are only a masquerade. Some day, some time, the pretence fails us and we have to face the truth. Like Sudha did. And I.

I had a glimpse of it, not when my parents died, for Sudha was there then, she was the link that ensured the continuity of my life, and soon after, there was P.K. as well. It happened to me when I saw Sudha's school certificate and knew that we did not share a father. That was a betrayal that cut away at the foundations of my life. Sudha never realized what this did to me. She had always known it, she said, she had not told me because—well, because my parents never had. And, she said, the truth was that she had almost forgotten that my father was not hers. He was our father, she never felt any other way.

She could not understand my reaction, she refused to accept my decision to go away, she refused to believe I meant what I was saying. When I told her I was going, she had the same stricken look on her face I had seen on her wedding day, when, bored, tired of sitting on the uncomfortable wooden folding chairs, I had walked out of the hall. She had come running out, frantic, looking garish and unlike her usual self in her wedding finery. And then she saw me, standing against a car, doodling in the dust on its surface and her face changed. But this time I was no longer a bored, confused child of eight, there was nothing I could do to wipe that look off her face.

'Where are you going?' she wanted to know, she had to know, and because I had to tell her something I told her I wanted to go back to Shivpur, the place my parents had come away from to escape the scandal that followed their marriage.

I had to go there after that, trapped into it by my own words, by Sudha's insistence on accompanying me. It was she who made a crusade of finding the house our parents had lived in. It was not easy, she had forgotten everything— she was only six when they left—and the few landmarks she remembered had disappeared. But she would not give up. In the evening when we came back to the seedy hotel we were staying in, she was irritable, exhausted, but the next morning she was ready to start the search all over again.

It was on the third day—I think—that she said, 'There it is.' Doubtfully. Then more confidently, 'Yes, that's it.' We stared at the house. I was disinterested and Sudha listless; it meant nothing to either of us. We went back to the hotel, flat and dull and sat in silence. And then I said it, what I should have told her much earlier if I had not been too much of a coward: 'I'm not going back to Bombay with you, I'm staying on here, I'm joining college here.'

She came out of her apathy in an instant and began questioning me: What was it? Was it something she had said? It couldn't be P.K., he was so good he would never hurt me, no, not even unknowingly. It had to be her. But I knew her, didn't I, she was quick-tempered, she admitted it, but surely I knew how little it meant?

From guilt I went on to annoyance and we began to quarrel, quarrels that went on and invariably ended in her desperate sobbing. I was frightened by her state, I had never seen my sister this way, not even after our parents died. I sent P.K. a telegram. He came at once with Ramesh and took charge of things immediately.

He persuaded Sudha, who had eaten almost nothing for two days, to eat and as a preliminary went to the market and got some lemons. A practical man, he bought a squeezer too, and I can remember him squeezing the juice, as earnest as any Gandhian disciple preparing for the end of Bapu's fast, while Sudha sat on the bed, legs folded under her, indifferent to everything, even the mess P.K. was making. But she drank the juice, I was astonished to see how greedily she drank it. (Later, when Viju was born, I realized she was pregnant then, which explained some of her behaviour, though not all of it.) By evening he had persuaded Sudha to let me have my way, made her agree to go back without me.

I was frantic for them to go and leave me alone, I saw them off with joy. I can still remember the crowds and noise on the station, the sound of running feet on the platform, the last-minute desperate cries of passengers, the raucous call of the vendors—*chai garam, chai chai.* Then the train left and I was alone. There was nothing left but the smooth gleaming rails. And a sudden hush, as if the train had taken away all the people, all the noise with itself.

I did not go back to the hotel that night, I did not want to be there, not even for a night, in the room that seemed to be redolent with Sudha's distress and grief. I spent the night there, on the station, on a stone platform built around a tree, watching in a dreamlike state the sleeping bundles on the floor and benches, hearing, once or twice, a child wake up and cry. Once, waking out of a doze I saw a train move out of the station in total silence, as if it was a ghost train. I got up and walked about until the first light brightened the sky, making the station lights look sickly and dim. I went then to the room P.K. had arranged for me to live in until the hostels opened. Unwashed, sleepless, I must have looked a sight, for I can remember even now my landlady's suspicious stare. But she let me in and I went to a tap in the backyard, filled a bucket with water and poured it over myself. And I felt released. Free.

Years later, I saw a Dutch painting. I knew nothing about paintings then; that it was a Dutch painting, that it was by Vermeer—I learnt these things later. But I was fascinated,

I can remember that, by the way the painter had captured a slice of time so that I was witnessing what he had seen, a bit of life in that narrow lane in a foreign land.

So I thought then. Now I know it was not just Time that the painter had captured; I was his captive too, caught inside that picture, seeing what the painter wanted me to see.

Only the creator is free, only the creator can be free because he is out of it all. I did not know this then. I know it now.

༚

ARU GOES HOME encompassed by a sense of humiliation. It is not merely the fact that she broke down before Gopal when she had determined to be in full control of herself; it is the recalling of how she had imagined it would be that mortifies her. She had been almost certain that Gopal would take her into his confidence, that the special relationship there had been between them still existed and he would reveal his feelings to her as he had not done to anyone else. She had seen herself reasoning with him, persuading him to change his mind, and then, coming back to announce that they could all go back home.

Home? What home?

She puts her scooter away, has a wash and changes without anyone noticing her, for which she is grateful. She does not want to talk to anyone about what has happened. She is glad she has not spoken to any of them about her visit, not even to Charu.

Charu senses something, nevertheless. Covertly she watches her sister getting ready for bed, the pillow set straight, the blanket unfolded, spread carefully in a wrinkle-free smoothness with a fold at the top, her slippers placed on the floor, side by side ....

'What are you staring at me for?'

Charu flushes guiltily, begins to say something, changes her mind and asks, 'Going to bed so early?'

'Yes.'

Charu does not react to the challenge in that single-word reply.

As Aru lies down, settling her head on the pillow, and pulls her blanket over herself, they hear Sumi call out, 'Aru.'

Aru closes her eyes as if shutting out the sound.

'A R U?'

'Damn!' She sits up with an angry jerk.

'I'll go,' Charu offers.

She returns to find her sister in the same position, the 'damn' expression intact on her face.

'What was it?'

'Nothing, really. Just some vague thing—you know how she is.' Charu yawns loudly, showing her tongue quivering in the cavern of her open mouth. 'God, I wish I could go to sleep and wake up late tomorrow morning. Oh well ....'

She has picked up her book and, with a weary sigh, is going back to her page when she is startled by Aru's voice.

'Why do you call her "she"?'

'What?'

'Why do you call Sumi "she"?'

'What do you mean?'

'Can't you say Sumi, or Ma, or anything else ... why do you say "she"?'

'Hey, cool it, Aru, what's with you?'

'Just because Papa has left her, it doesn't give you the right to be rude to her, it doesn't mean she's worthless ....'

'Have you gone crazy?'

'You ... think you can insult her ....'

'Shut up, Aru, just shut up, will you!'

Charu, too astonished even to be angry, sees that her sister is in a cold fury, she doesn't seem to be able to stop.

'You're showing your contempt for her when you say "she". Why,' and the question is propelled out of her with the force of a bullet, 'why do you call her "she", tell me that.'

'Oh, shut up, I don't want to talk to you when you're in this—this—this state.'

There is silence after that. Charu, tapping her teeth

with her pencil, picks up her book and turns her back resolutely on her sister. But the page is a blur, she can't read a word. It is a relief when Aru speaks in a more normal tone.

'Well, say it, go on, say it.'

Charu looks at her. Aru's body no longer has the tense look of a tightly wound spring.

'You saw Papa today, didn't you?'

'Yes.'

'It's no use, it's no use talking to him, I could have told you that. Listen to me, Aru, let's not get involved in their hassles, let's get on with our lives. All these things are not important.'

'Not important? Charu, you—you frighten me. They are our parents, it's our home and you say these things are not important!'

'They're important if you let them be. I won't. They can't mess up my life. I'm going on with what I want to do.'

'Five and a half years of medical college before you can start earning—where's the money to come from?'

'I've asked Premi-mavshi. Or rather, she asked me if she could help and of course I said yes. I'm not proud. As long as I can complete my studies, I don't care where the money comes from. I'm not like you and Ma. Make a note of that, I said Ma—not "she".'

Charu is grinning, her usual impish grin, but Aru does not respond. She is silent.

'You all right, Aru?' Charu asks hesitantly when the silence stretches between them.

'Fine. You go back to work. You're right, you just go on with your life, don't bother with all these things.'

Charu does not notice the emphasis on the 'you'. She is too relieved to have her sister back to her usual self. It seems as if they have returned to the normal level of their intimacy, but the sisters are conscious nevertheless, of a wedge-shaped shadow that has come between them.

Sumi has become aware of this, too. She sees that despite the girls having resumed, on the surface at least, the normal course of their lives, something has changed. They have withdrawn into themselves, each pursuing her own activity, interacting minimally with each other. Even the occasional bickering—over Charu's untidiness, Aru's obsessive orderliness, Seema's dependence—has ceased.

The three girls have changed in themselves, too. Aru's reserve has turned into a secretiveness. She goes out a great deal, more than she did before, and it is obvious that this has nothing to do with college or her studies. In fact, she has resigned from the Student's Council, something she had taken very seriously until now. Charu has become wholly single-minded and dogged, the intensity of her pursuit of a seat in a medical college frightening. Nothing else seems to exist for her, apart from her college, her evening classes and her books when she is at home. And though Seema, belying Sumi's fears, looks the most untouched, she keeps aloof from her mother and sisters, following Kalyani about, even holding her sari-end, as if she is reverting to that early infancy she can't possibly remember. It makes Sumi uneasy.

There's something else, too. Sumi has an odd feeling that the house is accepting them, like it did Kalyani and her daughters all those years back, making them part of itself. Sumi sees her daughters unconsciously, unknowingly, lowering their voices to the exact decibel required to keep them from being heard by their grandfather upstairs. And she thinks: I don't want my daughters to live with a hand clasped over their mouths, like Premi and I had to. And I don't want my daughters to live in a house where—where—but she can't pinpoint this until Hrishi spells it out for her.

Hrishi, who is in the same class as Charu, is now a daily visitor, picking her up for their special evening class and dropping her home after it. It is when Charu makes one of her usual jokes against him that Hrishi retorts, 'You know what you are? You're a clown. A female clown,' he adds.

'Why female clown?'

'Clowns are always males, silly.'

The girls begin to laugh at that, laughter that becomes uncontrollable at the dawning look of realization on Hrishi's face. Unnerved finally by their laughter—even Seema has joined in—he says, 'Tchah!' flapping his hands as if driving away a smell. 'Too many females here. It's like a zenana.'

And to Sumi, Hrishi's words echo something Gopal had said once—reluctantly, and only in response to her urging, her goading, rather—in explanation of his increasing silences, his withdrawal from them.

'It's not easy to be the only male in a family of females. You feel so—so—' he had hesitated and then in a rare, uncharacteristic gesture, propelled his fist into his other palm, as if breaking through something, 'you feel so shut out.'

They're right, Sumi thinks now, both Gopal and Hrishi, there's something wrong about a house with only females— or males. It's too lopsided, not balanced enough. There's already a change in our behaviour; there's a carelessness that lies, like a thin overlay of dust, over our lives. And ease, too, there's too much of it. There's none of the tension that's necessary to make us feel alive, to give us the excitement of living.

What Sumi likes even less is that Aru is becoming conscious of the situation in the house, of the queer relationship between her grandparents. Sumi has never spoken to her daughters about this, but now, living in the house, in the midst of it, there is no getting away from it. Things have changed since Sumi's childhood, Shripati is not the same to his granddaughters as he was to his own daughters, yet the oppression of his unseen self cannot but make itself felt. In this atmosphere, how can any of them, Aru especially, forget what Gopal has done, Sumi thinks.

But Aru has no intention of forgetting, no intention of letting Sumi forget, either.

'I think you should see a lawyer,' she says to her mother.

'You mean because of Gopal? Devi's been saying that to me, too, she wants me to meet Murthy's cousin who's a lawyer. But I don't see the point of it.'

'The point? The point is you've got to do something.'

'What? Get a divorce? I'm not interested.'

'But he owes you, he owes all of us, yes, you especially, he owes you—' lamely, 'something. He can't get away like this! He has to give us maintenance.'

Sumi laughs, she seems genuinely amused. 'Gopal has outsmarted the law. He's given us all that he had. And he has nothing now, not even a proper job. I don't think he's getting more than a bare subsistence from Shankar's press— so Ramesh tells me. So what can the law make him do?'

'Sumi, you're making it too easy for him, you're letting him get away with it. He's getting off scot-free. It's not right, he must be made to realize what he's done ....'

'How? By punishing him? Do you want to punish him, Aru? I don't. I'm not interested. I just want to get on with my life.' She puts an arm around Aru's shoulder. 'Let him go, Aru, just let him go. This is not good for you.'

But the feel of Aru's body, rigid and unyielding, tells Sumi that Aru will not let go.

'Let him go? As if he's a—a mere acquaintance or somebody with whom we've had a small misunderstanding? He's our father, Ma, he's your husband. How can you dismiss it so lightly? I don't understand you at all.'

But Sumi understands what Aru is doing: she's trying to reclaim, not her father, but a situation of which he was a part. I know she can never get it back, but she has to learn it herself. I can't do anything more.

Aru goes back to Gopal. He's in the press this time, working, he seems unsurprised to see her.

'This is a rush order, we've got to complete it today. It'll take me some time to be free.'

'I'll wait.'

When he comes to his room nearly an hour later, she is waiting for him. Shankar, following closely on his heels, is taken aback when he sees her. He looks awkwardly at the glass of coffee he is holding.

'Please, sir, you take this, I'll get another glass right away.'

'No, Shankar, I don't want any coffee. Aru, you ....?'

Though she recognises his unspoken desire that she should refuse it, too, Aru takes the glass from Shankar. Gopal emphatically refuses one for himself and Shankar goes away leaving them alone.

'Have some?' Aru holds out her glass.

Gopal smiles, shakes his head. Aru does not respond to the smile. She intends never to lose sight of the fact that he is an adversary. Accepting the coffee from Shankar was a blow struck at Gopal, and now, offering him some is also an act of hostility, not of friendship. Gopal recognises this.

It is a bloodless duel this time, both of them are unimpassioned and restrained. She does not ask him any questions, she tells him—how it has been for them, the feeling of displacement, the questions and innuendoes they have to face, the sense of shame and disgrace. She speaks to him of Sumi, of the change in her, of Charu and her desperation, her feeling of having been let down. She is finding it hard to stay cool now, anger is slowly rising in her, but she still holds it on a leash. She calls him a callous father—'it was Seema's birthday, you know that, you could have sent her a letter, she was waiting, we could all see that'—a cruel husband, an unfeeling man.

And then, finally, comes the question: Why did you get married at all, why did you have children?

Her eyes are fixed on his face, a cold and dispassionate regard.

There is a long pause, she can see he is deliberating his answer, finally deciding not to say anything at all.

'It's too late to think of that now, Aru. It serves no purpose arguing about these things.'

When she is sure there is no more to come from him, she speaks. 'I'm going to see a lawyer.'

There is no doubt what this is intended to be: it is a threat.

'It's not important what you do to me now, Aru. It's what you're doing to yourself that's wrong.'

'It's too late to think about me now, isn't it? Too late to show your concern.'

And on that little bit of childish spite she walks out. Both of them have been too engrossed in their conversation to notice that it has begun raining. Aru takes an angry pleasure in not wiping the seat of the scooter, in the discomfort of the wet seat. By the time she moves out of the small lane, the drizzle has become a downpour. She keeps going mechanically, her head down against the streaming rain, still in that world of hostility and pain. It takes her a while to realize that she has lost her way. Looking about, she finds herself in a place she has never seen, a lane lined by old-fashioned tiled houses that open straight on to the road. She makes a tentative turn and finds herself in equally unfamiliar territory. She comes to a crossroad and gets off her scooter, gasping slightly as the rain streams down her face, trying to find her bearings, to orient herself.

A motorcycle stops by her. 'Need any help?' the rider asks her in English.

She gives the person a wary look. But his visor is down and she can see nothing of his face.

'Yes,' she says, 'I'm lost.'

'Where do you want to go?' When she has explained, he says, 'Follow me,' and starts his engine. Suddenly he stops and peels off his waterproof jerkin. 'Wear this.'

'And you?'

'I'll be okay.'

She looks down doubtfully at the jerkin before putting it on. It's too large, the sleeves come way below her palms. She can feel, rather than see, the man's smile and she smiles herself as she rolls up the sleeves.

'Right, let's start.'

She finds her spirits rising as she follows him in and out of narrow lanes he seems very familiar with. A peculiar kind of exultation fills her as they move along the unknown streets, this unknown rider and she. The sound of the rain and of their two vehicles fills her ears to the exclusion of everything else, so that later, when she remembers this strange dreamlike ride, it comes back as if in a vaccuum, as if they were the only two persons on the road. She knows he is controlling his speed so that she can keep up with him, nevertheless when he finally stops, she is some way behind.

'Now,' he says when she comes up to him and can see that they have touched a main road, 'take that road, it goes straight to the City Station. And from there ....'

'I know my way now. And thank you,' she says, belatedly perhaps, for he has already restarted his engine, its sound drowning her voice. But he raises his hand as if he has heard her—or is he saying farewell? She watches his figure recede, become smaller and is just about to start her scooter when she remembers the jerkin.

'Oh my God!' She thinks of following him, tries to speed up, but it's no use, she has already lost him.

When she gets home she lets the jerkin dry on the seat of her scooter before she takes it in. For some reason, she does not want to talk to anyone about it. She bundles it into a plastic bag and pushes it into the lowest shelf of their wardrobe. For a while, each time she opens the wardrobe, she gets a whiff of the unfamiliar odour of a strange person and thinks of the figure on the motorcycle, riding ahead of her, heedless of the pouring rain, leading her out of those confusing lanes.

And then an uneasiness creeps in: I must return the jerkin to him. But how do I do that? Put an ad in the local paper?

Will the stranger who gave his jerkin to a girl on a scooter....
Your jerkin is with me. Come and get it.
Where are you, Sir Walter Raleigh?

Aru does not believe in fairy tales; her disconcerting questions, even as a child, had made this very clear. Nor is she going to start believing in them now. Nevertheless, the thought that she will meet the man some day, that they will recognize each other instantly, is a fantasy that she builds in her mind, one that she carefully tends and nurtures. The story always ends in mutual recognition. There never is any more.

Aru is indulging in sciamachy. She has the frustrated look of a person combating a shadow, a shadow that absorbs her anger and gives her nothing in return. As for me, it was not only her questions that daunted me, it was her look as well, the clear-eyed, judging gaze of the young female, weighing me up, finding me wanting. Don't look at me like that, I wanted to say. This look is for others, for other males, it's to protect you from them, it's not meant for me, your father.

But I could not say it. I'd opted out, I'd abdicated from that position, I cannot get back into it when it suits me. And so I said nothing. But her question comes back to me now, after she has gone and I know I was right in thinking of Aru's questions as the Yaksha's questions. How, unless you are a Yudhishtira, do you answer them both truthfully and wisely?

'Why did you marry? Why did you have children?'

It was fated. Kalyani said that. You were meant to come here, to live with us, to marry my Sumi.

If it was indeed preordained, it means that my leaving Bombay, my studying in Shivpur, my getting a job in Bangalore, coming to know about the outhouse behind Kalyani's house—all these were part of it. Or do we go back, even further back in time, to Sumi's ancestors leaving their homeland and coming here with the Peshwa's army, to my own family history ....

Preordained. Only the movies can elevate marriage to such a pedestal, making it the culminating event of a lifetime, of several lifetimes. Only Kalyani can believe that all these things happened so that Sumi and I could meet.

Why did I marry Sumi?

Because I met her—it's as simple as that. I knew it the night I escorted her and Kalyani back home after her school drama, the moonlight filtering through the trees creating a fascinating chiaroscuro on Sumi's face, while Kalyani walked between us, innocent and unaware of what was happening. Along with the knowledge, there was a frisson of danger too. I should have walked away from her then, as I had in Shivpur, turning my back on Girija and her demands. But this time I didn't. And I, who had been only a spectator, found myself getting obsessed by her presence, watching with immense pleasure the unshaded light of her person set against the dark shadows of her home.

Why didn't I leave? Is there, in fact, a plan we cannot grasp, and cannot overturn either, with our own puny actions? A predesigned pattern we cannot see because we are part of it? I remember trying to explain to Sumi that football is not just a mindless game as she thought it, it's not just a lot of grown men kicking a ball about, as she said. I tried to tell her that there is a plan behind all that aimless kicking, the seemingly haphazard passing. That all those actions which seemed futile and unconnected were in reality part of a plan, a working towards an end—a goal.

I think of this when I remember the conversation I overheard in the bus. Was that part of the plan? Would I have married Sumi if I hadn't overheard the conversation? I will never know the answer to that; to try and get at the truth now is impossible. I know this, however: it was when I heard them speak that my desire shaped itself into a definite thought. The truth, that I was going to marry Sumi, was already there, waiting for me. It was at that moment, after listening to them, that I came into collision with it.

They were in the seat just ahead of me, two young men of about my age, so absorbed in their talk that they gave the feeling of being in some quiet, isolated place by themselves. And I, sitting behind them, listening to them, became part of it too, a ghostly third in their conversation.

It was a long journey, from one bus terminus to another. The bus stopped at halts and crossroads, people got off and on, they shoved, scrambled for seats, swayed in the aisle, the conductor gave out tickets, called out the names of stops—all this must have happened. But for me there were only those two men and their talk.

They were discussing the feelings of one of them towards a girl, a neighbour, who was, I gathered, in love with him. She had made her feelings clear, subtly, yet, it seemed, unmistakably. It was the man who was not sure of his feelings. He was confused; his confusion hung like a cloud about him. He was speaking to his friend about it, asking him: What do I do?

'She's a good girl, I like her, but ....'

He spoke of what it was that was holding him back. 'She's not of our caste, she does not speak our language. What will my parents say?'

But I could guess that this was not the real problem, that the problem lay within him, making him unsure of himself. Or am I ascribing my own feelings to him? Sometimes I wonder whether I really overheard the conversation. Did I? Or did I imagine it, make it out of my own confused mind, my own ambivalent feelings towards marriage? And was I the other man too, telling me what I wanted to hear? 'Marry her,' the friend said, and he said it over and over again. 'Marry her, she's a good girl, she'll make you a good wife, I am sure of that. Marry her.'

No, I did not imagine it, I did hear it, the bus ride is still too vivid for me to have any doubts about that. But even today I cannot get over the strangeness of it, for they spoke as if for my benefit, the problem was mine, the advice for me. It was like hearing strangers relating my story, it was like hearing the end of my story in a strange place.

So I married Sumi. And I knew I was right, it was my body that told me this truth. I never had any doubts about my feelings for her. The night she came to my room, I told her to go back home, but the thought of her going away had been like death.

After marriage, there were no more doubts. I knew I needed her, her warmth, her humanness, her womanness. The life of the body—why do the saints disdain it so? It is through our bodies that we find our first connections to this world. I knew it when I saw Aru as a baby, her tiny mouth open, ceaselessly searching for the nipple, the milky fountain, for the softness and warmth of her mother's breast. Yes, for me it was right to live with Sumi, I know that even now.

And there were my children. Why did you have children? I could have answered that question: I wanted it all. And I did everything—caring for my babies, tending them, caressing them—with joy and passion. Those hours in the night when I was alone with them (it was always I who woke up, Sumi could sleep through a baby's hungry howling, but for me the smallest rustle, the tiniest whimper was enough), holding the small warm bundles in my arms, I was filled with an emotion I had never known until then.

The life of the body—yes, I revelled in it. Sumi's fragrant woman's body, the searingly clean little-girls' bodies of my children—these gave me great happiness.

But I glimpsed it even then, the truth that would soon confront me, I saw it when Sumi put the baby to her breast. For I knew, when I looked at them, that they belonged together as I never did. Even when Sumi was impatient, when she showed a flash of temper as she often did for being deprived of her sleep, they were together in that magic circle. Woman and child. And I was outside. A man is always an outsider.

I envied Sumi for this. And for this, too: for a woman, from the moment she is pregnant, there is an overriding reason for living, a justification for life that is loudly and emphatically true. A man has to search for it, always and forever.

I have faith and therefore I know who Krishna is, Sanjaya told Dhritirashtra.

I believe and therefore it exists. Stop believing and it is over in the blinking of an eyelid.

The body shrinks from annihilation—Camus is right when he says this. But there is no choice. The life of the body has to end. It was my body that told me the truth once again, my body that could lie beside Sumi night after night, quiescent, feeling nothing. After the earlier humiliation of my inability to sustain my excitement, of being unable to go on, this was peaceful. But I could not avoid the truth, I knew it was over.

When it is so possible, no, so easy, to argue out my case with the secret adversary who's always lying in wait for me in my mind, why was I struck dumb before Aru? Why could I not give my daughter the answers she so badly needs to have?

But how could I have said this to Aru: Marriage is not for everyone. The demand it makes—a lifetime of commitment—is not possible for all of us.

No, I can say these things only to Sumi. And I am still waiting for her to come to me.

૭

EACH TIME GODA comes to visit, she brings with her a stainless steel box of 'something I made just today—I thought you might like it ....'

'You are lying, Goda-mavshi. Do you think I don't know you've given up making sweets since Bhauji-kaka's diabetes? I also know what you're doing—you're trying to fatten me up.'

'And is that wrong? You need it. Look at you, look at those bones,' Goda says with the contempt of a woman whose own comfortable plumpness was always considered an asset.

Sumi knows it's true, what both Kalyani and Goda are never tired of telling her—that she has lost weight. But she feels that what she has shed is unwanted matter; what now remains is the essential. Her fine-boned body, which gives an appearance of fragility, feels full of energy. Whenever she looks into the mirror, which for so good-looking a woman she rarely does, she thinks: This is the real me.

Now that Sumi's face has lost its rounded contours, the resemblance between her and Aru is suddenly marked. An air of gravity links them to each other and, though neither of them realizes it, to Manorama, Kalyani's mother, whose picture hangs in the hall. There are sudden flashes of resemblance connecting the three women, the different generations, creating a sense of continuity in the house.

Sumi, unaware of this, has increasingly begun feeling an intruder in her parents' house. We're interlopers, she thinks, my daughters and I. Just passing through.

From where has this idea come to her? From her childhood? From the conversation between Kalyani and Goda? (Not from anything said, perhaps, but from the silences that seem to put the unsaid words in parentheses, emphasizing them, making them significant.) Or, from the walls of this house that seem to cry out that the very reason for their existence was a son?

A son is born to me, dear friend, a son is born to me.

It was Goda who sang the song at Nikhil's naming ceremony, a song full of joy, a woman sharing her joy in the birth of her son with her friends.

Nine months I bore the pain and now my house is filled with light.

Sumi saw it then, the adoration of the male child. It must have been this way in the stable in Bethlehem, in Nanda's house on the banks of the Yamuna in Gokul. The male child belongs.

'I have no right to be here,' Sumi says to her father. 'I feel a parasite.'

Each time she enters this room, it is like taking a step back into childhood. Nothing in the room has changed since then, except for the music system which is a recent acquisition. The same books are still piled on the shelves and on the low window sills. And, in some way, as it often happens, the room seems to have taken on, through the years, the personality of the man inhabiting it, so that there is something guarded about it, an air of reserve, the very light in it being carefully doled out by the long narrow windows.

'You don't know how easy it is to become a parasite.'

'Parasite? What do you mean?'

'There's Ramesh ready to give me money, and Devi and Premi, of course. And now you're asking me if I need any money. It's so easy for me to take it from all of you, to go on living here free, sponging on you.'

'Don't talk nonsense. This is your home. You belong here.'

His voice is stern, but the words penetrate her armour.

Her throat works, she is afraid she will lose control over herself.

'And don't speak of parasites.' He uses the English word as she had done. 'I would never encourage you to be one, I always wanted you to be independent.'

Sumi is never allowed to forget it, she is always reminded that the room entombs not just her father's ambition for himself, but his ambitions for her as well. She was to fulfil the ambition he had given up when he came back here at his dying sister's request, she was to take up where he had left off, become a distinguished lawyer, and—who knows?—perhaps a judge, like Premi's father-in-law, the man who had once been Shripati's colleague.

It had seemed an honour at first, a privilege to be allowed to enter this room, to touch the books, to open them. By the time she was a girl, dusting them was nothing more than a boring chore. And when she realized why her father was letting her do these things, it became the prisoner's stone-breaking duty; she wanted none of it. When she married Gopal, she walked out on everything.

'I'm looking for a job, Baba. I have some money right now, but I'll need a job soon.'

'A teacher's job? Have you got anything?'

'Only the vague promise of one. A temporary place. A teacher is going abroad for six months, her daughter's having a baby. But that, if I get it at all, will only be next term.'

'And in the meantime, if you need money, ask me. Look upon it as a loan if you want. Don't let pride come in your way.'

'Pride? What pride do I have, Baba?'

To her own surprise and consternation, the tears she had suppressed a little while back, gush out.

'That was stupid of me,' she says when she has managed to control herself. 'And don't worry, if I need any money I will ask you. But living here free, I think I can make what we have last quite a while.'

'The girls need things, don't they, clothes and all that, apart from fees and books?'

'I won't let them want, Baba.'

'Good. And why don't you call some of your friends home? That girl with the silly laugh—what's her name ...?

'Vani?'

'Yes, call her home. You need company.'

He's confused, he thinks I'm still a teenager, that I can find comfort in the company of friends. Yet, when I was at home, he disapproved of all my friends. Boys, especially. He saw me once with a boy and said, 'Remember my dignity.' And then I found Gopal right here at home ....

The sound of Hrishi's motorbike rouses her. 'There's Charu. Time for our dinner.'

'That fellow's rash. I don't like Charu going out on his motorcycle.'

'It saves her time, Baba. And, anyway, how else would she go for her evening classes? There's no bus going that way.'

'He shouldn't be having a motorcycle at all, not at his age. His parents spoil him.'

'Let them.'

'What?'

'Let them spoil him. He's their son after all.'

He seems taken aback by her retort. For a moment, he stares at her silently.

'I suppose you think I'm a stupid old man,' he says after a pause.

'Old, yes, stupid, no.'

He goes on as if she hasn't spoken. 'I can't believe it myself, that I'm old. I look at my hand,' he holds out one and there is a distinct tremor in it, 'and I think—but that's an old man's hand! Is it really mine? Strange how quickly it all happens—it's over in a flash.'

She closes the door gently behind her when she goes out. Baba doesn't like any noise—the knowledge is part of her. Yes, I thought I knew him, but this—he's never spoken like this before. And as she stands there, thinking of her father, a strange thing happens. It is like a visitation, an apparition that she sees, not all at once, but gradually, developing before her like a sketch, the lines finally becoming a recognisable figure.

Kalyani. It is Kalyani she sees standing before the closed door, banging on it with her open palms, shrieking out something, slumping at last on the floor, her head resting against the still closed door. All the sounds fading away, finally leaving a silence that enclosed the thudding of a heart. The heart of a child who stood there terrified, watching her mother lie in a huddle. No sounds at all except this throbbing rubadub rubadub. And the child going down stiffly, holding on to the banister, her wet palms making a sliding sound on the smooth surface, her legs wobbling, thinking—I didn't see it, I saw nothing, nothing happened.

Now, after all these years, it can no longer be denied. It did happen. I saw it, I saw my mother lying there. And a little later I saw Goda helping her down, and Kalyani, as if foreshadowing her old age, bent, clinging to the banisters, her face spent and hollow.

Who was it had told her once about a person walking through a glass door? Sumi can't remember, but the story has stayed with her and comes back to her now. 'And can you believe it, afterwards there was the shape, the exact shape of that person in the glass. The edges were bloodstained, tiny drops of blood, it looked quite pretty really, like small red beads decorating the glass.'

Sumi hadn't believed the story then. Surely, she had argued with whoever it was had told her this, no one could walk through a sheet of glass! Even if it was a new unoccupied house, they'd have drawn a chalked cross on the glass, wouldn't they? And even if such an unlikely thing were to happen, let's say you don't notice the glass because you're in a hurry, or looking the other way and you run into it, surely the glass would break and shatter into bits! Punching the shape of your body in the glass? What kind of an impossible story was that?

And yet the image of a blood-edged human shape has remained with her. And now, remembering Kalyani banging wildly, vainly, at the closed door of her husband's room, she thinks—yes, it could happen. You can walk out leaving your own blood-edged shape behind.

But why am I thinking of the past, and my mother's past, at that? Today, now, this moment is enough for me; she had said this to Gopal once.

'But, Sumi, even this needlepoint of a moment, this now, is receding from you as you speak of it, it is becoming the past. How can you disclaim the past? It is never possible.'

She had laughed then at Gopal's sophistry and argued against him. Once it's over, I've finished with it, she had said.

No, that's not possible, it's never possible. Gopal was right. Kalyani's past, which she has contained within herself, careful never to let it spill out, has nevertheless entered into us, into Premi and me, it has stained our bones, Premi's more obviously perhaps, but mine as well. And will this, what is happening to me now, become part of my daughters too? Will I burden them with my past and my mother's as well?

'In our children, my dear Copperfield, we live again.'

But do we also, like limpets, like the Old Man, climb on to their shoulders, taking a free ride on their lives? She thinks of this when Goda, a dedicated matchmaker who takes a creative pleasure in arranging marriages, speaks to Kalyani about a 'boy' who's come from the States and wants to get married before he goes back. Though the conversation is between Kalyani and Goda, the girls seem to understand that it is directed at them.

Charu enters into it head-on, asking 'Will I do, Goda-ajji? Amma, you had better give her my photograph and yes, my horoscope too. I hope you have one ....'

'Silly girl! Everything is a joke to this child.'

'I'm not joking, I'm dead serious. Goda-ajji, do you think I'm not a suitable girl? What's wrong with me, tell me that.'

'Really, Kalyani-akka, this girl is ....'

'It's Aru's turn first. Yours comes after that. Until Aru is married, we're not giving your photograph or horoscope to anyone.'

'Crushed! I think it's terribly unfair. Why do I have to wait for Aru? You better hurry up, Aru, or else all these wonderful boys will have got married and ....'

'I'm never going to get married.'

Aru's tone, unlike Charu's, is wholly serious, her face makes it clear that she means what she says.

'Aru, you shouldn't talk that way.'

Aru says nothing, just gives Kalyani a level look. And it is Kalyani's eyes that fall, Kalyani who changes the subject.

I must move out of this house, Sumi thinks, I must look for a house for my daughters and myself, I can't go on living here. But how and where do I begin to look for one?

Sumi finds a most unlikely ally in her search for a house. It is on an impulse that she enters an estate agent's office, impelled into it by the sight of the board outside, thinking— yes, of course, I can get a house through an agent. When she enters, however, her heart sinks at the sight of the overweight, coarse-looking man in the tiny cubicle. She almost turns round to go out again, but the man, speaking into the phone, takes her in with a quick shrewd glance and gestures to her to sit down. His conversation on the phone sounds more like a quarrel, his voice rude and sharp, the words and language scarcely concealing contempt.

'What can I do about it? You should have thought of it earlier.' Finally saying, 'It's your problem, not mine,' he puts down the phone and turns to her.

Sumi is to realize later that he talks to everyone in exactly the same way, there is nothing personal in his acrimony, it's part of him. Now, however, she is put off. And yet, to her own surprise, she finds herself listing her requirements when he asks her, 'And what do you want, madam?'

He doesn't seem to be listening to her, he's fiddling wth some papers on his table, tapping his fleshy beringed fingers on it, impatient, as if waiting for her to finish and go.

'Right,' he says when she has done. 'We'll do it.'

He always speaks in the plural, she realizes this, too, later, though the only other person in the office is a boy who takes pleasure in being ruder and surlier than his boss.

'Yes, we'll do it.'

She's reluctant to leave on that uncertain note but he is already dialling a number, obviously finished with her. She stands up, still waiting. He seems surprised to find her not gone.

'You have your own transport? Right, come tomorrow. This time. I'll show you some houses.'

She is certain he will have forgotten all about her, but when she goes to him the next day, he is ready and waiting for her. The first day sets the tone for their joint search, which is what it becomes. He speaks to her in English, calls her may-dum, she speaks in Kannada, calls him Nagaraj-avare. Neither gives in; she is careful never to lapse into English, only occasionally fumbling for a word. If he does slip into Kannada once in a while, he corrects himself almost immediately.

She soon learns that they are speaking different languages in more ways than one. 'This is a good house, madam. One room, hall, nice kitchen. It is correct for you.'

But when she gets there, she finds the hall is only a passage, the room airless and narrow, the kitchen has no sink ....

'Good house, madam, no problem of security.'

And it's just two rooms in the midst of a nest of similar two-room homes.

And so it goes on.

He listens with unflappable composure to all her questions, her complaints. Only once does he retort, and then not with anger.

'Madam, you want a house worth Rs 5,000 for 1,000. Who will give it to you?'

She begins to realize that he is evasive, devious. He takes

her to see houses to which he does not have the keys, promising he'll get the keys the next day if she likes the house. And they peer through the windows like a pair of voyeurs.

'Nagaraj-avare,' she says in exasperation once when he takes her to a wholly unsuitable house, 'I have three young daughters going to school and college. I can't possibly live in a place where there are no buses, not even a proper road.'

'Madam, I will try to get a good house for you and your daughters, but you also have to adjust a little bit. See, it is like this. My wife goes to buy a sari. They keep showing her saris and she says, show me this colour with a different border, this design in another colour. But in the end she buys a sari, doesn't she? She wears it, doesn't she? She begins to like it, doesn't she? A house is like that. Start living in it and it becomes yours, you will like it. People who build houses for rent don't build for you. If you want a house with everything the way you like, you will have to build your own.'

Build your own house?

That evening she begins doodling on a piece of paper, doodles that soon become a sketch. A sketch of a house, her perfect house, it is supposed to be. But a strange thing happens. When it is done, she finds she has drawn a sketch of this, the Big House. She destroys it and starts afresh, but once again it is the same. It is as if there is a tracing of this house already on the paper, on any paper that she begins to draw on and the lines she draws have no choice but to follow that unseen tracing.

Sumi has so far kept her house-hunting crusade secret from everyone, even her daughters, but Aru and Charu see her with Nagaraj and it is out. The girls are so aghast at the thought of her going about with a man like Nagaraj that the fact that she is looking for a house is almost forgotten.

'Ugh, Ma, how can you! Going about with a creep like that! That cap of his and those dark glasses! And that shirt! My God!'

'Don't be such snobs,' Sumi says reprovingly, but she knows what they mean. She had felt that way herself at first; now she knows him better. And their relationship has changed. For one thing, he has begun speaking to her in Kannada which makes their conversation more natural. And if, because of the language, there is a kind of brusque familiarity in the way he talks to her, there is nothing offensive about it. He treats her, in fact, like a nutty relation towards whom he has some duty.

'Don't tell people your husband is not living with you,' he suggests when she has explained her household to a prospective landlord. 'People think wrongly, sometimes they take advantage of you.'

Something, she realizes, he has never done. In fact, it is only now that he reveals his knowledge of the fact that she will be living alone.

'What do I say? Do I tell a lie?'

'Say he has been transferred. That he is working abroad—America or Dubai or something.'

Ever her rejection of his 'correct' houses does not seem to anger him any more. She wonders whether his patience, surprising in a man normally so rude and impatient, comes from some soft sentimental core in him that responds to her plight, to the fact that she has three daughters. (She has seen his children's names on the spare tyre of his scooter.) Sometimes, in her more cynical moments, she thinks the change in him dates from the day he saw the Big House.

'Rented house?'

'No, it belongs to my parents.'

'When you have this, why do you go searching for houses?'

'I want something of my own.'

Silly fool, his look had seemed to say.

Now here he is, once again promising her a house.

'I know you will like this one. I am showing you first because I think it is right for you, very safe for you and your daughters.'

She has learned not to take his professional spiel seriously, but a note of excitement in his voice, unusual in so phlegmatic a man, promises something positive.

'They are an old couple, they want a decent family—like yours. They are more interested in good people, in decent company, than in money. I told them about you and they are willing to adjust a little about the rent, maybe even the deposit.'

When she sees the house, a brand new apartment built above an old home, she is hopeful for the first time.

'It's perfect,' she says when they have gone through the house. 'I'll take it.'

For a man who rarely smiles, it is as if he is beaming.

'Right, we'll make it final. If we don't do it, someone will come tomorrow with money and we will lose it. You have your cheque book with you?'

'Yes, but I may not be able to give them the entire amount today.'

'No problem, give some, now. If they like you,' and it's like some magic formula, this mantra of liking, 'they won't mind.'

'Ramchandra Rao at home?' he asks the woman who silently takes the keys from him.

She shakes her head.

'Will he be back soon? Can we wait here?' Without waiting for an affirmation, he tells Sumi, 'You sit here, madam, with Amma. I'll wait outside.'

The woman does not sit; she stands leaning listlessly against the door, scarcely aware of Sumi.

'If I could have some water ...?' Sumi asks.

They will like you, he had said. But she doesn't even look at me.

But when the woman returns with the water, she sits opposite Sumi and watches her with an intent look that is as disconcerting as her earlier indifference.

A Matter of Time • 81

'How many children do you have?'

The question comes the moment Sumi puts the glass down.

'Three.'

'Sons? Daughters?'

'Daughters.'

'We have only one son.'

The sense of something wrong makes itself unmistakably felt. Sumi feels a prickling of her skin, a premonition of something fearful coming.

'He died three months back. In a car accident. He was returning from Mysore.'

There is nothing that can be said to a person who looks this way, who speaks this way.

'We built the upstairs flat for him. He was to get married. If we live together, Amma, he told me, there will be problems. But I don't want to go far away from both of you. He said that. I don't want to go far away, he said ....'

Sumi's hands begin to shake. Don't, she wants to say, don't tell me anything; but it is as if she has been struck dumb. The woman cries with dreadful ease, like a person who has had an enormous amount of practice. Sumi, unable to remain still any longer, puts out a hand, but even before she can touch her, the woman says, 'Go away'. Sumi draws her hand back. 'Go away, just leave me alone.'

Sumi is starting her vehicle when Nagaraj, hearing the sound, crushes the stub of his cigarette under his foot and comes rushing to her.

'What happened?'

'Nothing.'

'Why are you going? He'll be here soon, I told you we have to ....'

'I don't want the house.'

'What!'

'I said I don't want the house.'

'But what happened? Did the woman say something?'

Can't he hear her moaning? She is desperate to get away from the sound.

'I don't want the house. Is that quite clear?'

He stares at her. There is no doubt she means what she is saying.

'All right. Do what you want. I can't waste any more time on you. It's impossible to deal with you. Namaskara!'

He claps his hands together with such force, the sound is like a shot.

She has gone some way before she realizes she does not know the way back home. She has followed Nagaraj to this place and there are no landmarks she can remember, to orient herself. She is coasting along slowly, looking at the signboards on shops, hoping for some clue, when she sees the board.

'Shree Manjunath Press. Prop. C.D. Shankar.'

Without thinking, she enters the gate. Three children are playing in the courtyard. The oldest, a girl, seeing her instantly asks, 'You want Gopalsiruncle?'

She does not at first understand the girl, the three words running into one making of it a strange, unrecognisable name.

'Yes.'

'He is up there. Go up, aunty.'

The door is open. Gopal is at the table reading and having his meal at the same time. The different containers of a tiffin-carrier are spread out before him and he is eating directly out of them. He looks up at the sound of her steps. For a moment his face gives her the impression that he has not identified her. Then he closes the book and says, asks rather, in a puzzled sort of way, 'Sumi?' And then again, 'Sumi.' He gets up, pats the bed with his left hand and says, 'Come, sit.'

She feels the need to explain. 'I was passing by. I saw the board and came in.'

'What are you doing in this area?'

'House hunting.'

She has a strong, almost overpowering desire to talk to him about it, about the woman and her grief, but he does not follow this trail and she is forced to let it go. In a while, she realizes she could not have spoken to him about it, anyway.

They have not met since the day he left home, since the night he told her of his desire to get away. A burden of unsaid things lies between them, but neither is able to speak of these; they suddenly seem irrelevant. Yet they have to talk, for silence is even more dangerous, more treacherous. And so they speak of Shankar and his family, of the children playing outside, of Gopal's work in the press.

The conversation between them is spasmodic, punctuated by the clink of his stainless-steel containers, the voices of the children in the courtyard calling out numbers—'tonty-two tonty-three'. A film song floats in from somewhere in the locality. There is a tension between them that both are aware of, and their dialogue is clipped, a parody of a husband and wife speaking at the end of the day.

Sumi can see the effort Gopal makes to speak of something personal.

'Ramesh told me you're likely to start on a job soon.'

'Hopefully. Do you know Aru's thinking of consulting a lawyer?'

'She told me that.'

'She was here?'

'Yes. She's on your side, do you know that?'

'This is not a war, I don't want the children to take sides, Gopal,' she flashes out.

'It's inevitable. Don't you remember Yudhishtira's "we are five Pandavas against a hundred Kauravas. But when an enemy comes, we are a hundred and five against the enemy"? I'm the enemy now. She can't help seeing it that way.'

He has finished eating, he begins piling the containers together. 'I'll be back in a moment, I have to wash my hands.'

She has been looking around the room, not examining it like Kalyani had done, but with a feeling of *deja vu*. And like Gopal himself, she connects it to his room in the outhouse.

> *I like a bird that flies in,*
> *perches in the courtyard*
> *and then flies away*
> *the very same instant.*
> *So should one live.*

Gopal used to sing this Purandaradasa song, I can remember him singing it. This is how he lived in our outhouse room, it is how he is living here now. Does he still sing it? What does he think of when he comes to the lines, 'like children at play/who build a mud house and then/tiring of the game/destroy it and go away'? Does he think of himself?

Restless, she gets up and starts moving about. The children are singing a song now, she can't catch the words for a while. Then, as the voices rise to a crescendo, she gets them: 'We'll catch a fox, put him in a box and never let him go.'

The voices rise in triumph on the 'never', emphasize it gleefully.

'My God!'

Smiling, she moves to the window, but she can't see the children. Only a small patch of the yard is visible—a woman's blue sari vanishing as she moves away, a flash of light on a gleaming surface, the wheel of a scooter. She moves to the other end of the window and now it's a pile of coconut fibres that comes into the range of her vision. And empty coconut shells, a jerry-can lying on its side—all the rubbish of a household. It's like seeing Gopal's life, tantalisingly disjointed, bits and pieces she can't put together, can't make any sense of.

And then she hears his voice. He is responding to someone, perhaps a servant woman, offering to wash up for him. The children call out to him and she hears him laugh. And, as if his voice knits everything together, she can suddenly see the substance, the reality of his life apart from her and their children. All these lives, contiguous to his, spell out the actuality of their separation.

We can never be together again. All these days I have been thinking of him as if he has been suspended in space, in nothingness, since he left us. But he has gone on living, his life has moved on, it will go on without me. So has mine. Our lives have diverged, they now move separately, two different streams.

She comes back into the room and sitting at the table, idly begins turning over the pages of the book Gopal was reading when she entered. A book of poems. She begins reading.

Gopal, coming in, finds her resting her head on the table.

'Sumi!'

Her face, when she raises it, is tearless. They stare at each other in silence.

'I must go,' she says.

He does not speak, he does nothing to stop her.

This is the moment I was waiting for, the moment of accounting. But when Sumi came, it was not to call me to account; in fact, she seemed distracted, only half aware of me, blown in by some violent feelings I had no clue to. I could only sense her distress; something had happened, but she did not, perhaps she could not, share it with me. And I felt I had no right to ask her, either. Nor could I ask her why she left as abruptly as she did.

Sumi has changed: they have said it to me—Kalyani, Aru, Devaki, Ramesh—in varying tones of sadness, reproach and anger. Changed from what? Is there one inviolate self, deviation from which becomes change? It was Sumi who made me think of this when, laughing at her own idea, she spoke of Draupadi's disguise as Sairandhri, the queen's maid.

'Don't you think this was something she had often wanted, to be by herself, to sleep alone, to be free, for a while, of her five husbands?'

Why not? Sumi is right, it's very possible. (But only a woman could have thought of this.) To have the pleasure, the liberty of being alone, her own mistress, not to have to share her bed every night with a husband—yes, she must have longed for it. And therefore, perhaps, the role of Sairandhri, when she had to adopt a disguise.

We had followed the thought with pleasure, I remember it now, Sumi and I, losing ourselves in surmises. What about Arjuna becoming Brihannala? Yes, that was easy; Arjuna, tired of the male world of war and violence, of relating to woman only as lord and conqueror, became Brihannala, the eunuch, so that he could enter the gentle world of women, of music and dancing and become an insider in this world.

Myriad selves locked in one person. I can see Sumi before the dressing-table, one of those with three mirrors. And the triptych of images in the three mirrors, each image slightly different. From which self has Sumi changed?

I think of the girl on the stage acting the bereaved mother, Kisa Gotami, with all the stage accoutrements of grief: hair loose, white sari and tear-choked voice. And the other Sumi, the girl I saw flashing about her home, was there too, darting out of those eyes, in the face framed in those two sleek wings of her hair, asking us, her audience: Am I not doing this well? Am I not a good actress?

And then the girl, my landlady's daughter, walking home with Kalyani and me, staggering a little in her sleepiness, floating on the cloud of euphoria of her success on the stage. As we moved out from under the shadows of the trees into the bright moonlight, I saw her face—the make-up inexpertly wiped off, patches still clinging to the corners of her mouth and nose, behind her ears, under her chin, the eyeblack smeared round her eyes, traces of it on her cheeks. Innocent, clownish, vulnerable—a self towards whom my mind leapt out in a startled tenderness.

But of all her various selves, it is the Sumi I saw that evening by the river who seems to me the essence of her being, the Sumi I always see lurking behind the person she presents to the world.

We were visiting Hegde, Sumi and I, and Aru was with us. I can remember my disappointment when I met Hegde; it was as if in the ten years since we'd last met, he had become a much smaller man. It was my fault, of course, that I had expected to see the larger-than-life hero I had made of him in our college days. He seemed much subdued too, as if chastened by his prison term during the Emergency. A man, he gave me the impression, who had accepted his lot as headmaster of a school in a small town with no regrets, no more ambitions left in him.

But I soon realized that the old Hegde still lay within. At Sumi's remark that he looked a little like the pictures of Shakespeare (and it's true that with his high forehead, long nose and slightly exophthalmic eyes, he had a look of the Bard), he jumped effortlessly, almost with glee, into his old arguments about the continuance of our bondage to the British—cultural now, not political, and therefore much worse and more difficult to fight. But through it all, his unreserved pleasure in my visit, in meeting my wife and child, revealed itself; reviving the old comradeship lit a spark in him, almost brought back the fiery, opinionated Hegde.

He took us to the river in the evening. There were others with us, the local doctor, I think, another man who never spoke, I can't remember who he was, and their wives. But it is only Sumi I can think of when I remember that evening. She was—what is the right word for the way she was, that evening? Joyous? No, it was more than that. Irradiated perhaps, as if a spotlight was shining on her. None of us could take our eyes off her. Even Hegde, the die-hard bachelor, Hanuman as he was called in college, seemed bemused by her; his eyes kept lingering on her face in an innocent, childlike wonder.

Yes, that was how she was that evening. I can remember Aru—only two then—putting her arms around her mother's neck, whispering in her ears, and Sumi laughing, a laughter holding so much happiness within it that it spilled over, spread, and the women were laughing with her, too. A little later the women went into the river—Sumi persuaded them—and though we decorously turned our backs on them we could hear the sounds of their splashing, the laughter and the frolicking. And the silent man, as if this brought back some remote past of which we had all been a part, began to sing. I can remember the song too—it was part of the enchantment of that evening. It was a song strung in the language of women, bringing to your mind pictures of girls, pots on head, going to the river for water.

'Come, sister, let us go ....'

The women's voices were silenced when the song began and they joined us a little later, sitting with us this time, as if the song had erased the dividing line between us. Sumi's face was tranquil, all the effervescence settled down, leaving behind a clear sparkle like that of crystal. And her skin, the skin for which I had so often tried to find a comparison and failed, was glowing after her bath, reflecting the pearly glow of the evening.

The sun sank as we sat there and it was the hour of twilight, poised between day and night. The world was bathed in a mellow light, a light that had a kind of distilled clarity so that everything, even the smallest blade of grass, was clearly and distinctly visible. A little later we went to the temple by the river, so tiny a place that it was no more than a shelter for the two idols inside. We stepped over the high, broad stone threshold and were instantly engulfed in darkness. And a chill that reached out to us from the stone walls, from the stone floor under our feet.

Someone rang the bell, as if to announce our arrival to the gods, and it clanged and reverberated in that small space. My heart began to beat a loud tattoo in response to that boom boom, I felt it expand in my chest, suffocating me. Aru was in my arms and she clung to me convulsively, I could feel her breath, warm and sweet on my cheeks. The smell of oil hung heavy and cloying in that low-roofed space, the lights dim to the point of extinction. Suddenly they spluttered—the priest had come in on seeing us, I could see his fingers moving about the wick; and then there was a steady glow. He lit the other lamps, too, and the lights shone clear and steady, an aureole about them. And it was as if the gods had suddenly moved forward into being amongst us, there was a palpable sense of their presence in our midst.

Venkatesh and Padmavati—the priest spoke of them with affection and familiarity as he made his preparations for the aarti. When the aarti began, the silent man began to sing, again a Purandaradasa song, this time that most beautiful and joyous song, resounding with the word 'Ananda'. His voice had a resonance like the bell, but strangely, now there were no echoes. I had the fanciful thought that the gods were accepting the song as their *naivedya*, absorbing all of it, leaving nothing behind but the sweetness of the word 'Ananda'. And Sumi's face, with its diaphanous veil of light and shadows, flickering as the aarti lamps moved, was as serene as the stone face of the goddess.

That night, in Hegde's bachelor home, I drowned myself in Sumi. Ananda, Ananda—the word swung in my mind like a bell, it pealed and echoed in it. I repeated the words of the song to Sumi, worshipping her from head to toe and it was not sacrilege but an echo of the same supreme joy Purandaradasa had found in his Lord, Vithala. I felt my being drown 'in hers, I was close to that great mystery, the otherness of my self. And I got it, a glimpse of the purest joy, the purest metal, untouched by any base alloy.

And then Aru woke up and cried and Sumi got up and went to her. And lying there, feeling bereaved, as if my child had been torn from me, I thought—the bliss is only for a moment. We can never possess it. It touches us and goes on, it is never ours.

And when Sumi returned, how strange it is, she had the face of the Sumi I saw here, in this room, today, as if she was there even then, waiting for me, the Sumi who raised her tearless face from the table.

Ananda. The word comes back to torment me. How could I have imagined myself to be that Sananda Govinda whom Jayadeva sang of, how did I think I could hold love and joy within me forever?

ॐ

THE FAMILY

Whatever wrong has been done by him,
his son frees him from it all;
therefore he is called a son. By his
son a father stands firm in this world.

—*Brhad-aranyaka Upanishad* (I.5.17)

IT WAS THEIR preoccupation with the past that brought Gopal and his landlady, Kalyani, together. And yet, no two persons could have viewed the past so differently. For Kalyani, everything is preordained, we are only the instruments. Even Bhagiratha's bringing the Ganga down to earth is not, as it is to Gopal, a magnificent act of human determination, but the story of a man playing out his destined role. In Gopal's view, however, the plot of humankind evolves through our lives, it is the human will that sets things in motion. Even if the pattern that finally emerges is nothing like what was intended, even if the human will fails in achieving its object, it can never be discounted. Human history, according to him, is fired by human desire. 'The beginning lies in desire'—what the *Natyashastra* says about the plot of a drama is for him, true about the drama of humankind as well.

And yet, however different their thinking, sometimes, somewhere, the two theories collide, criss-cross one another. Gopal is not immune to the fascination of strange, unknown forces operating on our lives, shaping them in spite of ourselves, while Kalyani is conscious, too, of certain human actions that shape events. Kalyani's family document is one of the points of conjunction. If each sees in it her/his theory validated, nevertheless, both of them realize that there is something more to it, something that, if not contradicting the theory, is yet the exception that proves the general rule.

'You married me because of my family.'

Sumi had said it to Gopal, not accusingly, not even reprovingly, but laughing at him, at the idea. And Gopal had to admit to himself, to her, that there was some truth in it. After hearing Kalyani's family history, he could never look at Sumi without seeing the subterranean stream of the past running under the clear runnels of her young girlhood; the honeycomb texture of her being was, for Gopal, soaked in the history of her family.

'Two pearls have been dissolved, seven gold mohurs have been lost and of the silver and copper the total cannot be cast up.'

The aftermath of Panipat. That disastrous defeat which changed the history of the country. These words which had conveyed the news of the disastrous loss of the hopes of an entire people were what had propelled Gopal into studying the history of the Marathas. It fascinated him, the story of these people who, from their hilly, coastal homeland, set out to conquer and spread themselves through vast territories from the Punjab to Cape Comorin. And Kalyani's family was part of this history. For a man whose own history stopped, as he saw it, with the bodies of his parents crushed against a wall, this thought fascinated him, it set his imagination alight.

Kalyani showed him her family document only after she realized that Gopal's subject was history, that his interest lay in Maratha history. He knew, from the way she spoke of it and handled it, that it was sacred to her. It had been written sometime in the first half of the 19th century by one of the family. Additions had obviously been made later; the eulogising of a nondescript person gives the hint that it was his son who did it. But the basic facts, the early history, is clear and unmuddled.

Vishwasrao, the man with whom the family history begins for Kalyani, came down South with Madhavrao Peshwa on one of his expeditions to the Karnatak. The date is not mentioned, though Gopal makes it to be 1766. It was when the army, in the course of its march, was camped on the banks of the Kaveri that Vishwasrao, bathing in the river one early morning, found a stone idol of Ganapati. A significant event which changed his life, for not only was Ganapati the Peshwa's family deity, the battle which was fought a few days after this resulted in the Peshwa's victory. Connections were inevitably made between the finding of the idol and this victory and the finder's fortunes were made. Vishwasrao was asked to install the idol in a temporary shelter, to stay there as its guardian, and as a reward and incentive was granted all the lands surrounding that area.

And so, even after the army left, the family stayed on. Madhavrao Peshwa died, Maratha power was splintered, threatened by the British and later, the territory went back to Haider Ali following an agreement with Raghunath Rao, the then Peshwa. But all this made no difference to the family; they were too deeply entrenched by then as powerful landlords and collectors of revenue for the region.

The hero of the family document is undoubtedly Vishwasrao. His role in Peshwa Madhavrao's entourage is not very clear, but whatever he was, Vishwasrao was obviously a very clever man and an ambitious one, who missed no opportunity to retain and enlarge his power. Praise, however, is not reserved for him alone; it is indiscriminately distributed by the writer of the document among many others. If Vishwasrao is the hero of the story, there are other claimants to minor stellar roles. Such and such a one, the document states, was a great soldier, a hero who died in the service of the Peshwa, this man was a learned scholar honoured by one and all, this one was charitable and generous, while another was a saintly man who, giving up all material possessions, ended his days in the Ganapati temple.

(Of the women, there is nothing. They are only an absence, still waiting to be discovered, something that only Aru will notice later. But that is altogether another story, it has no place here.)

Kalyani believes implicitly in the document. To her, the men are what the document says they are—heroic, generous, learned, saintly. Gopal, not blinded by family loyalty and pride, could see the holes and inconsistencies in the story told by this Vyasa. Without mentioning exactly what Vishwasrao's position in Madhavrao's entourage was, the impression is created that he was close to the Peshwa, that he was part of his inner circle. (A great deal is made of the fact that Madhavrao, on a later expedition, worshipped at the temple and gave money for its extension and maintainence.) Which, Gopal knows, is not true; he has not been able to find Vishwasrao's name in any of the records of the expeditions.

He was, this much can be conjectured, one of a large family of children, with a streak of adventure (or desperation?) that made him forsake his meagre family lands and follow the Peshwa on his expeditions. There was enough family spirit in him though, for him to get two of his brothers to join him later and share his prosperity. Though he was not a soldier, the record makes frequent mention of his bravery. (Gopal finds it intriguing that a Brahmin family should take pride in claiming martial qualities. Proof of Toynbee's theory of mimesis of the creative minority?). One of his sons, however, died fighting in a battle—most probably, the battle of Chinkurali. But their glory really rested on their prosperity, and that prosperity on the initial bit of luck in finding a stone idol, in the grant of lands that followed and in becoming revenue collectors for the region. And, of course, keeping on the right side of the rulers—whoever they were.

Though the document speaks with fervour of Madhavrao, after his death the family did not stay loyal to the Peshwas. The truth was that if they were to survive in this foreign land which they were preparing to make their own, they had to make their peace with the local rulers and become their loyal subjects. It took all their diplomacy, all their guile, to stay afloat, until they reached a stage of prosperity when it was they who were courted by successive rulers. And then they belonged.

Traitors? Kalyani would scorn the word. And Gopal is

inclined to agree with her. In that era of flux, when the Marathas, Haider and his son, Tipu, the Nizam, the local Mysore rajas and the two foreign powers were all fighting for control, when rulers changed in quick succession, what did loyalty mean? When bits of kingdoms were bought and sold, when rulers bartered away land in exchange for peace, to whom was loyalty owed? And in any case, the family stayed loyal to the things that they considered mattered—to their caste, their status and their ideas of themselves. They clung tenaciously to their language, Marathi, and each generation imported brides from the 'homeland' so that the original language should not be lost or corrupted. (Though eventually, inevitably, it was.) The generation after Vishwasrao's sons gave up the pretence of soldiering and settled down to being landlords, using the soldiers who had decided to stay back, as labourers. Knowing that being guardians of the temple gave them privileges and a position no ruler dared deprive them of, they held on to that, though the work of actual worship had long since been handed over to another family. The family name Bhat, which they had adopted after finding the idol, was dropped, later generations calling themselves just Rao.

And so the family took root, settled, prospered. How could they not, Gopal thought, when he visited the village Ganeshkhed. (This was before he married Sumi.) Sitting on the narrow embankment of a culvert, Gopal could hear the canal singing sweetly as it flowed along the roadside. In the distant fields, where they had set fire to the sugarcane roots, he could see the flames, creating a beautiful pattern as they moved forward on their devouring crusade, a pattern that spoke not of destruction, but of preparation for the next crop. How, indeed, could they have failed to prosper, with such fertile lands within their grasp?

By the time of Gopal's visit, the fields were no longer family property; the temple too, though it still stood, was just bare stone walls, no longer a place of worship, defiled, it was said, by a suicide within its precincts. The family house was long since in ruins and none of the family lived in the village. They had moved to Bangalore before this century began, in the train of a Narayanrao, who had been taken into government service by the then Diwan. Narayanrao had built another family home in Bangalore. A temple, too, wholly unlike the simple stone setting for the stone god on the banks of the river in Ganeshkhed. A garishly decorated god and temple that Kalyani and Goda speak of with pride and nostalgia. Yes, truly the family prospered.

Thinking of this while he waited by the roadside for the bus to take him back to Bangalore, Gopal became aware of the voices of a group of boys wading in knee-deep water. He could not see what they were doing, only that it was not play but work; their voices told him that. The words came clearly to him through the evening hush and he realized that they were speaking Marathi. Almost unrecognisable, wholly changed from the language as it once was perhaps, nevertheless it was Marathi. And Gopal was startled into the thought: why, they are part of it, too. The history that Kalyani is so proud of belonging to, the history which she reads with such pleasure on her family document—it is their history as well. The ancestors of these boys were as much part of a conquering army as Vishwasrao had been. Yet they remain here, still scratching out a meagre living from the land, while Kalyani's family, having got all they could from it, moved on to richer pastures. And this, not merely because of a stone idol that lay in the river waiting to be picked up. It is the knowledge of what they had been that made the family privileged, it is the writing down of it that gave them the consciousness and set them apart. To be ignorant of your history is to be deprived of it.

'Life must be lived forwards, but it can only be understood backwards.'

Kierkegaard's words have often made Gopal wonder: but what kind of an understanding does knowledge yield?

When Gopal became a student of history, it had seemed to him that there was a truth that lay at the end of the road, waiting to be revealed to him. It did not take him long to realize the futility of this hope. Historians, even the most brilliant of them, especially the most brilliant of them, are like magicians. With flamboyance they draw your attention to what they want you to see, take it away from what they want to conceal. 'Look!' they will say, 'the Queen of Spades.' And you see the Queen of Spades. All else is concealed in the darkness of a deliberate deceit.

'History exists in the final analysis for God.' Camus is right. Yes, that is how it is. Only God, or whoever it is standing outside this game, can see the whole of it. For the rest of us, a story in which we play a role ourselves, can never be clear to us. Only a Vyasa could write a story in which he played a role, and at times a not very noble role, with such detachment and clarity. It is not surprising then, that in Kalyani's construct of the family story there is no room for any minute details. She sees it like a mural on a large scale, the figures larger than life-size, the flaws and inaccuracies too minute to be noticed.

Yet, for Kalyani, her picture is the true one. And why not? After all, we can lay claim only to our own truths. The 'higher truth', as the Rig Veda calls it, is always beyond our grasp, that reality continues to evade us. Even the 'inferior truth' of facts is treacherous. And therefore it is, perhaps, that we prepare carefully edited versions of our lives to present to the world. For ourselves too. Except that we know they are there, the alterations, the deletions; but we ignore them, these squiggles, these jottings in the margin, we pretend they are not there, we tell ourselves we have changed nothing.

People have a right to their own history; they need their myths as much as the facts, perhaps even more. That Meerabai drank poison and lived, that Purandaradasa was converted by God in the guise of a mendicant, that Tukaram's poems emerged intact from the river after thirteen days—these beliefs are part of people's lives; to do away with them is to make a rent in the fabric of their lives.

Thus had Gopal argued with himself when he decided

to retract the theory he had worked out in his article, after his accidental discovery of some erotic poems. To connect these to the devotional poems of a saint-poet, to reveal that it was the same man who had written both, to replace the myth of the pure untarnished saint with the truth of a passionate human being who stumbled his way to sainthood—suddenly it seemed wrong. I have no right to do it, he had thought. People have a right to their own history. To deprive them of it is to take away their own idea of themselves.

And yet, even when he had articulated this to himself, Gopal had known something that he could no longer ignore: that he was indulging in sophistry. 'Their own history'—yes, that is where the problem lies. Gopal knows, he has long realized, that we have a very complex relationship with the past. Whether we are resisting it, reliving it, ignoring it, or trying to recreate it—all these things often at the same time—we are always, in some way, trying to reshape it to our desires. Therefore, this idea of 'oneself' is, actually, what we want ourselves to be.

Kalyani, plunging into the past with her granddaughter Aru, will try to refashion her family history out of carefully chosen material, leaving out everything that is dark and discomforting. Nevertheless, Aru will get a glimpse of the part that Kalyani has written out; like a cloud looming in the distance, she will know it is there, even if its shape is not very clear.

The truth, perhaps, is that whatever we do, we are always giving the past a place in our lives.

৵

CONVERSATION BETWEEN KALYANI and Goda during Goda's weekly visits follows a regular pattern. It begins with Goda's recital of complaints about her husband, Satyanarayan, to which Kalyani responds with sympathetic, energetic clucks and a constant repetition of 'you poor thing'. To anyone who knows what the lives of the two women are, it would seem odd for Kalyani to pity Goda. (And even odder, perhaps, for Goda never to reciprocate.) But Kalyani's habit of sympathizing, of protecting 'poor Goda' began in their childhood, for Goda's life, so comfortable now, had a very unpromising start. Losing her mother at birth, she became in effect an orphan when her father married soon after and relinquished his baby daughter to the care of his wife's brother and his wife. Soon, he seemed to forget the very existence of this motherless child.

In her uncle's house, where there already was an only child, Kalyani, Goda could have been neglected, she might have been unfairly treated, made conscious of the difference between her and the daughter of the house. But that never happened. Goda was much loved by her uncle and aunt and in turn wholly devoted to them. Between her and Kalyani there was the strong bond of sisters, a bond that stood even the stress of Kalyani's mother, Manorama, making much of Goda, often showing her greater affection than she did her own daughter, so that outsiders were sometimes misled into thinking that it was Goda who was the daughter of the house.

It was a happy childhood for Goda. Her luck held in marriage too, for Satyanarayan was, still is, an easy-tempered man, a good provider and cheerful companion, laying his jokes at Goda's feet like a homage, and even today, after forty years of marriage, devoted to his wife.

And yet each week there is this recital of Satya's peccadilloes, from his cheating on his diabetic diet, to his insistence on driving their old Fiat (named, by their grandson Hrishi, 'More Hit Than Miss') and his extravagance in buying, according to Goda, all the magazines on the stands, both English and Kannada.

Since Sumi's return, however, things have changed. Satya has taken a back seat and it is Sumi's and Gopal's marriage that is most often spoken of. In whispers. Listening to them, Sumi sometimes has a picture of her marriage moving slowly through this dark tunnel of whispers to the yawning silent darkness into which Kalyani's own marriage has disappeared. Today, interrupting the two women, Sumi catches the quick flashing look they exchange, the sudden silence that follows.

'Don't stop,' she says crossly. 'Go on, you can speak of Gopal and me, I don't mind.'

'Sumi, why do you think ....'

'Actually, we were speaking of Devi. Has she rung you up? She told me she would.'

'No, she hasn't.'

Sumi doesn't believe Goda, but that night Devaki does ring up.

'Sumi, I'm having a party this Saturday, I want you to come.'

'What's the occasion?'

'None. We've become too dull. That's what Vasu says. And he's been grumbling that it's all my fault, that I don't think of anything but my work these days. Isn't that just like a man? It was he who pushed me into starting this business. But you will come, won't you, Sumi?'

'Yes.'

Sumi hears the little sigh Devi gives at her assent, as if she's been holding her breath, a sigh that belies her casual tone.

'Lovely. Hrishi will pick you up.'

'What, sit behind that maniac in a good sari? No, thank you, I'll come on my own.'

'And let me confess,' it comes out in a rush, 'I've invited Gopal, too.' Sumi is silent. 'Do you mind?'

'Mind? Why should I? But let me tell you that if it's for us to meet, we've already done that.'

'Oh!' A pause. 'You have?' Another pause. 'Well, all right.'

Devaki is back to her usual brisk tone. 'I want both of you to be here.'

'Has Gopal agreed to come?'

'Well—he didn't say he wouldn't, he said he'd try....'

He won't come, Sumi thinks, and she is sure that Devaki, for all her professed confidence, is not so sure, either. Her eyes, even as she greets Sumi, are darting around anxiously.

'My God, Sumi, that's a beautiful sari. You look gorgeous.'

'Good enough to seduce Gopal?'

'Don't be silly. It's Kalyani-mavshi's sari, isn't it? These old saris make me drool.'

'You're looking very smart yourself.'

The blossoming of Devaki after marriage into a chic young woman is like a modern-day Cinderella story. Seeing an old picture of the three of them, Sumi, Premi and Devaki, Charu had exclaimed, 'I can't believe this is you, Devi-mavshi.'

And Devaki had laughed at herself in the picture—a skinny, awkward girl in glasses, wearing a short, straight dress that showed her knobby knees, scowling, as if conscious of the unpleasing image she was presenting to the camera.

'I look a sight, don't I? I always wonder where Amma used to get me my frocks from. They were uniformly hideous. And what about your mother, Charu? Look at her in her parachute!'

But even the 'parachute' (their word for the long shapeless skirts yoked to a bodice that girls had worn then) could not hide Sumi's grace.

'Oh, put those picture away someone, I can't bear to see myself,' Devaki had exclaimed.

But her easy laugh had made it clear that, unlike Premi, who could never look at her younger self without feeling a knot of pain inside her, Devaki felt comfortably distanced from the awkward girl she had been.

It has been a long journey. Devaki had been the dark one in a family of fair people, the 'Madrassi' in the North where she grew up, the odd Hindi-speaking girl who did not know her own language well enough when they came home. Conscious of her shortcomings (my mother never let me forget them, she says wryly), Devaki had deliberately remade herself, successfully lopped all the awkward corners off herself. And with marriage to Vasudev Murthy, a successful architect from a distinguished family, she had gained confidence, fitted herself easily into the kind of life Vasu wanted. And now, with her becoming a 'woman entrepreneur', she has moved into an independent role of her own.

But Devaki's feelings for Sumi haven't changed from what they were in their childhood. Sumi was the daughter of Kalyani-mavshi who lived in the Big House. A fact that made them, in some way, superior. It was Goda who had implanted this consciousness in them; though, as she grew up, Devaki began to wonder about it—why were they superior? Certainly Devaki and her brothers were better dressed, they went to better schools and they had, when they settled down in Bangalore, a nicer home. But Devaki granted Sumi superiority ungrudgingly, without any reservation. Sumi was her childhood idol, the way she would like to have been herself. Beautiful, graceful, effortlessly, almost without wanting to, gathering friends around herself.

The breakdown of Sumi's marriage has hit Devaki hard.

Her efforts to talk to Gopal, to make him see reason have failed. And so this attempt at reconciliation. She is anxiously waiting for Gopal, afraid he won't come. She has almost given up on him when, finally, he does.

He enters when the party has reached a stage in which the guests have spread themselves in groups over all the three rooms Devaki has opened for the evening. Nobody notices Gopal at first and he stands listening to Murthy speaking about the conversion of his old family home into its present form.

'This hall—you can't believe the way it was—just a cramped little room, you know, which you entered through a narrow, dingy passage. And so we knocked out the wall here, pushed that one out, put in those two windows,' his hands move in generous arcs as he gestures and points, 'you should see the beautiful light that comes through them in the evening ....'

Suddenly he becomes conscious of Gopal who has been listening as if he has never heard this before. For a moment, Murthy is at a loss; the two haven't met since Gopal walked out on Sumi. Then he resumes his host's mask and exclaims, 'Gopal! Good to see you.'

He grasps his hand with just that little bit of extra pressure to show that Gopal is more family than guest. Or is it to make it clear that in spite of Gopal's behaviour he bears him no grudge?

Introductions are made and Gopal notices that as far as Murthy is concerned he is still a university teacher. Gopal lets it pass, it does not seem important enough to be corrected. Murthy efficiently moves him on to other people, other groups, and though Gopal seems composed and wholly at ease, he is feeling dazed, overcome by the room, the crowd, the buzz of voices. Accustomed as he has now become to the sweaty smell of the 'boys' working with him in the press, the strong cooking smells that come to him from the kitchen of Shankar's house and the fumes of the vehicles that roar in and out of the courtyard, Gopal is overpowered by the heady smell of women's perfumes and flowers. To talk to so many strange persons, after the hermit-like solitude he has lived in, seems too much of an effort.

And then he sees Sumi. She is sitting erect in a tall chair, her profile delicate and sharp against the glitter and colour of a Tanjore painting on the wall behind her. A light just above, which illuminates the painting, casts a kind of glow about her head giving her a misty, unreal look. He can see that she has made herself up, something she does only for parties. There was, Gopal remembers, something joyous and celebratory about the way she got ready for such occasions.

He can see her now, sitting before the mirror, looking earnestly at herself, drawing the lipstick carefully across her lips, pursing them together, a thoughtful look on her face as if she is tasting the lipstick. And then, standing up to wear her sari, her left hand deftly making the pleats, drawing her breath in so that she can tuck them in, patting them flat, smoothing them down. That sari she's wearing, it must be Kalyani's, I can see she's ironed it herself in a hurry, the creases are still there. I can see her impatiently pushing up her bangles each time they fall down to her wrists as she irons, the same two bangles she has worn since we got married, the pattern eroded with the years. 'I must remake them,' she says every time she notices them. And then, 'No, they're your mother's, Sudha gave them to me, what does it matter if they're worn out?'

Suddenly Gopal catches himself and controls his thoughts. I thought I'd left it all behind, but I haven't, it's here with me still and at the sight of Sumi everything comes back. It's as if she's brought me the ring and I move from nothing to everything in a flash. Dushyanta had only those few days in the ashram to remember when they put the fish-stinking ring in his hands, but for me it's years, nearly half my lifetime, all my lifetime it seems to me.

'Gopal!' Devaki has noticed him. And then there is Sumi smiling at him, without embarrassment, introducing him to the young man she was talking to. She wanders away a little later and Gopal is once again amazed and awed by her ease with strangers. Gopal himself is already bored, there's nobody there he wants to speak to, except perhaps— Sumi? I must get out of here, he thinks, but Hrishi comes to him with a plate and then it's too late.

'Well?' Devaki asks Sumi when they are by themselves in the kitchen.

'Well, what? Devi, I knew you were a romantic girl, I can still remember those awful mushy romances you used to read, but surely now that you're a businesswoman, you've changed? Did you expect Gopal and me to fall into each other's arms in your living room?'

'Don't be funny. It's not that. But ... but ... Damn it, Sumi, you know what I mean.' Devaki's tone is impatient, but her eyes are misty.

Sumi does know what Devaki is hoping for. She also knows that the unshed tears in Devaki's eyes are as much for Gopal and their marriage as they are for Sumi herself. To both Premi and Devaki, Gopal and she were 'the lovers', the touchstone for all lovers henceforth. And there was Gopal himself, who could cross the barrier between the sexes with ease, who was able to do something most men found hard—present his whole self to a female, not just a part of himself.

'You silly girl, why are you crying?' Sumi removes Devaki's glasses and gently wipes her eyes with her own sari.

'Don't! You'll spoil your sari. And maybe I'm crying because you don't. You don't even talk about it, Sumi.'

'I've never been able to cry easily, you know that. And what do I say, Devi? That my husband has left me and I don't know why and maybe he doesn't really know, either? And that I'm angry and humiliated and confused ...? Let that be, we won't go into it now. What's for dessert, Devi? And what pretty bowls! New?'

'Dessert? It's payasa.'

'Goda-mavshi's.'

'Of course. And yes, these are new, I got them made recently. I suddenly realized what a lot of silver junk we had at home, so I converted all of it into this. Amma was furious.'

'I can imagine that. "Each little spoon has its history. These are Hrishi's little teeth marks, and this is where Hrishi's little fist hammered away and Kalyani-akka gave you this when you were a girl—Devi, how could you?" Yes, I know exactly what Goda-mavshi said.'

They laugh together and it's as if they have successfully skimmed over the thin ice of Sumi's uncomfortable confidences. They go out with the sweet and Devaki moves smoothly into her party patter as she goes around with the tray.

'It's my mother's theory that payasa should always be eaten hot, to chill it is sacrilege. And you add a spoon of ghee on top, it should look like you've kept a shining silver rupee on the payasa. No, really, jokes apart, Amma's payasa is nectar, "absolute amrut", my father calls it. Nobody can make it like her.'

Sumi quickly and silently serves out her tray, taking the last bowl for herself. Pushing aside the slight skin that has formed on top, she begins to eat. Her hair has come loose as it always does after a while, there is a thin film of sweat on her face. She seems deep in thought as she eats, but Gopal, watching her, knows she is absorbed in the pleasure of the moment, savouring the milky sweetness of the payasa, crisping the nuts daintily between her teeth. Someone comes to her, Sumi smiles, pats the chair beside her in her usual gesture and Gopal thinks, she is very attractive, she can get married, maybe I should divorce her, set her free.

He gets up to go but is buttonholed by Murthy who, slightly drunk, has reached the stage of exaggerating everything—his gestures, his laughter, his emotions. He becomes very familiar and affectionate with Gopal, refusing to let him go, insisting Hrishi will drop him home. He keeps calling out for Hrishi, but Hrishi, noticing his father's state, ignores him. Suddenly furious, Murthy walks after him and Gopal taking his chance slips out.

By the time Devi and Murthy drive Sumi home, Murthy's mood of belligerence has given way to a maudlin self-pity.

'I'm a failure, my only son has no respect for me, look at the way he behaves, he just doesn't care. Can't he see how much I respect my father, even at this age I can't imagine disobeying him, what's wrong with this generation ....'

'Oh, stop it, Vasu. You know your relationship with your father is a different story altogether. You can't compare ....'

'Yes, take his side, pamper him, it's your pampering ....'

'Not again!' Devaki sighs in exaggerated exasperation. 'Hrishi is at an awkward age, that's all. Now what?' she says in irritation as Murthy cries out, 'Stop, stop.'

'There's Gopal.'

Sumi, a silent passenger so far, comes out of her dreamlike state and sees Gopal walking steadily by the side of the road, head down, absorbed in his thoughts, unaware of the car that has suddenly stopped.

It's only when Murthy shouts out, 'Gopal, hey Gopal,' that Gopal slowly turns around to see them.

'Come on, we'll drop you.'

Gopal gestures as if to say, 'I'm all right, you go on,' and without a word begins walking again. Murthy hesitates, looks at Devi who gives Sumi a quick glance in the mirror, puts the car into gear and moves on.

A little later Murthy says, 'I'm cold.' And gives a little shiver as if thinking of Gopal walking in the chilly night wearing nothing but a thin shirt. Sumi says nothing and Devaki and Murthy are silent too, their arguments forgotten.

It is a misty morning. Sumi, coming out of the bathroom to the back veranda, finds that Prasad's and Ratna's house is no longer visible. The trees are just spectral shrouded shapes. She can hear Shyam's and Shweta's voices, but coming to her through the grey muffling cloud of the mist, they no longer seem the voices of real children. Kalyani comes from the backyard, a clutch of curry leaves in her hand. She changes her garden slippers for her indoor ones at the bottom of the steps and climbs briskly up, making 'brrr' sounds. She is wearing the old brown man's sweater she always wears at home. It's too large for her; lost in its depths she looks even smaller than she is.

She sees Sumi standing and says, 'It's chilly. Wear something warm.' A slight vapour forms around her mouth. 'And come in and have your coffee.'

But Sumi continues to stand there, listening to the sounds from inside, the girls' voices, the monotonous hum of Kalyani's radio, the clatter of cups. A ray of sunshine breaks through the mist, feeble, but enough to transform a spider's web in the wooden trellis into a sparkling, diamond-studded gossamer fabric. Sumi can see the spider still working on it, scuttling to the centre and then back. Over and over again. Busy, she thinks with a smile, with the business of its life.

'Sumi. Coffee.'

'I'm coming.'

'You look cold,' Aru says to her mother.

But it's she, sitting huddled in a shawl, legs folded under her, skirt pulled down to cover her feet, who looks as if she's feeling the chill. Now she gets up and wraps her shawl round her mother, her hands staying for a moment on Sumi's shoulders. It is like a hug, and to Sumi, more warming than the shawl. Kalyani enters with Sumi's coffee, and Charu who has been reading, rocking herself slightly as is her way when reading, looks up at her mother for the first time and says, asks rather, 'Well?'

She has the same expression Devaki had when she said 'Well?'

In fact, all of them, yes, even Seema, are looking at her just as expectantly. So they knew about it, it was planned that Gopal and I should meet.

'How was it?' Charu prods her mother impatiently when Sumi does not respond.

'Devi's party? Good. As always.'

'Was Papa there?'

'Yes.'

'Hrishi said ....'

'Poor Hrishi is in disgrace.'

'What has he done?'

'Nothing. Been his usual self. Irritating his father ....'

'Hrishi's an ass.'

'Did you two talk?' Aru interrupts them. 'Papa and you, I mean?'

'Yes, of course. We are on talking terms, you know. We aren't *gatti*.'

The childish phrase, the one they had used as children for not being on speaking terms, brings no smile to Aru's face.

'Aru, that was neither the time nor the place for any kind of serious talk.'

'But, Sumi ....'

'And guess what, Amma?' Sumi deliberately turns away from Aru and her questions. 'I met one of your—sorry, I should say our relations.'

'Who?'

'A young man called Rohit.'

'Rohit? I don't know any Rohit.'

'He doesn't know us, either. But Devi said he's—now, whose son did she say he was?'

Sumi throws herself with enthusiasm into a 'now what was his name?' dialogue with Kalyani. And Aru, realizing her mother will not give her any answers, walks angrily away.

'Lalita. Yes, that's the name. Devi said he's Lalita's son.'

Kalyani is still puzzled. 'Lalita? Who's Lalita?'

'How do I know? You should. But wait a minute, Devi told me that, too. Lalita is the daughter of—of—God, what's wrong with me? I know it'll come, it has to. Daughter of—I think I have it. It ended in pati.'

'Raghupati?'

'That's it. Lalita is Raghupati's daughter.'

Charu, who has seemed to be intent on her book, puts

it away with a thump and calls out to Aru who, clothes piled on her arm, is on her way to her bath.

'Listen, Aru, we got it finally. Rohit is Lalita's son and Lalita is Raghupati's daughter. Right, Amma?'

'So who cares?'

'I do, if you don't. Tell me quickly, Amma, I can't wait any more—what is Rohit to us?'

Sumi stands transfixed by the words, and the lines that she had read in the book on Gopal's table that day, suddenly erupt into her mind.

> *What could my mother be*
> *to yours? What kin is my father*
> *to yours anyway? And how*
> *did you and I meet ever?*

The tears she had controlled then, the tears she had disdained in Devaki's house, suddenly threaten to claim her. She barely has time to get to her room before they burst out of her with an uncontrollable violence. They flow so copiously it's as if there is a deep well inside her, a spring that has been tapped by the words of the poem.

Charu finds her mother sobbing as she has never seen her do before, she sees the wildness, the madness of being lost in a strange world in her eyes and she is terrified.

'What is it, Ma? What is it? Please, Ma, tell me what's the matter.'

Her agonised pleas finally fade away into silence as if she realizes the futility of asking and she is content to hold Sumi close and rock her. She rocks her, as if she is the mother and her mother her child, until both of them are soothed into a tearless calm.

❧

'AND WHAT IS he to us?'

Aru takes up the question Charu had asked Kalyani, in jest, almost in mockery perhaps. 'Did you and Goda-ajji find out what this chap Rohit is to us?' she asks Kalyani that evening.

Kalyani gives Aru a wary look. Is she serious? Does she really want to know?

'Go on, Amma,' Aru prods her grandmother, 'you know you're dying to tell me. Is he a cousin or isn't he?'

'Cousin!' Kalyani is contemptuous. 'Cousins are only in English. An English lady who came to our house once kept calling Godu and me cousins. Godu was almost in tears. Kalyani-akka is my sister, she told her.'

'Well, if he isn't a cousin, what is he?'

Kalyani gets herself into a tangle of relationships and names which makes no sense to Aru. 'Here,' she offers, 'let's write it down, perhaps that'll make it clearer.'

When the names are linked by lines, the kinship becomes suddenly clear, it jumps out at them. Even Kalyani is fascinated by the sight.

'My grandfather had begun a family tree, but he could never complete it.'

'What happened?'

'I don't know. He began with us, with my father actually, and he wanted to go on until he got to Vishwasrao, but ....'

'Who's Vishwasrao?'

And so Aru, for the first time hears the story of her own

past—of Madhavrao Peshwa and Vishwasrao, of the finding of the idol, the building of the temple and the family settling down around it. Encouraged, perhaps, by Aru's silence, Kalyani moves on to her favourite story, the discovery of the 'other Ganapati idol' by her father Vithalrao.

'The other Ganapati?'

'You know, the one in the niche above our front door....'

'You mean the one outside?'

Aru's interest, fairly languid so far, suddenly quickens; now she is indeed well and truly caught. Sumi, coming upon them, finds Aru listening with fascination. Her responses—the drawing in of breath, the widening of eyes, the 'And then?' that punctuates Kalyani's narration—are those of a child listening to a story. Sumi wonders whether Kalyani needed this audience to bring the incident out of the past for her, for she herself has never heard it. Nor had she any idea that Kalyani could tell a story so well. As Kalyani speaks, the incident comes alive—Sumi can almost see the shaded grove of trees behind the family temple in Ganeshkhed, dark and secret even during the day. The tap-tap of a hammer loud and clear in the silence. And Vithalrao, attracted by the sound, coming upon a man working on a block of black stone, so engrossed that he scarcely looks up at the intruder.

It is when Kalyani speaks of her father's 'vision' that Sumi is surprised—not at what Kalyani is saying, but at Aru's response. There is none of the scepticism she would have expected; the question Aru asks is a straightforward 'looking for information' kind of one. 'A vision? What kind of a vision?'

And now, for the first time, Kalyani falters. She hesitates, she cannot convey to Aru the full extent of this, the family miracle. For Aru has no idea of the kind of man Kalyani's father was; he was not a religious man, nor a believer in idols and rituals. And yet there it was—in place of the block of stone the man was working on, he saw a Ganapati idol. Not there, but in a niche above the front door of the house he was building—a niche that he hadn't planned for.

'And the question my father asked the man—that, too, came out of nowhere into his mind, as if someone had put it there. He had no intention of asking it, no idea—he told me this once—that he was going to ask it.

' "Will you let me have the idol when it's complete?"

'This, not knowing that the man was, in fact working on an idol. But the man nodded. And spoke for the first time.

' "Come back in three months."

'My father went back exactly three months later,' Kalyani goes on, more easily now, having successfully negotiated the 'miracle'. 'And there it was, the idol, just as he had 'seen' it—down to the minutest detail.

'And then my father brought it home and installed it in the niche he had got ready by then. My mother was not too pleased about it. It's too high, she complained. How do we do our puja? But my father said it was just as well. He doesn't need any pujas, just leave him alone, he said. My mother didn't give up, though. Twice a month, a servant climbed up a ladder to clean it and put some flowers on the idol.'

And so Bora, Sumi thinks, is following a tradition when, standing on a ladder, he cleans the idol with Nagi assisting and Kalyani watching. He wipes it with a wet cloth until the god emerges glossy and shining, clear of his filmy veil of dust and cobwebs, his pot belly gleaming, one leg daintily crossed over the other. Finally, putting a dot of kumkum on the forehead, Bora tucks a hibiscus behind one ear and another in the loop of the trunk. Then, climbing down the ladder, he looks with satisfaction at his work before folding his hands reverently.

Kalyani, too, perhaps unconsciously imitating her mother whom she must have seen doing this as a child, folds her own hands and mutters, 'Look after us, Ganapati, protect us.'

'He doesn't do such a good job of looking after the women in the family, does he?'

Sumi's question takes even her own self by surprise. As

for Kalyani, she seems stunned. She stares at Sumi for a while, silent, as if she is thinking of a rejoinder. Finally she says, 'What can even the gods do against our destinies?'

Even the gods cannot fight human destiny—it's a queer, strange logic that defeats Sumi's understanding. But the dignity with which Kalyani speaks blocks out any response. And when Kalyani goes away, Sumi turns to the idol and thinks: maybe, in a way, though this is not how Amma meant it, she's right. It's only a piece of stone after all.

But as if the god has now come out of his anonymity for her, Sumi begins to notice things about the idol. A kind of patient, dignified sadness on the face. A sense of incongruity about the figure. It isn't the elephant-head that seems wrong; on the contrary, the wonderfully proportioned, large flapping ears, the tusk, the trunk, the very wrinkles on it—all these are so beautifully sculpted that they seem absolutely lifelike. It's the human torso, with its exaggerated pot belly, the rows of necklaces on the flabby chest and the short legs that seem wrong. For some reason the creator, the silent man in the dark grove of trees, springs into Sumi's mind. Did he put something of himself into this? What was he trying to say? Or did the two of them, the sculptor and Vithalrao, create this god between them?

The discomfort that the story has aroused in Sumi has apparently not touched Aru. Obviously she has not thought of it as anything more than 'an interesting story'. That it is in any way connected to her, that these people Kalyani speaks about are part of her life, is something that occurs to her only when Kalyani says abruptly, 'You look like my mother.'

'I do?' Aru is at first startled. Then she grimaces slightly, showing that she is not flattered by the comparison.

'My mother was a beautiful woman,' Kalyani says reprovingly as if she has read the thought in Aru's mind.

'Beautiful?'

Aru's disbelief comes from her impression of the picture of Manorama in the hall. A stern, if rather voluptuously rounded face, almost blank in its inscrutability—is she beautiful? Perhaps, Aru thinks, that was the way people presented themselves for a picture in those days, for Vithalrao in the companion picture is just as serious and grave as his wife. In fact, the thick gold chain, giving the hint of a pocket watch, and his gold-rimmed glasses add even more weight to the sense of solidity he conveys. And yet there's something, a glint of humour in the eyes perhaps, that hints at a man consciously presenting the facade that is expected of him for such a picture. The lips, half-hidden under a bushy moustache, lifted in a small quirk at the corners, add to this impression. Whereas Manorama seems to be all of a piece : the pose *is* the woman.

'I don't see any resemblance,' Aru demurs.

'You would if you dressed better.'

Kalyani looks disapprovingly at what she calls Aru's ragpicker's clothes—a cotton skirt of indeterminate length and a T-shirt two sizes too large for her.

'Silk saris and diamonds, eh, Amma? And a helmet on my head when I'm riding the scooter!'

But Kalyani is in no mood to be sidetracked. 'You should have seen my mother's saris. She never wore anything but silks. Such silks! And her diamonds—you could see them flashing a long distance away. My father used to say you didn't need a lantern at night if she was with you.'

The floodgates of memory have been opened and Kalyani can't stop. Goda, who has joined them, is puzzled at first. What is Kalyani-akka about, she wonders, speaking of the past to this child? But she is soon drawn into it; it becomes a duet, Goda's panegyric even more extravagant than Kalyani's.

'I've never seen anyone as beautiful as Mami. She was as fair as milk. And so tall—she was like a queen, wasn't she, Kalyani-akka?'

'But she didn't like that. She hated her height.'

'I know. I remember Mama teasing her, saying that if they'd known how tall she would grow, his father would never have chosen her.'

'She cried when he said that—remember, Goda?'

'She didn't like jokes about such things. Especially about their marriage. It made her furious. Her anger was—my God!'

When Kalyani and Goda speak of Vithalrao and Manorama's marriage, their voices carry the ring of people retelling myths, of troubadours singing of love, of storytellers relating the wondrous things that happened in the past. Sumi, overhearing them, thinks of Kalidasa's *Kumarasambhavam*. Just so did the poet sing of the marriage of Shiva and Parvati, making of it a magical, awe-filled story, yet one that falls within the realm of belief because it sings of love, of the love of a man and a woman. And you think—this is how it must have happened.

The two women speak of the marriage as a miracle. What else, they seem to imply, can explain this marriage between the daughter of a poor village Brahmin, who often had nothing more than the coin with which he tucked in the extra length of his dhoti, and the educated intelligent son of a well-to-do man from Bangalore?

Kalyani calls it destiny. It will be much later that Aru will realize that Kalyani uses the word destiny for a great number of things. Here, it carries within it the truth that all the characters in this drama were unusual people. Not just the two main characters, Vithalrao and Manorama, the hero and heroine they may perhaps be called, but the others as well. In fact, the hero and heroine don't matter so much in the story of an arranged marriage. It is the parents. There was Vithalrao's father, who didn't hesitate to do what could have damned him in the society he lived in, and maybe did: make an offer to a girl's father for his son. That he noticed her confidence, self-assurance and intelligence more than her shabby clothes, speaks volumes about the kind of man he was.

Manorama's parents didn't come out of the usual mould,

either. It was her mother who had sent her daughter to Yamunabai's 'school', such as it was, at a time when schooling for a girl was something that could come in the way of her marriage prospects. And she did this in spite of the fact that Yamunabai and most of her students were not Brahmins. (Yamunabai, actually, is the most unusual character in this story, though for long her role will remain unknown. It was Yamunabai who was really responsible for the metamorphosis of a sulky overworked child, trapped in the drudgery of looking after her younger siblings, into the girl who caught the attention of the visitor from Bangalore.)

Manorama's mother was an honest woman as well, for it was she who induced her husband to write a letter to Vithalrao's father about the disaster that struck, just a month before the wedding was to take place: Manorama 'grew up'.

To her father, a man who prepared the yearly Hindu almanac, both for the little extra money it gave him and because he found the calculations immensely fascinating— to this man, Time was something to be calculated, divided and charted on paper. That it could work on humans, that it had made his daughter a 'woman', came to him as a total surprise. He was not too unworldly, though, to know that by making this revelation he was risking the marriage which was to him such a godsend. He was a poor man even by the standards of the time and he had four daughters, of whom Manorama was the oldest, to be married. Nevertheless, he wrote to the groom's father confessing what had happened. And promptly came a reply saying that it made no difference at all. The wedding would take place as planned.

And so they were married. Kalyani and Goda give a deep sigh when they reach this point and so much does it seem like the ending of a fairy-tale that Charu adds: And they lived happily ever after. So indeed it would seem from the response of the two women.

'The past comes to us filtered through our memories.' Aru remembers having read this line somewhere and she sees the truth of it when she watches Kalyani and Goda reviving, perhaps reliving the past. For, even while the past seems to flow rich and thick between them, there is, at times, a queer sense of disharmony. Not when they speak of Vithalrao, for Vithalrao emerges from their stories as a warm, affectionate man with a sense of humour. No, there is no dissonance here. It is when they speak of Manorama that there is the hint of a discord, a sense of something missing, something held back.

When the two women speak of Manorama, and they continue to do so, as if having once invoked her, they cannot easily let go, they seem to be churning the ocean, out of which Manorama emerges, full-blown, in her silks and diamonds, like Lakshmi on the lotus. But the slime in which the lotus is anchored is not spoken of. The girl in the patched skirts and running nose, a younger sibling constantly sliding down her skinny hips, never appears in this story. In fact, Manorama's natal family remains cloaked in silence.

It is possible, of course, that the two women know little, maybe almost nothing of Manorama's childhood, for Manorama ruthlessly cut herself off from her family after her marriage. (And perhaps, in the process, denuded herself of her childhood, of the innocent part of her being.) It seems strange, it would seem strange to any woman, that she deprived herself of that emotional sustenance that only a girl's own family can give her. The songs, the stories, the legends that have sprung up around women's 'mother's homes' as a fountainhead of love and caring grew out of a reality: a woman's need for love that took account of her as a person, not as a figure fitting into a role. 'When I was a girl ...' a woman wistfully says and it is as if that girl is the real her.

But Manorama rejected this. The fact that her mother died just a year after her marriage made it easier perhaps, for her to distance herself from them. Not that she broke off ties completely. She gave what help she could, specially during any crises; but she rarely went home, nor were any of her brothers and sisters invited to visit her, except a younger sister, and that only once. And, this was much later, the youngest, a boy left motherless at the age of one. It is possible that Manorama had a soft corner for this motherless child. Or, perhaps this boy, born after her marriage, was the one child she had never carried about, and therefore brought her fewer reminders of a past she wanted to forget.

Whatever her reasons, he was the only one of her siblings to visit them. A silent, withdrawn boy, Vithalrao discerned both intelligence and ambition in him. He decided to help him, sending him to a good school, later to college, and when he had done his law, getting him into the office of a friend of his, a renowned lawyer in Bombay. And when the time came, Manorama had no qualms about reminding him of what he owed them, what he owed her, his elder sister. Vithalrao was unhappy about what his wife was doing, but knowing her determination, he had no choice.

It does not take Aru very long to realize that when the two women, Kalyani and Goda, speak of the past, they are playing cat's cradle, skilfully transferring the thread from hand to hand, from finger to finger, creating a design between them, a design that allows certain facts to slip through. Clearly, there are stories concealed in the interstices of silence. One of these is of Kalyani's marriage to her own uncle, Shripati.

Kalyani, in the relating of her memories, goes back to the earlier part of her life, making it seem as if she was only a daughter, as if there was no more to her life than that. Yet the part of her life that she has edited out is there, the dark looming cloud of its absence making itself felt, even to Aru, who knows nothing about it.

'Kalosmi'—'I am Time risen to destroy the world.'
Listening to Kalyani and Goda speaking of her

grandparents, Sumi gets a sense of the power of time. Time, not as the destroyer, though, but as the creator. Kalyani and Goda, she thinks, unlike people at a seance, who want to conjure up the spirits of the dead, are bringing the old world alive, recreating it out of their memories. And Sumi thinks: will this happen to us, too? Kings and queens had their chroniclers; for ordinary mortals, there are only the children—if they live long enough, that is, for their parents to become a distant, nostalgic memory. But will our children, in this post-Freudian age, speak of us this way, one day? Will time remove all the dross, leaving only the gold behind?

That Goda and Kalyani should be partners in this exercise in nostalgia seems perfectly natural to Sumi; it is Aru's involvement that surprises her. In a way, it is a relief. Aru's withdrawal from all of them, her frequent absences from home, for which she often gave no explanation, had made Sumi uneasy. Even worse, perhaps, had been the days when Aru stayed home; she spent her time by herself in her room, her face, when she finally emerged, flushed, slightly swollen, making Sumi wonder: Has she been sleeping or crying?

This new occupation has brought the girl back into the family circle. And closer to Kalyani with whom she has had a troubled relationship. But Sumi, if less anxious, is nevertheless puzzled. What is there in this for Aru? Is it an escape? Is she looking for something?

If she is, it is a purely impersonal search, for Aru reminds her mother of a jeweller picking up stones, grading them for size, colour and purity, putting them in different heaps, for some use that only he, the jeweller, knows about. I could have done this, too, after Gopal left, Sumi thinks— retracing my steps, picking up things, thinking—is this it? But she has turned resolutely away from even her immediate past, she is preparing herself for the future, for the job which she is soon to start on.

Sumi has given up the idea of making a separate home for herself and her daughters. She has not gone back to

Nagaraj, not since the day she watched the bereaved mother break down. Ultimately, however, it was not this memory that had put an end to her search for a home of her own, nor her father's appeal to her to not move out— though that had been disconcerting enough. To have the feeling that he was appealing to her had made her acutely uncomfortable. Power and authority, which had always flowed out of him, suddenly seemed poised between them. And will I, some time soon, be in control? Unthinkable!

But this had nothing to do with her decision to continue living in the Big House. It was, once again, the economics of the situation that had made the decision for her.

Ironically, it is after she has come to this decision that Ramesh comes to her with a proposal, a proposal which, if she could have accepted, would have made it possible for her to have a home of her own.

Ramesh looks as if he has been nerving himself to this, he finds it hard to begin, to explain what he has in mind.

'My God, Ramesh!' Sumi exclaims when she finally grasps what he is trying to say. 'I can't possibly take money, that kind of money, from you.'

'But it's your money, didn't you hear me, Sumi? It's yours. My father intended Guru to have it, but, poor man, he never had enough. That flat in Bombay is as much Guru's as it was my mother's, don't you see? And Guru got nothing out of it.'

'You know, Ramesh,' Sumi's tone is reflective now, 'I've begun to think that what Gopal has really done is to take sanyas. I'm surprised none of you have thought of that. But look what's happened—it's not he who's going around with the begging bowl, it's I who am doing that.'

'Begging bowl? What a horrible word, Sumi.' Ramesh is stammering slightly, as he always does when he is angry, a rare occurence with him. 'This isn't charity we're offering you. We are not giving you even half the value of the flat, we can't do that. It's only a token.'

But Sumi knows it's a way of helping her out. She also knows that though Ramesh says 'we', including his sisters in his intention, he will be be doing it alone.

'What will Chitra say?'

'Chitra has nothing to do with it. I don't interfere in her family affairs, and she doesn't interfere in mine. That's how it has always been with us.'

'Don't think I'm being high minded, Ramesh. It isn't easy for me to turn my back on money. I want it, my God, I want it so badly! I want so much to feel secure, I want to know that my girls won't lack for anything. It's so stupid of me, Ramesh, I never imagined such a thing happening, I never prepared myself for this. I gave up teaching when Seema was born and ....'

'Look, Sumi, don't think too much about it. I'll deposit the money in your account, maybe we'll make it a joint account with Aru. Let it be there, you can use it in times of need—perhaps for the girls' weddings?'

'Weddings! Now you're talking like Amma.'

Sumi laughs, but the topic of her daughters' marriage is one she cannot really ignore. Kalyani and Goda won't let her forget it. It's always on their minds, in their conversation, something which seems to them both a problem (who'll marry them?) and a solution to Sumi's problem. Sumi, like Aru, is amazed by Kalyani. How can she, of all people, think of marriage with enthusiasm? She's angry, too. Gopal and I never thought of our daughters' marriage, never as a problem, anyway. Maybe we should have taken out marriage policies in their names like so many parents do, maybe we should have ....

But suddenly one evening, Sumi realizes that what lies at the core of Kalyani's uneasiness is not money but something else.

There's a call from Devaki for Hrishi, who, after bringing Charu home from the class, lingers, joining the girls in their conversation while they set the table for dinner.

'My mother? What does she want?'

It's not a long conversation. Devaki apparently does most of the talking, with Hrishi vainly trying to get a word in and making faces at the girls while he listens.

'My mother's gone mad,' he says when he puts the phone down, looking slightly dazed. 'Just because I'm a little late, only half an hour, mind you, she imagines I'm drunk or lying dead on the road, or Godknowswhat.'

'Poor baby.' Charu makes infant-soothing sounds. 'Can't it go alone anywhere then? Does it need its mummy to look after it, the poor little thing?'

'Oh, shut up, Charu, I've had enough from my mother, now don't you start.'

They all laugh at him, but Sumi, who picked up the phone, cannot forget the edge of anger in Devaki's voice. It's not because Hrishi is late, it's because he is here, with us, with Charu. I've seen her looking at Hrishi and Charu. Devi loves me, she is fond of my girls, less of Charu than of Aru, perhaps, but it's not that. It's the idea of Charu and her only son, that's what she doesn't like. With their position and money, she's more ambitious for Hrishi. But she's so wrong. Charu and Hrishi have grown up together, they're easy and comfortable with each other, but there's nothing of the male-female in their relationship, they're like two friends of the same sex, they don't think of each other that way.

But in this Sumi is wrong, she is mistaken about Hrishi's feelings, anyway. In fact both Sumi's older daughters are fated to be pursued tenaciously by the two young men who set their hearts on them. Rohit now enters the scene and he makes his feelings for Aru quite clear, there is never any attempt to conceal them from anyone.

Goda brings him home. 'This is Rohit, Lalita's son,' she says, modestly triumphant, and then explains his presence. Rohit is an architect; he heard about the Big House from Murthy, when, meeting him professionally, they stumbled upon their kinship.

'He wanted to see it very much and Devi asked me to show it to him. So I brought him along ....'

Rohit, entirely composed, listens silently, smiling occasionally when he thinks a response is required. His silence acquires solidity and substance against the background of Kalyani's and Goda's patter, Kalyani's especially. The presence of her kinsman seems to have gone to her head, she can't stop talking. As she takes him round the house, she tells him all her stories, she makes him join her in standing reverently before the pictures of her parents in the hall, she gives the history of each room they enter and repeats her father's jokes with an enjoyment that makes it seem they are still pristine fresh to her.

Rohit is an exquisitely well-mannered young man and if a small smile surfaces occasionally, he suppresses it. Kalyani's words flow over him, he can't take in everything she says. But he notices how, each time they enter a room, she lifts her feet to the exact height required to cross the high wooden threshold. He sees the way her hand brushes a wall, a door, as if communicating through them with the house, he hears the inflection in her voice when she speaks of her father. And something comes through that Murthy has not been able to tell him: this house is a living presence for Kalyani.

When they get to the front hall, Rohit takes in the magnificent staircase and is ready to go up when Kalyani stops him.

'There's nothing upstairs.' Rohit's look of disbelief pushes her into adding, and for the first time she seems uncomfortable, 'just a small room. My father wanted to build more rooms upstairs, but—but his father died and he lost interest somehow. Come and sit down, Rohit. Goda will have got the coffee ready by now.'

Rohit, however, manages to slip out of the house and stands staring up. Yes, there it is, just one room as Kalyani said. Ugly and incongruous. Like a stopper on further growth.

He is still gazing at the room and thinking of its oddity when he hears the sound of a scooter, of girls' voices. Charu, getting off, sees him first and moves to him with a puzzled look.

'I'm Rohit.' So complete is his self-possession that she automatically replies, 'I'm Charu,' but it's obvious she expects him to explain his presence. Rohit, however, is looking past her at Aru who has removed her helmet and, relieved of its weight, is shaking her head so that her plait comes free and flies about her face. She turns to Charu, a smile on her face, and is on the point of saying something when she sees Rohit.

'This is Rohit.' Charu mischievously mimics Rohit's matter-of-fact tone, but to her astonishment, Aru, after only a moment's pause, adds, 'Oh yes, Lalita's son,' and then laughs at Charu's amazement.

'Lalita ....?'

'Rohit! Coffee is ready. Oh, there you are, girls. Come and have your coffee.'

Through all the confusion of serving the coffee and snacks, Rohit's eyes keep moving to Aru's face. But it's only when they have all settled down that Kalyani introduces her granddaughters to Rohit.

'Oh, but we know him. He's Lalita's son.'

'But ...' Rohit tries to say something.

'And Raghupati's grandson.'

'And whose great grandson is he, Aru?'

'I don't know. Ask Amma.'

'Narasikaka's.'

'But—but ...' Rohit, clinging desperately to his formal politeness, finally gets in, 'how do you know all this?'

'Ha! Mysterious, isn't it?'

'What do you mean? You're family, aren't you? Even if you are Narasikaka's branch, you're still part of the family.'

'What was wrong with Narasikaka, whoever he was, Amma?'

'He was a son of a bitch.'

Charu splutters. 'Don't mind our ajji, Rohit. She's the soul of tact really, most of the time, anyway.'

'Really, Amma!'

'What's wrong with speaking the truth? Ask Goda about him. Remember, Goda, they used to say he brought his keep home once, brazenly wearing some of his wife's jewellery which he had given her!'

'Keep! God, what a word to use.'

Rohit is at first bewildered by their swift reactions and responses, but Goda and Kalyani soon draw him into the net of intimacy they create. Rohit relaxes and forgets to look at his watch, though his eyes keep stealing to Aru's face every now and then. When he gets up to go finally, he seems reluctant to leave.

'Come again, Rohit.'

'There you are, Rohit! Forgiven for being Narasikaka's descendant.'

The girls laugh at Kalyani, they don't realize that for her, and for Goda too, the ancient feud still lives on. They don't understand that the two women are, in fact, keeping alive the hatred of Narasikaka, transmitted to them in their childhood by Manorama. To Manorama, it was this uncle of her husband's who was the villain of the story; for it was he who brought pressure on Vithalrao to marry again, when it was clear that Manorama, who had finally given birth to a daughter after a series of miscarriages, would have no more children. Failing in this, he tried to induce Vithalrao to adopt a son, preferably one of his own grandsons.

But Vithalrao, a modern man in the real sense of the word, rejected both. 'Why should I leave my property to a stranger, to someone else's child, rather than to my own daughter, no,' looking at Goda, 'to my own two daughters?' he would say. (And Goda's sari goes promptly to her eyes when this is quoted.)

Manorama, who had been terrified that her husband would marry again, never got over this fear. It was as if that deprived childhood which she so resolutely ignored, was always close to her, so close that a nudge was enough to push her back into it. To add to her insecurity, that main crutch, the one most women depended on, a son, was denied to her. All that she had was a daughter, Kalyani, who would get married and become part of another family.

'I was a clever girl,' Kalyani said once. 'I was very good at Maths like my father. He wanted me to become an engineer—can you believe that? You will be the first woman engineer in the country, he used to say.'

And yet Kalyani was not allowed to complete her schooling. She was taken out of school and married off by Manorama to her own brother Shripati. Perhaps, after this, Manorama felt secure. The property would remain in the family now. Her family.

৽

PREMI, WHO HAS carried within her the sense of extreme crisis she had encountered on her last visit, is surprised when she arrives, to see how normal everybody looks. Kalyani starts off, almost immediately, on her usual complaints, but after the silence Premi had encountered on her last visit, this seems almost welcome.

'Why couldn't you have come a day or two earlier? I know you had to be in your own home for Diwali, but you could have tried to be here for Bhau-bij—of course, it doesn't occur to you that Nikhil has three sisters here. And I suppose you've come with a return ticket as usual!'

Premi's attempts to give reasonable answers founder on Kalyani's refusal to understand Premi's position as the only woman in her family.

'I have to go back on Sunday, Amma, Nikhil's school reopens on Monday.'

'Nikhil's school! What class are you in, Nikhil?'

'Third standard,' Nikhil replies promptly.

'Third standard! And his mother says he can't miss school for a few days!'

'Nikhil, you stay back, beta, let your mother go.'

'And my school?'

'Throw it in the dustbin.'

'Chuck it into the sea.'

'We'll make a nice, fine chutney out of it.'

Nikhil, sitting in a tall chair, his palms placed flat on its arms, his legs dangling, moves his gaze swiftly from face to face, enchanted by this nonsensical conversation.

'I want to stay longer here, Mama,' he declares when Shyam and Shweta join them. 'Hundreds of people here.'

'Hundreds, Nikki?'

'Thousands.'

Nikhil's presence, as always, livens them up. He is shamelessly pampered by everyone, but perhaps because he is never just a passive receiver, he somehow manages to remain unspoilt. His affection for them, for his aunt Sumi especially, makes him radiate happiness at being with them. Even Shripati does not mind his frequent incursions into his room and Nikhil, running up and down the stairs, creates a link between the room and the rest of the house, so that they seem to come together, even if only temporarily.

Gopal's first question, when Premi visits him, is also about Nikhil. 'Why haven't you brought him?'

Premi hesitates. She has not spoken to anyone about this visit; the fact that none of them has referred to Gopal has made her chary of mentioning him.

'Well, never mind. Bring him on your next visit.'

Gopal smiles at her as if he has understood her hesitation. And for Premi, it happens again, as it does each time she meets Gopal after a long interval. The picture of Gopal she has held within her, of the thin, withdrawn young man whom she had, as a girl, watched secretly from a distance through the trees, clashes with the man Gopal is now, the man he has become. And there is a jolt, she has to make a slight adjustment, like after wearing her contacts, before the two pictures dovetail into one.

This time she notices that he has lost weight; his clothes hang on him, making him look gaunt. But he is genuinely pleased to see her and unlike her, is wholly at ease. Yet in a few moments he gets up and says, 'Let's go out somewhere. I'm sick of this place.'

She gets into the rickshaw with him with a sense of girlish excitement. 'My treat,' she says childishly when they settle down on the hard, rickety chairs of a garden restaurant.

'Sure. You owe me one anyway.'

'I do?'

'You promised me a treat when you passed your finals, remember? And then you got engaged and married, all in a month, and forgot about it. But I haven't.'

'Do you know what the truth is, Gopal? When I came home after my finals, I didn't know it myself, that I was to marry Anil, I mean. Anil doesn't believe me, but that's the truth. Amma didn't know, either. I was the one who told her. But,' she smiles, an awkward, strained smile, 'why am I speaking of all that now? What will you have, Gopal? A dosa for me.'

In spite of her disclaimer, she goes back to the topic herself after the waiter has gone away with their orders.

'It was the same about my going to Bombay to do medicine. Baba got the forms for me, he told me to fill them up and said I was to go to Bombay. I can't help thinking that Baba sent me away to punish Amma. Sumi and you had just got married, remember? I think he wanted to tell Amma—you let Sumi get away, so you can't have your other daughter, either. You think it's far-fetched? Yes, I can see you do. But you don't know Baba. I do, I can believe anything about him.'

Gopal's silence makes her falter, then she deliberately changes the subject.

'You can't imagine how exciting it used to be, coming here when we were children. "Going to Cantonment" was the biggest treat we could have. Goda-mavshi and Bhauji-kaka brought us here each time they came home for a vacation. They would take us out, give us treats, buy us clothes. Choose anything you want, they would tell Sumi and me. But somehow, I always felt Goda-mavshi was worried about spending too much—she's a bit of a kanjoos like Amma—and so I'd choose something not very expensive. But Sumi never seemed to care, she bought what she liked, without thinking of the money. And then I used to lie awake at night, thinking—why didn't I choose something else? Why did I go in for something cheap?'

Gopal, laughing with her, thinks of how different the two sisters make their childhood out to be. The only lack Sumi complains about is books. 'I used to steal books,' she had confessed to him once. 'I would borrow them and if the girls didn't ask for them back after a time, I would tear off the first page, write my own name on them and keep them. After all, if they didn't miss them, why shouldn't I have them?'

But Premi's memories, even the few she can speak of, are only of deprivation and fear. Looking at Premi, 'the picture of Bombay chic' as Charu calls her, in her expensive cotton sari, her beautifully groomed hair, her simple but expensive jewellery, Gopal has always felt that she is constantly reminding herself of how far she has got away from the child Premi.

'Okay,' Gopal breaks into the silence. 'You can say it. Go on.'

'Why did you do it, Gopal?'

He does not pretend not to understand her question but plunges into an answer straightaway, as if continuing an unspoken argument that has been going on between them under the surface of their conversation.

'Why did I do it? I can give you so many answers, but I've begun thinking that the plain truth is that I just got tired.'

'Tired? Of Sumi?'

Gopal takes no notice of the shock in her voice, he goes on as if she hasn't spoken.

'You remember the Yaksha's question to Yudhishtira: what is the greatest wonder in this world? And what Yudhishtira's answer was? We see people die and yet we go on as if we are going to live forever. Yes, it's true, that is the greatest marvel this world holds, it's *the* miracle. In fact, it's the secret of life itself. We know it's all there, the pain and suffering, old age, loneliness and death, but we think, somehow we believe that it's not for us. The day we stop believing in this untruth, the day we face the truth that we too are mortal, that this is our fate as well, it will become difficult, almost impossible to go on. And if it happens to all of us, the human race will become extinct.' He pauses and goes on, 'It happened to me. I stopped believing. The miracle failed for me and there was nothing left. You've got to be the Buddha for that emptiness to be filled with compassion for the world. For me there was just emptiness.'

'I don't understand you, Gopal. You mean this is why you left Sumi?'

'Well, let me put it this way. I could no longer believe that there is a meaning to my life, a happy culmination waiting for me at the end of it. Can you imagine what living with such a person would be for my children? For Sumi?'

'No meaning to your life?' Premi gets hold of that phrase. 'Oh Gopal, what about your children?'

'For you, it's Nikhil, isn't it? But not for me; to think of being the purpose of my parents' life would have been too heavy a burden for me to carry. Can I then burden my children with that load? No, Premi, the meaning has to be found in your own life.'

For the first time, he is speaking to me as a person, not as Sumi's kid sister. He never saw *me* and in a way I liked it for it made me invisible and I could watch him easily. I was a little in love with him then. A little? No, as much as a girl of thirteen can be. I was awake the night Sumi went to his room, I knew she had gone and where, I had seen them look at each other. I slept on her bed that night as if it would make me Sumi—I remember that. In love? I don't know, but Gopal was the man against whom I measured all other men.

Yes, Anil too. He had scarcely looked at me before we got engaged, I was only the awkward girl, the daughter of a family friend who spent occasional weekends in their home. And then we got engaged and he played his role of

fiancé to the hilt. But to me there was something false in
the picture, there was some irritant in it that hurt me, like
a piece of grit in the eye. He said the word 'love' often, as
if it was a magic word that could convert all the things he
did—the phone calls, the gifts, the going out together, the
endearments—into something real. But they never became
real. For me the real thing was Gopal looking at Sumi.
Everything else was trash. It was only when Nikhil was born
that I knew what love really meant. It was only then that
Anil became real to me; he was the father of my child.
Perhaps you can make a lie the truth by acting on it for
years. But Gopal says he found out his life was a lie.

'You don't know what you're doing to your children,
Gopal. I know how it can be, believe me, it's terrible. Once
Sumi said to someone, "My father is a lawyer" and I was
surprised. Do we have different fathers then, I had
wondered? I knew nothing at all about him, see? Except
that I was scared of him and that our family life was—it was
different, not like other people's. I never brought any of
my friends home. What if they asked me about my father?
What if they asked me—why does he ring a bell? Why
doesn't he talk to you and your mother? And when the
girls spoke of their parents, even of their quarrels, I felt
like a leper. Don't do this to your girls, Gopal. And Sumi's
just forty, she has a long way to go.'

'She says she's getting a job.'

'That's not what I meant,' Premi flashes at him. 'It's not
money that she needs, it's a normal family life.'

'A normal family life?'

Premi responds to the questioning tone with acerbity.
'You know what I mean. She needs you, she needs a
husband.'

'And for a long time I haven't been that to her.'

Premi looks at him open-mouthed and then
understanding, flushes, the colour flaming in her cheeks,
her ears.

'For quite some time I had a strange feeling about

Sumi. It's like when you think you recognize someone, you tap them on the shoulder and when they turn around you see it's no one you know.'

'But you loved her—you did, didn't you?' She is pleading with him.

'That seems irrelevant now, it's not the point at all.'

'Irrelevant? My God, irrelevant!'

'Why are you so angry, Premi?'

Perspicacious as usual, Gopal has divined the anger behind her grief. It's true that she's angry—and not only with Gopal, but with Sumi as well. At their carelessness in throwing away what they had, uncaring, it seems to her, of the value of what they have discarded.

'Don't take this so hard, Premi. Things will work out somehow. I said it to Amma, too. I mean it.'

'You don't know what you're saying. I go to bed with this burden of Sumi's life, I wake up with it. You can't do this, Gopal. And why? For no reason, for nothing at all. Why, Gopal? Why?'

'Premi, don't. I don't like to see you crying. And you have your own life.'

'But you're part of it, Sumi, you and the girls—oh God, how can I not think of them, of you?'

'Please, Premi.'

She tries to control herself and in a while does. They sit in silence for a few moments. When she speaks again, she is calmer, her tone more businesslike.

'Do you know Aru wrote to Anil asking him for legal advice?'

Gopal sits staring into his palm as if he hadn't heard her.

'Aru has to go her own way,' he says at last. 'I can't do anything about it.'

When they get up to go, she seems drained of all energy. Her body droops as if she can't bear the weight of it. He puts an arm around her, holding her close, giving her support until she straightens herself. It is, she remembers later, an almost wholly impersonal clasp.

'We're a cursed family, Gopal. I'm frightened for our children.'

'They'll be all right, you've got to believe that.'

The irony of this advice, coming so soon after what he has told her about himself, escapes her. But Gopal smiles at himself.

The conspiracy of silence that has been spun about Gopal's name is now, to Premi's relief, pierced by Aru who says, 'Let's go for a loaf, Premi-mavshi.'

It's obvious she wants to talk to Premi by herself—Nikhil has gone to spend the day with Jai and Deep—and that she has planned it. She leads the way to a restaurant, but once inside, she suddenly hesitates and asks, 'Is this okay?' With a touch of endearing naiveté she adds, 'I always wanted to come here. You don't mind? It's a bit expensive ....'

Premi smiles at Aru's anxious face. 'It's fine. It won't make me bankrupt.'

'The rich aunt—sorry, Premi-mavshi, you hate us saying that, don't you? But I don't like anyone spending too much money. We don't have to eat much.'

'Don't worry, Aru. Have what you want.'

But neither of them wants to eat and they settle for a coffee for Premi and an ice-cream for Aru.

'You met Papa, didn't you? What did he say?'

'The same things he said to all of you, I guess. Some things that make sense, a lot that don't. I'm wondering whether I asked him the right questions. Maybe, if I had, I'd have got the right answers.'

'Now you're talking like Papa, Premi-mavshi,' Aru retorts crossly. 'That's absolute rubbish. What right questions? There's only one—why has he done this? Actually, to tell you the truth, I'm no longer interested in his answer. What difference does it make to us, anyway? I only want him to realize he can't get away scot-free. He shouldn't be able to do this and just walk away. Did Anilkaka show you my letter?' she asks abruptly.

'Yes.'

'And he says it's no use going to the law?'

'No, he says it's more sensible not to. It won't help.'

'But, Premi-mavshi, I want to make a point. I don't understand Sumi, I truly don't.' She looks directly at Premi and Premi realizes she is in dead earnest. 'I've been thinking about marriage a great deal, Premi-mavshi. What's there in it? I mean, look at Amma and now Sumi ... What do you get out of it?'

'There's Nikhil.'

The reply is spontaneous, Premi has spoken without thinking. The next moment she flushes like a girl caught out in an admission she hadn't intended to make. But Aru, intent on some thought of her own, scarcely notices her aunt's confusion.

'And look at Goda-ajji and Bhauji-kaka—they're always scrapping. At their age and after so many years of marriage! And she's constantly complaining about him to Amma.'

In this, Aru is less than fair to Goda's marriage. She has missed out—how can she not, at her age?—the interplay of feelings that spell out that marriage.

'But tell me, Premi-mavshi, I never thought about this until we came to live with them—what really happened between Baba and Amma? Do you know?'

'Hasn't Sumi told you?'

'She said something vague about their having lost a child. It made no sense to me. Why should losing a child make them this way? Do you know what happened?' she asks again.

Premi does. So does Sumi, though her knowledge is less complete than Premi's. Strangely, they have never spoken of it between themselves. It was part of their lives, as was the situation between their parents, the oddity of which they began to realize as they grew up. As children, they accepted it; children accept everything as long as it can be absorbed into a routine. Even the small neglects and cruelties, once familiar, become less painful.

And so their ideas, as vague as Aru's are now, were never spoken of, never discussed, never questioned. Where was the need? To Premi, the shame of it had mattered more than the knowing of what really happened. She could not, she could never speak of it to anyone.

But Sumi had mentioned it to Gopal. Once. By this she had committed herself to him, to an intimacy that neither of them could ignore. (Gopal can still remember the day, the moment: Sumi flitting about his room, restless, touching things, finally sitting on the windowsill, gathering herself into an absolute stillness, saying, 'we had a brother'.)

And then, after her marriage, Sumi turned her back on the shadow in the family; but Premi, who had so much more desperately wanted to escape, walked right back into the family secret, the family history, with her marriage. For it was Anil's grandfather with whom Shripati had been working, it was Anil's family that had sheltered Kalyani until her father came and took her away. And it was Anil's mother who told Premi the whole story.

Premi had never revealed it to anyone until now, but the hunger for information she sees in Aru's eyes, the feeling that it is necessary for Aru to know what happened between Kalyani and Shripati to make sense of their situation, loosens Premi's tongue. Her coffee gets cold as she talks, Aru's ice-cream congeals into a mud-coloured mess. Premi has an odd feeling of reliving the day, of bringing something out of the recesses of her memory, so clearly can she visualize the scene: Kalyani, the baby on her lap, luggage piled about her, a little girl playing about and a boy ... the boy ....

No, it can't be a memory, how can it be? She was only a baby then, she was the baby on Kalyani's lap. It's a picture she has created for herself through the years since she heard the story, a picture so vivid that each time she goes to the railway station she thinks she can point out the exact spot where it happened.

'Amma was coming home to Bangalore for the holidays

when it happened. It happened at V.T. station—she lost him there.'

'Lost?' Aru repeats the word. 'Lost? You mean, really lost? Not dead?'

'No, not dead, not then at least.'

'Oh my God!'

'Baba had gone to check the reservations, leaving Amma with—with the children. When he returned, the boy wasn't there.' Aru waits for more. It comes grudgingly. 'He was never found.'

'And then?'

Premi is silent, she shrugs as if to say, 'what more can there be?' But Aru, her body leaning forward, her face tense, insists on a reply. Premi forces herself to go on.

'This happened in the afternoon. At night someone came to Anil's house—you know Baba worked with his grandfather—asking them to go to the station. Amma must have given them the address. She was still there, sitting on the platform, her luggage and children about her, waiting for Baba.'

'Where was he?'

'They didn't see him for nearly two months. He was searching, he went about the city like a madman, they found this out later, searching the streets, railway platforms, beaches, even hospitals and mortuaries. He never found him.'

Again she stops. This time Aru has nothing to say. Premi goes on. 'They—Anil's grandfather—sent word to Amma's father. He went to Bombay and brought her back here. Baba has not spoken to her since the day it happened.'

'He ...' Aru hesitates, 'was he older than Sumi?'

'The boy? He was a year younger than Sumi. I believe he was the same age as Goda-mavshi's Satish, they were born within a week of each other.'

'So how old was he when it happened?'

'Four. Sumi was five and I ....'

'Four? But surely—I mean, he could have spoken ....'

'No, he couldn't have done anything. He was mentally

retarded. I believe he was—he used to be quite violent. He was very well grown physically, Amma found it hard to manage him.' And now Premi seems to be speaking to herself. 'He will be nearly forty now—if he's alive. Each time I see a beggar, I think—maybe that's my brother. There's an idiot near the Siddhi Vinayak temple. I've stopped going there now, because whenever I see him, I think—that's him ....'

'Don't, Premi-mavshi, don't!'

Aru pushes her plate violently away and leaning her elbows on the table, covers her face with both her hands. The melodramatic gesture, so uncharacteristic of Aru, disturbs Premi. She puts her hand on Aru's arm and gently asks, 'Aru?'

Premi can see the effort with which Aru recovers. 'I'm all right.'

They hold hands for a moment. Aru lets go and returns to her questions.

'Didn't Amma explain what happened? What did she say?'

'Nothing.'

'The baby was crying—that was the only thing she said.' Premi can remember her mother-in-law telling her that. The baby was crying. Was that her explanation? Her justification? Did she blame me for what happened? And was that the reason for the hand pressed painfully on my mouth, for all those painful nudges, the sharp nips and hard slaps that were so much a part of my childhood, so that even now my body seems fearful, shrinking from imaginary acts of violence?

'No, Amma said nothing at all.'

'Premi-mavshi, do you think she did it deliberately? I mean, he was hard to manage—you said that, didn't you? Do you think she let him wander away and said nothing?'

Premi's reply is so prompt it is obvious she has often asked herself the same question.

'I don't think so, Aru. How could she? No mother could possibly do such a thing. It was an accident.'

'But he was retarded ....'

'Specially because he was retarded. You don't understand. I know, I've seen mothers with retarded children—they're so vulnerable, the mothers are so protective ... No, it's impossible. And Aru, don't think too much about this. It's the past, it's over now.'

'Is it?'

Late that night, Charu, on her way to the kitchen to get herself a cup of coffee, finds the light on in the hall. She goes in to switch it off and sees Aru on the sofa, apparently sleeping. Yet the moment Charu gets near her, she opens her eyes.

'What's the matter? Can't sleep?'

Aru sits up then and tells Charu the story. And ends with the same question she had asked Premi. 'Do you think she did it deliberately?'

Charu is shocked into an instant 'No! How can you even think of such a thing?'

'Baba obviously thought she did. If not, why did he ...' she searches for the exact word, 'cut himself so completely away from her? Thirty years? No, more than that. Imagine not speaking to your own wife for over thirty years.'

'But Aru, he was her son.'

'A retarded child she couldn't cope with. Think of all the things she could have done, but didn't: she could have yelled out, she could have asked someone for help, she could have sent Sumi after him ....'

'But Aru,' Charu repeats lamely, 'he was her son.' And more confidently, 'You know how she loves children, babies specially.' Yes, they've seen her with babies, with Ratna's sister's baby, chirruping to it, lifting it high, bringing it down and putting her face gently against the baby's delighted one.

'Yes, she loves babies. But you know babies are different.'

Aru is unable to explain more clearly what she means: that babies are Nature's trap, the fly-paper to catch women and pin them down to the nurturing role Nature needs them to take on for her purposes.

'And if she didn't do it, why didn't she explain, why didn't she defend herself?'

It's the injustice of it that Aru minds, Kalyani's silence that she finds inexplicable.

'She must have been scared. You know how Baba is, even I find myself tongue-tied sometimes.'

To Aru that is no excuse. It's important to her that you speak out, state the truth, that you stand up and defend yourself, that you refuse to be misjudged. Aru is at the moment reading Erica Jong and the words 'to name oneself is the first act of both the poet and the revolutionary' have filled her mind, keep resounding in it.

The sisters argue about it. They do not know it is a futile exercise, that they are trying to reach a conclusion, some conclusion, without knowing the history of the relationship between Shripati and Kalyani. They know nothing of the reason .for the marriage, of Shripati's reluctance, of Manorama's appeal to Shripati's sense of gratitude, of the cruelty that made Kalyani accept a feared uncle as a husband. They have no idea of the hopelessness that lay within the relationship, that doomed it from the start.

'She should have stood up for herself.'

'How?' Charu asks matter-of-factly.

Aru is unable to elaborate, but she is sure that the strategies can be found, they should be found. And then suddenly her belligerence gives way to despair.

'When I was a child, I used to think that as you grow older, you become wiser, more sensible, that you can cope with things better because you know so much more. But look at all of them ...' her voices rises, 'what a muddle, God in Heaven, what a muddle! What's the point going on if that's all we can do, go on muddling forever? It seems pointless. I'm not sure I want to go on.'

'Hey, you can't give up. What will I do then?'

Charu's tone is light, but Aru can see fear in her eyes. She smiles at her.

'You? You'll go on and do all the things you want to do—become a doctor, boss your patients and staff, make money, get married—to Hrishi?'

'Help! That silly kid.'

'Well, whoever. And you'll have two kids, boss them about, put the fear of God into them—and into your husband, of course ....'

Aru goes to bed smiling, but in a while she begins to think about Kalyani again, about her silence and will she ever break it? (She will, later, much later, and it is to Aru that she will speak. But even then she will not be able to bring herself to speak of that act of public desertion, of those long hours on the station platform with her children, surrounded by curious strangers, as if that is a memory so painfully blotted out that to bring it back to life would be as painful as the process of childbirth.)

And then Aru's thoughts go on to her grandfather, of what he did to Kalyani, what he is still doing to her. She tries to stoke her anger against him, but it is impossible. She can't think of the cruel husband Shripati, only of her grandfather alone in his room, of the way he looks up when she enters, of his pleasure in her company. She thinks of all his little arrangements in his room, which seem so pathetic to her, of how his fingers tremble when he folds his clothes and smooths them down. And anger ebbs away, leaving her flooded by pity instead. She turns to her father then and this is much easier; the flame of anger burns bright and steady in her.

This ambivalence in Aru soon becomes apparent to Sumi; the signals she sends out now are totally confused. Aru seems to have lost her earlier single-mindedness and in a way, Sumi is relieved by this. She has been disturbed by the thought that Aru has begun to see her mother as a victim, that, in fact, she has begun to see a victim in every woman, a betrayer in every man. I don't want her to live, to start her life, with that kind of a generalization. It's unwholesome, Sumi thinks.

Sumi is an uneasy witness to Aru's intense reaction to Premi's story about one of her patients, the pregnant wife of an AIDS patient, who, aware of his condition, married the girl so that he would have someone to look after him later. Aru's horror and pity find an echo in Sumi, who also sees in the story something else—new dimensions of betrayal and cruelty in the woman-man relationship. She does not speak of this aloud though, and she wishes Premi hadn't related the story in Aru's presence, not at this time anyway.

But it is in her relationship with Kalyani that Aru reveals her ambiguous feelings the most. The change in her behaviour towards her grandmother, since Premi's revelation, is marked. She veers from being protective and sympathetic to provocation—a kind of gentle needling, as if she's gingerly testing the sharpness of a blade with her fingertips.

The truth is that Aru is puzzled. Brooding over the impenetrable mystery of Kalyani's mind, she is now continually watching her grandmother. She finds it hard to connect that despairing woman left stranded in public to this Kalyani, chuckling over the radio, scolding Nagi, teasing her when she comes in a new sari, bullying Shyam and Shweta into eating when she finds them sitting outside their locked door, like a couple of refugees, waiting for their mother to come home.

And there is the day Charu comes home after finishing the last paper of her preliminary exams. Euphoric, she flings her books away and throwing her arms around Kalyani exclaims, 'And how are you, my dear granny?' Speaking in English. And it is in English that Kalyani replies, an American-accented English at that, an attempt at it, rather.

'I'm fine, I'm okay.'

Charu stares at her transfixed, mouth open, then suddenly grinning, chucks her grandmother under the chin saying, 'Cho chweet, Amma.'

'Get along with you.'

But Kalyani is obviously delighted by the effect of her joke.

'You think your grandmother can't speak English, eh? Let me tell you, I went to an English school for a few months, yes I did, a posh school where we wore the smartest uniforms. I can still remember my History lessons ...' And to the accompaniment of their laughter, she recites, 'Babar the Brave, Humayun the Kind, Akbar the Great, Shahjehan ....'

And while Charu questions her, 'Why did you leave that school, Amma?' Aru stares in amazement at Kalyani. Thinking of Premi's story, she wonders: can she have forgotten? Can you possibly forget such a thing? When Goda's son Satish, home on his annual vacation, visits them, noticing Kalyani fussing over him, Aru thinks: Does she remember her son when she sees Satish? Is Satish the mark on the wall against whom she measures that lost son of hers? And when Kalyani signs her name, carefully spelling out 'Kalyanibai Pandit', Aru is amazed. How can she still have his name, for God's sake? Or, and this is the most bizarre thought of all, has she forgotten all that happened, has she put it away where it belongs—in the past?

Until one day when the curtain lifts, giving Aru a glimpse of Kalyani's mind, just a glimpse, but enough to prove that all of Aru's assumptions have been wrong.

It begins with a conversation between Kalyani and Goda, an argument really. About names again, for the two women having picked up the threads of the past, seem reluctant to put them down. It's the name of Kalyani's and Goda's grandmother, the woman who died young.

'Indubai,' Goda calls her.

'Who's Indubai?'

'Why, Kalyani-akka, what do you mean? She's our grandmother.'

'Rubbish. Her name was not Indubai. They called her Indorebai because she came from Indore.'

'What was her name then?' Goda is unusually belligerent and Kalyani, prepared to give battle, falters. She can't remember. She knows it wasn't Indubai, she's sure of that, she's determined she'll prove it to Goda.

'Does it matter, Amma?' Sumi asks when she sees her going through piles of papers, old diaries and letters. But Kalyani won't give in, she's sure she'll find the name somewhere. Suddenly, in the midst of a chore, she says, 'Sitaramkaka! Why didn't I think of him earlier? He'll know.'

'Sitaramkaka? Who's he?'

Learning that he was the family priest in Kalyani's house when she was a girl, they are incredulous. 'You think he's still alive?'

Kalyani knows he is. She met his grandson Giridhar, with whom the old man lives, just a few months back. He was still going strong then, Giridhar said. 'I think I'll pay him a visit,' she says.

The old man's grandson, Giridhar, is himself nearly sixty. And the child, toddling unsteadily in the hall, is his grandchild. Which makes the baby—what? The old man's great grandson? Aru, who has accompanied her grandmother, quails at the immensity of his age.

But there's nothing awesome about the old man who's lying propped up on a hard pillow, the picture of a well-tended child. He looks heart-breakingly clean, as if his bones and his eyes have been scrubbed the same way as his clothes. He stares at them blankly while Giridhar's wife tries to prod him into an awareness of the visitors.

'It's Kalyaniamma, Ajja. I told you she's coming. Remember? Surely you remember Kalyaniamma?'

The old man comes suddenly out of his apathy, nods vigorously, laughs and mumbles something they can't make out.

'He's so good sometimes.' The woman sounds like the disappointed parent of a child who's refused to perform before guests. 'He understands everything we say. I don't know what's the matter with him today.'

Over coffee and large plates of snacks, Kalyani explains the purpose of their visit. Aru, listening to her, is embarrassed. It seems absurd, intruding into the lives of these strangers—strangers to her, if not to Kalyani—in search of something as unimportant as a name from the past. She is amazed that the family doesn't seem to think so; on the contrary, they gather around listening in fascination to Kalyani, pressing food and coffee on them with much warmth and goodwill, they apologize over and over again for the old man's inability to give Kalyani what she wants.

In spite of the chaos resulting from so many people in the house (there are three generations—no, four, if you include the old man) living together, there is a sense of cohesion. And if the furniture is shabby and the house untidy, there is a feeling of lavishness in the house, not of opulence or luxury, but of plenty, of comfortable living. Giridhar, the fountainhead of all these comforts, is obviously a very successful accountant, yet there is more than a hint of patronage in Kalyani's attitude towards him, towards the whole family. And Giridhar too keeps repeating, 'It's all your blessings, Amma, yours and your parents'. If your father hadn't helped my father to study, we would never have got all this.'

Giridhar's wife, the one the old man most easily relates to, makes another attempt to rouse him before they leave. This time Kalyani talks to him as well.

'Don't you know me, Sitaramkaka? I'm Kalyani, Vithalrao and Manoramabai's daughter.'

The old man titters as if she has made a joke. The woman pats his hand gently and says, 'All right, ajja, all right.' Suddenly the old man's eyes fall on Aru.

'Who are you?' he asks clearly.

'I'm Arundhati.'

'She's my granddaughter, Sitaramkaka. My Sumi's eldest daughter.'

The old man doesn't seem to hear Kalyani. He's still looking at Aru.

'Kalyani.' The name emerges clearly.

'Yes, yes.' Kalyani is excited. 'I'm Kalyani, Manorama's daughter.'

'Poor child,' he says, still speaking to Aru. 'She was so

frightened. Poor child.'

'Let him be,' the woman says when, having lost interest in Aru, he goes on mumbling 'poor child' to himself. 'I don't think he will remember anything today. Go to sleep, ajja.'

They leave him lying flat, eyes closed like an obedient child, arms by his sides.

Kalyani's silence on the way back, a silence that gives Aru the feeling of a shutter having come down, continues even after they get home and it is left to Aru to tell the others about their visit.

The next day, however, Kalyani is back to normal and Aru, returning home, finds her in a state of frenetic excitement.

'Giridhar rang up. His grandfather woke up today, absolutely clear and lucid and when they asked him for the name, he told them.' She pauses for dramatic effect. 'You'll never believe this. She was Arundhati.'

'What!'

Kalyani is satisfied, triumphant, crowing over Goda when she comes in the evening. Nothing can mar her pleasure, not even Aru's doubt.

'How do you know it's the right name? He heard my name, remember? Perhaps that's how it got into his head. He could have got things mixed up. He called me poor child, remember?'

'He said that? To you?' Goda asks.

'Yes, he kept saying—"poor child, she was so frightened." '

Kalyani and Goda exchange a quick glance and to Aru, who sees the look of shared complicity, it is clear they know what the old man meant. Amma knew it yesterday, which is why she was so silent. 'Poor child'—was it Amma he meant?

But Kalyani says nothing and Aru will hear the story later, from Kalyani herself, though not all of it, for Kalyani will blame herself, absolve her mother of all wrongdoing. She was disappointed in me, she will say, she expected me to be like her, but I was too timid, too dull, she will say.

Timid, yes, and unsure of herself. And, with a mother like Manorama, with a sense of inadequacy as well. It was this that made the letters so pleasurable to her. They made her feel admired and appreciated. Kalyani was fifteen then, and pretty in a dainty, fragile kind of way. The young man who watched the girls going to school obviously thought her very pretty. And so the letters, one each day, which came by way of a little boy. There was nothing in the letters to identify the sender, they were unsigned. And innocent. Romantic in a poetic kind of way. Kalyani was enchanted. But Goda, two years younger, was troubled. It seemed wrong somehow. And finally, when the letters came close to asking for a meeting, she spoke to Manorama about it.

At first Kalyani was, oddly enough, relieved to have the burden of her secret taken off her. And totally unprepared, therefore, for the intensity of her mother's anger. Manorama made it seem that Kalyani had done something obscene, she asked her questions the girl did not understand and could not answer. Terror drove her into dumbness and to her mother her silence confirmed her guilt. Vithalrao, realizing that his attempts to shield her made things worse, withdrew. Even the family priest was touched by the girl's plight, but no one dared to speak to Manorama.

That was the end of Kalyani's schooling. Manorama never let her go out of the house after that and within a year she was married. Even today Kalyani speaks with regret of her lost education.

'I envy these girls, don't you, Goda? They are so free.'

'You want to wear pants and ride a scooter like them, eh, Kalyani-akka?' Goda teases her but she knows what Kalyani really means. For if anyone knows the whole story, it is Goda. She was a spectator, a guilty one and the thought still haunts her: why did I speak to Mami about that letter?

And yet Kalyani is right in playing down everything but her mother's disappointment in her, for it was that which played the biggest role in her life. Manorama wanted a son; instead there was Kalyani. Not an unloved child, no, never that. But for Manorama, she became the visible symbol of their failure to have a son. And then, she fulfilled none of the dreams Manorama had for her daughter. Her daughter, she had thought, would be beautiful, accomplished, she would make a brilliant marriage that would be Manorama's triumph, that would show them, the family, all those women who had treated Manorama, the daughter of a poor man from a village, with such contempt. Instead there was Kalyani, who could do nothing that pleased her mother.

Except once, when she gave birth to a son. There was great rejoicing then. Vithalrao, joking, had called it a red carpet lying-in. It was literally that, for there was a beautiful red carpet by Kalyani's bedside for her to put her feet on, the moment she got out of bed. And the fire under the huge copper pot burned all day, so that Kalyani had hot water to wash even her little finger. The naming ceremony was the occasion of a lifetime. The house was full of guests, fragrant with flowers, gleaming with silverware. The poor were fed and the dustbin in the street was overflowing with used banana-leaf plates for two whole days.

But the child turned out to be an idiot and Kalyani came back home, a deserted wife, with her two daughters.

Kalyani is forever speaking of miracles, she sees them everywhere, even in this matter of a name.

'When we named you Arundhati, the name didn't come out of nowhere, it was put into our heads, I'm sure of that,' she says with sibylline sagacity. (Ignoring the fact that it was Gopal who chose the name.)

The family smiles at her predictability, they humour her, none of them believe in her miracles. They don't seem to realize that the real miracle is Kalyani herself, Kalyani who has survived intact, in spite of what Shripati did to her, Kalyani who has survived Manorama's myriad acts of cruelty.

Manorama died unforgiving, she never relented in her anger towards her daughter. There was more to it than the disgrace of her coming back home, a rejected wife. Manorama's treatment of her daughter led to a breach between Vithalrao and Manorama, the first since their marriage. Vithalrao was a changed man after Kalyani's return home. To everyone's surprise, the man of science turned to astrology and a different astrologer came home every few days. It was as if Vithalrao was searching for someone who would tell him, 'your daughter will soon be reunited with her husband, they will live happily together.' If it was a search, it was a solitary one, for he never spoke to anyone about it, he never associated his wife with it.

The rift between them never healed. Vithalrao had a stroke soon after and for this, too, Manorama held her daughter responsible. She would have liked to punish her by keeping her away from her father, but that was not possible.

It was painful for Manorama to see the man Vithalrao had become. She had enthroned her husband, put him up on a pedestal; it did not matter to her that he did not want to be there. She never realized that he laughed self-deprecatingly at the position he was forced to occupy by his wife. His collapse into a broken, suffering human being was hard for her to take. His tears—and he cried a great deal—horrified her. 'Stop it,' she would say, scolding him with a rough tenderness. 'You shouldn't do this, stop it.'

But Kalyani was never embarrassed by his tears. She gently wiped them away as if he was a younger sibling, patted his hand and sat silently by his side until he recovered. He seemed soothed by her presence, something that filled Manorama with an angry grief. A few days before his death he kept repeating some words none of them could catch. It was Kalyani who finally understood what it was he was trying to say. 'Put me down.' He wanted to be put down on the floor; it was as if he knew that death was coming and he had to prepare himself for it.

Manorama refused to accept this. No, Kalyani was wrong, that wasn't what he was saying. And she wasn't going to allow them to move him from the bed. The fact was she was terrified, she wouldn't let him go, she refused to understand that Vithalrao wanted to die, that he was straining after death. Kalyani, unable to bear her father's agonised pleas, had him removed from the bed and placed on the floor when Manorama was away. She was rewarded by the peaceful look on his face. He died in a short while and to Manorama, it was as if Kalyani had killed him.

'You are my enemy, you were born to make my life miserable.' The words echoed in Kalyani's ears every night.

Yet in her own last illness, Manorama would let no one but Kalyani look after her. Even Goda, towards whom her favouritism became more blatantly obvious, was not allowed to do anything for her aunt. Kalyani is the only one who knows what she had to endure, for Manorama in her last days was not only tyrannical, she became suspicious and fearful, charging Kalyani with trying to kill her as she had her father.

And then she wrote to her brother, a fact that Kalyani learnt from Goda. It was when the builders came to build a room upstairs that Kalyani realized Shripati would be coming back to live with them. She lay awake at nights, terrified, waking out of fearful dreams when she did finally fall asleep, her body drenched in sweat. Shripati came home and, as if she had been waiting for this, Manorama died soon after.

Aru tries to connect the two women, the Kalyani left stranded by her husband in public and this Kalyani who seems to have exorcised all her ghosts. And fails. How can she not fail when she knows nothing of the long journey that lies between these two points, of the different points on that journey? Later, when they spend much time together, Kalyani will speak to her of it, of some of it. And strangely, she will speak without bitterness, as if she has, indeed, exorcised her ghosts.

But certain things will remain: Kalyani's mulishness, as Goda calls it, in refusing to wear her mother's diamonds or saris, the furtive air with which she mends clothes, as if expecting her mother to come upon her and say, as she so often had, 'haven't you anything better to do than this beggarly occupation?'

The truth is that Kalyani, her mother's despair, the girl who had seemed such a weak, feeble creature, was the one who defeated her mother after all. Manorama had taken charge of her own and her husband's life, she had given it a shape that was to dazzle everyone. She herself took an enormous pride in her husband's position and her own public activities, which included instituting, with her husband's support, a school for girls: The Yamunabai Pawar School for Girls.

But Kalyani destroyed all this. When she returned home, a deserted wife, and, as Manorama saw it, a disgrace to the family, Manorama gave up everything, she never took part in any public activities again.

ॐ

'GARDENING?'

Kalyani is surprised to see Sumi in the kitchen garden, planting bulbs in the bed she's got Bora to prepare for her. The soil here is rich and wet and yields easily to Sumi's probing fingers.

'What's that you're planting?'

'Those white flowers, they're delicate and fragrant—I don't know their name ....'

'Tuberoses?'

'No, Amma, they're bigger, gladioli-size, but more delicate ....'

'Saugandhika?'

'Maybe. I don't know. One of the girls gave me the flowers—I liked them, so she got me these bulbs today. Let's see what comes up.'

'If it is Saugandhika, we'll have to wait till Shravan.'

'That's eight months—well, that's not very long to wait.' Eight months—not very long to wait? Kalyani thinks of the twelve-year-old Sumi who had been so captivated by the Tillanna—its perfect heart-stopping rhythm, the exquisite, almost mathematical perfection of its poses—that she had joined a dance class right away. And left it within a week.

'They say I have to wait years before I can dance the Tillanna,' she had said.

And now she says—'eight months is not a very long time to wait.'

'Perhaps it's some other flower and we'll see it earlier,'

Kalyani says with some vague idea of being comforting.

Sumi, smoothing the earth, patting it flat, thinks, yes, who knows what will come up? And as she is washing her hands at the tap, the story of the Princess and the tree that grew in her backyard comes into her mind.

Now, who was it who had told her the story? It couldn't possibly have been Kalyani, she had never been a teller of stories—not then. But if Sumi can't remember the storyteller, she can remember the story very distinctly. Suddenly the characters seem to come out of her childhood into the present, bringing their story with them.

The king. His much-loved only daughter who ate rice and curds every day. And the tree that grew in the backyard where she washed her hands after each meal. The child growing up into a beautiful princess (naturally—could a princess be anything but beautiful?) And her declaration that she would marry the man who could identify the tree. All the suitors failing, except one. And that one the palace gardener's son who had seen her washing her hands at the spot every day. It's a 'Rice and Curds' tree, he said. And so won the princess's hand.

Goda—suddenly Sumi remembers it was Goda who had told them this story. Only Goda-mavshi could choose a story with such a prosaic undertone to a romance. Yes, she'd have no problems yoking the romantic to the mundane. (Sumi remembers protesting, 'But, Goda-mavshi, there can't be such a tree!' And Goda's stern rejoinder, 'Why not? How do we know?' Yes, she was right. How do we know, how can we ever know that a thing does not exist?)

Perhaps, Goda-mavshi's simple purpose had been to overcome Sumi's dislike of rice and curds. But, and Sumi smiles to herself, there are so many more morals in it, some just right for today. There's the importance given to a tree, to the identification of it, there's the dismissal of the aristocracy, the triumph of the common working man ....

And yes, it occurs to Sumi, there's more to it then this. To think of it, why did the princess insist on such a queer condition? Had she fallen in love with the gardener's son and—Sumi feels a quickening excitement at the thought—plotted the whole thing, knowing this was the only way she could get him? She knew her father, she must have been sure this was the only way to trick him into giving her what she wanted. Yes, she must have been a clever young woman, indeed. And, perhaps, a passionate one? Had she watched the gardener's son at work, noticed his muscles gleaming in the sun and decided she would have him for her husband?

A clever young woman, anyway, who used a man's own weapons against him. The stratagem would never have worked with a woman; no woman would fall into the trap of honouring one's word, of giving a blank post-dated cheque. Would Kausalya have sent her son Rama into exile because some time, long ago, she had promised a man she would give him any boon he asked for? What a dangerous weapon such a promise was! Things change with time, people change, circumstances change; nothing is constant. And therefore, you can never make a promise for the future. (And yet, if you cannot expect constancy, on what do you base human relationships?) No, Kausalya would never have made such a promise; and even if she had, she would have refused to honour it. Was honour worth all the tragedy that followed?

These ideas and the story of the gardener's son come together in Sumi's mind when she hears one of the teachers in her school speak of wanting a play for the inter-school play competition.

And so 'The Gardener's Son', which Sumi writes out in two nights. An ordinary fairy-tale with the Princess's subversive tactics woven into it. The teacher in charge of dramatics, desperately looking for a play, grabs it and the very next day they choose a cast and start rehearsing the play.

Working with the girls, rehearsing them, Sumi finds herself filled with exhilaration. It's not just that she's broken through the barriers the girls had put up against

her, a new teacher: it's the girls' laughter as they read out
the lines, the fact that they have caught on to what Sumi
has made of the fairy-tale, the fact that she, yes, she has
done this.

'What do you think happens afterwards, Miss?' one of
the girls asks. And Sumi thinks of it on her way back home.
Yes, what happens when the gardener's son gets power and
becomes the King? He shuts his wife out of that power, of
course; that's inevitable. But will she be able to find a
weapon against him as she did against her father? A
weapon that will not destroy herself as well?

It's a good thing fairy-tales end where they do. Wisdom
lies in knowing where to stop. Sanskrit drama is right:
there should be no tragedy. If we are to construct a world,
why not shape one with the hopelessness left out, why not
end with the hope of happiness, the promise of realization?
Bhavabhuti reneged against the rules in his
Uttararamacharita, he looked beyond the safe family portrait
of Rama, Lakshmana and Sita, with Hanuman kneeling at
their feet, and look what a tragedy he conjured up! And
then, unable to bear the burden of it, he made a U-turn
and came back to a commonplace, saccharine, utterly
incredible happy ending. No, better to leave things alone,
end with the word 'Shubham'. 'All's well'. And so, I will
leave the Princess and the gardener's son to enjoy the
fruits of their plot, I will not go beyond that.

Reaching home, Sumi is putting her vehicle away when
Aru comes out to her with a swiftness that reveals she has
been waiting for the sound of her mother's moped. Sumi
feels a throb of anxiety at the sight of Aru's face.

'You're late.'

'We were rehearsing ... What's the matter?'

'It's Seema.' Sumi's heart skips a beat. 'She's not well.
She's just started her periods.'

'Oh, is that all? For a moment, you scared me.'

Yet when she sees Seema in bed, lying on her side, her
skirt rucked up showing the back of her thighs, she looks
so childish, so vulnerable, that for the first time Sumi feels

the burden of mothering girls.

'Seema?' She opens her eyes and looks blankly at her mother. 'Are you all right?'

'No, I'm sick, I have a pain, I'm feeling dirty, I stink, I hate it.'

'It happens to everyone.'

'So?' Sumi has nothing to say to that. 'And it will go on and on until I'm old.'

'Seema, it's not so bad.'

'Leave me alone.'

I can't reach her. How did I cope with Aru and Charu? Was it easier because Gopal was with me? But Gopal was no use, he was just angry and embarrassed, he felt uneasy with the girls for a while ....

'Seema, you're not sick. This is growing up.'

There's a stubborn silence.

'I don't want to grow up,' she says finally. 'And they say I can have a baby.'

'They? Who said that?' No reply. 'That's not true. You're just being—prepared. But you can't have a baby unless you want it.'

What am I saying? Seema herself was born when I didn't want a baby. And it's no use, anyway. Seema curls herself into a ball and goes into a fit of crying.

'Seema, listen to me ....'

'Go away, I want to sleep, I want to be alone.'

The tone is not a child's, it's an adult's and Sumi goes away. Seema has a right to cope with things in her own way.

A little later, however, Sumi sees Seema sitting up, drinking a cup of Bournvita Kalyani has got her, listening with childlike interest to Kalyani's stories of how it was in their days.

'We had to sit out three whole days, we couldn't touch anything. My father didn't believe in it, it's nonsense, he used to say, it's not dirty, it's natural. But my mother wanted us to observe the staying-apart ritual. And so, on those three days we sat apart, Goda and I, all day, but the moment father came home, we behaved as if we'd done everything as usual. We couldn't sit on the sofas, of course, and we didn't eat with the others. Poor man, my father never guessed. Such a clever man, but ....'

Surely, if he was such a clever man, he did guess, Sumi thinks sourly. And then she's ashamed of herself. I shouldn't mind that Amma could do what I couldn't. Yet the soreness remains and later she says to Kalyani, 'Now, don't you encourage Seema to imagine herself ill and stay away from school.'

But to everyone's surprise Seema goes to school the next day and, except for a slight awkwardness in her movements, seems to have gone back to her usual self. Yet there is a change. In the evening she tells Sumi, 'I want to see Papa.' That she has some purpose in her mind is quite clear. She is also sure about what she wants: Sumi is to take her—she firmly rejects Aru's offer to do so—and once there, she is to leave her alone with Gopal.

Sumi is standing in the yard of Shankar's house when Shankar drives in.

'Madam!' He's astonished to see her. 'Why are you here? Is Sir not in?'

She explains about Seema.

'Come in, then, Madam.'

He is so distressed by her standing outside that she agrees.

'Manju,' he calls out to his wife. 'Take Madam inside, will you?'

It is obvious from the plates and glasses strewn all over the house that there has been a festive meal that morning. The house is still redolent with festive cooking smells.

Manju leads her to a vigorous-looking woman. 'This is my mother-in-law,' she says. And to her, 'Amma, this is Gopal sir's wife.'

Under the old woman's directions, Manju gets Sumi a heaped plate. When Sumi demurs, the old woman argues, she insists Sumi eat everything, but Manju quietly takes the plate away and gets Sumi a glass of coffee. The coffee is good, hot, frothing and sweet and drinking it, Sumi feels her fatigue draining away from her. While the old woman talks to Sumi, probes, rather, she watches Manju moving about, takes in the grace of her movements, the sense of repression that she gives. She neither sits down, nor does she speak to Sumi, leaving the role of hostess entirely to her mother-in-law. Only when Sumi gets up to go does Manju come to her, with the ritual plate of kumkum, paan-supari and coconut in her hands.

'When are you going back to your husband?' the old woman asks abruptly. 'You should be with him. Look at his state! It's all right to stay with your parents for a while, but that's not your home. When my daughters come home, I don't let them stay long. Go back to your husband, he's a good man. If you've done wrong, he'll forgive you. And if he has—women shouldn't have any pride.'

'Please don't mind my mother-in-law,' Manju waits until they are out of the room before speaking. 'Old people think they can say what they want, they can hurt your feelings, it doesn't matter.'

Manju's tone is so bitter that Sumi comes out of her own thoughts, the insistent drumbeat of 'how-dare-she, how-dare-she' and sees the distress on Manju's face, the misty sheen of incipient tears in her eyes.

'It's all right,' she says.

'And please don't let my husband know what his mother said. He respects you and Gopal sir so much ....'

'It's all right, Manju.'

Outside the house, in the open air, she feels a little better, released from the fearful anger and pain. On an impulse she puts her hand on the younger woman's arm.

'I won't tell your husband, I promise. And don't feel bad for me.'

However, Shankar himself picks up the thread of his mother's talk. 'Madam, have you seen how Sir looks? He's lost so much weight, I'm worried about him ....'

'Shankar,' and Sumi speaks in English, 'I can't do anything for Gopal. He's going his way and I have to go mine.'

The utter weariness of her tone silences Shankar and they stand without speaking until they see Gopal and Seema descending the stairs. Seema is ahead and Sumi notices that she's given up wearing her little girl's socks and shoes, that she's wearing heeled sandals instead. Her legs look shapely and dainty, the legs of a young girl, not a child's. Has she been crying? Sumi can't see her face in the fading light, only the way they come down, Gopal and she, as if unaware of each other, giving the sense of a great distance between them.

On the way home, in the rickshaw, only an arm's length away from other vehicles, Sumi has a sense of the city converging on her. The noise and the tumult fill her ears and instinctively she moves closer to Seema to assuage her panic. But Seema, staring straight ahead, seems as much a stranger as the rickshaw driver, oblivious to everything but the moment when the lights will change and he can move on. And suddenly Sumi's anger turns from the old woman to Gopal. He had no right to do this to me, to let the world into our relationship. And what did he say to Seema? What did she ask him? Why doesn't she tell me anything, why doesn't she talk to me? How do I reach her?

☙

ROHIT IS NOW a regular visitor. Unaware of the past, wholly disinterested in early animosities, confident of his future, Rohit is enchanted by this family he has stumbled upon, especially by the eldest girl, with a stately name that fits her like a glove. Rohit is no romantic, he is a practical young man with his feet firmly planted on the ground; but to see Aru in that house brings to his mind the magic of fairy-tales, of kings, queens, princesses and enchanted castles. He makes no attempt to conceal his interest in her; it's there, right out in the open for all to see. Walking in now on the three sisters who are looking at some pictures, exclaiming and laughing over them, his eyes linger on Aru as she collects the pictures and puts them away. Aru is conscious of his look, as her heightened colour and the slight stiffness of self-consciousness reveal. She is mortified by her own reaction and when Rohit asks her, 'Can you give me a lift?' she is brusque and rude.

'Where's your car?'

'Gone for servicing.'

'I'm not going your way.'

'Drop me at the Circle. I'll get a rickshaw from there.'

'All right, come on, then.'

It's a grudging concession but Rohit settles himself composedly on the pillion as if he hasn't noticed it.

'Did you say something?' she suddenly turns around and asks him just as she gets ready to start the vehicle.

'Me? No. You must have heard the beating of my heart.'

He's perfectly serious, there's not even the glimmer of a smile in his eyes.

'Is that supposed to be "ha ha funny" as Charu says?'

'No, I'm serious.'

His face is still grave. Aru gives him a puzzled look and turns away. Rohit is careful not to touch her, he sits erect like a soldier on parade, arms folded across his chest, keeping his balance perfectly, even when they bump over the uneven stones outside the gate.

Kalyani who has been watching them, gives a small sigh when they move out and turning round to go back into the house, sees Charu behind her.

'What happened to the boy from the States, Amma?' Charu innocently asks. Kalyani flips her palm downwards in a contemptuous gesture as if to say 'Who cares?' and Charu laughs.

The truth is, as Aru has already noticed, old skeletons are harmless. Their bones have crumbled into fine dust and you can sift through it without fear or distaste. It's the newer skeletons you have to be wary of, they're the ones you've got to keep securely locked in cupboards, be careful that they never get out and show you their deathly grins.

'Why did you tell Rohit about Gopal?' Kalyani questions Sumi.

'That we don't live together? You think he doesn't know it? Amma, everyone knows it by now. What purpose would a lie serve?'

'He'll tell his mother about it. They'll all know. Rohit will never come back.'

'Does it matter if he doesn't? Why are you so bothered, Amma, about the opinion of people we've had nothing to do with for years?'

But to Kalyani's astonishment and delight, not only does Rohit come again, he brings his mother with him when he does. Kalyani is in a flutter. It is an event for her. She talks too much, gestures too extravagantly, springs up and walks about, forgetting what it was she had got up for.

'I should have known. I got the coconuts plucked today and it always happens this way—the day we do it, one of the family comes home. Remember, Goda, the last time we took down the coconuts, it was your sister-in-law who dropped in?'

'And the time before that, it was Chitra's mother ....'

While they speak, Kalyani and Goda are wordlessly exchanging their impressions of their visitor. Lalita, who has what looks like an impregnable self-assurance, seems a most unlikely mother for the sober, quiet, Rohit. In her rich silk, ornate jewellery and vivid eye make-up, she is too elaborately dressed for such a visit. But the loudness is not vulgar; rather, it has the over-emphasis of the actress or dancer, the likeness to an artiste heightened by her total control over her physical self.

It turns out that she is, in fact, an artiste. She is a veena player, she expects them to have heard of her—'I've played on the radio, even once on TV'—though the fact that they have not, makes no dent in her self-confidence; she takes it in her stride. Her curiosity about this family is the only chink in her armour. It is obvious that she has heard about them, much before Rohit renewed contact, and the subtle air of condescension, the hint of patronage she shows Kalyani, which Kalyani fortunately misses, reveals that they have been regarded as 'those poor things', unfortunates who need to be pitied.

Sumi's entry distracts Lalita; she gives her an intent, puzzled look. 'Have we met before?' she asks after Kalyani's introduction.

Sumi, tired, in need of a wash, hesitates, says, 'No, I don't think so,' and goes in.

Kalyani, who has been on the defensive since Sumi's entry—what has Lalita heard about her? What is she going to ask?—suddenly plunges into talk about 'Premi, my doctor daughter'. When Sumi joins them, her face glowing and damp after a wash, Kalyani is well into Premi's family by marriage: 'Her husband's grandfather was a great lawyer, a friend of Sardar Patel', and 'her father-in-law was a judge, you must have heard of him?'

Poor Amma, Sumi thinks, Premi and Anil's family—this is all that is left for her to brag about. But Lalita isn't really interested; in fact, she's scarcely listening. Her curious eyes have gone back to Sumi's face. Suddenly, interrupting Kalyani, she exclaims, 'Of course! Now I know. I saw you in the play last year. You were with that group ... What's the name?'

'The Players. Yes, I was.'

There is a subtle shift in Lalita's attitude; something has been defined which brings Kalyani's family out of the 'poor unfortunates' class. And when it is discovered that Chitra, whom she knows, is related to Sumi, her tone becomes even more friendly. The real woman, kindly, if self-absorbed, emerges from the pose of a visiting dignitary. Absent-mindedly she begins to munch the chaklis she had spurned earlier as she talks to Sumi about her younger daughter who's 'crazy about the theatre'.

'She wants to make a profession of it, she says, she's already acted in a TV serial, but we think she's too young ....'

'How old is she?'

'Sixteen.'

'Sixteen. Ah, that's the age! When I was sixteen I could act a little, dance a little, paint a little, write a little and I thought that together they added up to genius. Oh yes, I was going to be someone great.'

'Look who's being modest!' Aru says it mockingly, but her tone is belied by the way she puts her cheek gently against her mother's face.

Kalyani is easier with Lalita now. No longer trying to impress her, she launches into her family stories. And to Goda's great embarrassment and Lalita's amusement, she tells them the story of Vidyapati, Lalita's uncle, who fell in love with Goda and wanted to marry her.

Goda, blushing like a girl, tries to prevent her, repeating,

'Stop it, Kalyani-akka, who's interested in all this,' but Kalyani is unstoppable.

'My mother said "never!" but my father said, "let's ask Goda herself." '

'And what did you say, Goda-ajji?'

'She? What else would this silly thing say? "Whatever you say, Mama, whatever you say, Mami."' Kalyani imitates, or thinks she does, Goda's voice. 'But my mother would never agree. And just a year later Vidyapati died. He got galloping TB and died in three months. And my mother said, wasn't I right? What would have happened if we had let him marry our Godu?'

Sumi notices Goda's involuntary shudder, the way the colour drains from her face, her hands clench into tight fists, as if she feels the dreadful flap of the wings of widowhood brush past her. And Sumi wonders, is this what has helped Kalyani to endure everything, the fact that she is a wife and not a widow? The fact that she has the right to all the privileges of the wife of a living husband? Sumi remembers the tray of kumkum, paan-supari and coconut Manju brought her, she thinks of the old woman's words, 'What is a woman without her husband?'

Is it enough to have a husband, and never mind the fact that he has not looked at your face for years, never mind the fact that he has not spoken to you for decades? Does this wifehood make up for everything, for the deprivation of a man's love, for the feel of his body against yours, the warmth of his breath on your face, the touch of his lips on yours, his hands on your breasts? Kalyani lost all this (had she ever had them?) but her kumkum is intact and she can move in the company of women with the pride of a wife.

Sumi remembers now what she had heard once, that it is prostitutes who are invited to thread a bride's black beads, because a prostitute can never become that inauspicious thing—a widow. A prostitute is never a wife, yet she is eternally every man's wife. Clever convoluted thinking, twisted logic, but right, if you believe in the first

premise—that to have a husband living is everything. But—
oh my God, oh my God!

And then again, where does this leave the idea of love?
Is that only a phantasmagoria that writers and poets have
trapped within words? But, no, it's not only Shakuntala
and Dushyanta, or Romeo and Juliet; flesh-and-blood people
have, through the years, pledged it, consummated it, died
for the thing they call love.

For a brief while, Gopal and I were part of this eternal
story too. We fell in love. I fell in love with his physical
being first, I have to admit that, with the spare clean lines
of his body, his eyes that crinkled at the corners, the way
his face moved from being earnest and adult in repose to
a boyish innocence when he smiled. I was captivated by all
these things; to me they were Gopal.

But this passes. We don't need to be saints to turn away
from physical pleasures. We don't have to go such a long
way, either, as Yayati did, to realize that a time comes when
the pleasures of the body pall. They taste flat, insipid,
perhaps even bitter. We want love to last, we think when we
begin that it will, but it never does; it transforms itself into
a desire for possession, a struggle for power.

What lasts then? The loss of the familiar rustling by my
side at night is what I mourn, not our lovemaking. I feel
cold without the presence of Gopal in my life; sex has
nothing to do with it, no, nothing at all.

My father gave up everything and turned to solitude.
Sometimes I think he turned his back on his wife because
he was frightened of himself, of what he could do in his
anger. I have sensed it in him, a kind of suppressed
savagery. Or maybe that was only an excuse which helped
him to get out of a marriage he had never wanted. Who
knows the truth? I only know that, sometimes, he seems to
me as much a victim as Kalyani.

Aru will never agree. Perhaps Aru is right. Put into the
context of here and now, Kalyani is more of a victim than
he is. And yet, when Aru speaks of the 'sins of patriarchy',

I am uneasy. She is only quoting, I know that, I imagine it is the Biblical ring of the words that appeals to her. Nevertheless, it makes me uneasy. For things are never so simple. We can never know all the incalculables hidden in the human heart. Why did my father come back? Was it his sense of responsibility towards his wife and daughters? To return to a wife he had spurned, to give up the ambitions and career which had become his whole life—no, that is something I can never understand. Has he learnt it now, the enormity of the thing he has done? Is that why he said to me, 'Let your girls learn to stand on their feet. Don't worry too much about getting them married'?

But I do worry, I have begun to worry about their marriage. I know they will stand on their own feet, I have no fears for Aru and Charu, not on that count. But marriage? Will Aru learn that love, however brief, however unsatisfactory, however tragic, is necessary? Will she realize that without that kind of a companionship some part of us withers and dies?

Yes, Sumi is anxious about Aru. She can no longer ignore the reality of Rohit's feelings towards Aru. She can no longer smile, as she has done until now, at Kalyani's comments and hints—not after the day she comes upon Rohit and Aru in the hall. She has an unexpected sense of intruding when she sees them together. And she is struck by the look on Rohit's face. His pose of casual sophistication has fallen away from him and he looks wholly vulnerable. But there is nothing ridiculous about this lover's look on his face. On the contrary, his consciousness of his vulnerability gives him both dignity and stature.

And then, as Sumi takes in Aru's taut body, the look of startled anger on her face, Rohit sees Sumi. He changes in an instant into the Rohit she knows.

'He spoke to me of Papa, of Papa and you,' Aru explains when he has gone, having given Sumi an invitation to his older sister's wedding. 'How dare he?'

'He meant well.'

'Meant well! It's none of his business. Honestly, Ma, you're as bad as Amma.'

I'm not thinking of your marrying him, you're far too young for that, Sumi wants to say. Just don't reject his friendship, don't reject it because he's a man.

But Sumi says nothing except, 'Are you coming for the wedding?'

'No, thanks.'

'You don't have a hope of staying away. Amma won't let us off.'

Sumi is right. Kalyani is very earnest about their participating in this family wedding. It means something to her that none of them, except Goda, can understand.

'So the family feud is over, eh, Amma?' Charu teases her grandmother.

'What family feud?'

Yet, when Kalyani gets her jewellery home from the bank and allots pieces to each one of them, Sumi understands: the family feud is not over. Kalyani wants them to attend in all their finery, to show the family that all is well with them, that there is nothing wrong. The girls' excitement, their exclamations over the jewellery, peppered, of course, with Charu's jokes, mislead Kalyani into believing that they will go to the wedding with her. She is crestfallen when she finds out on the morning that Sumi is the only one accompanying her.

'I don't understand these girls. When we were young, we would never miss a wedding. And if we were allowed to distribute flowers or paan-supari—why, that was heaven for us!'

'They've agreed to go for the reception. You can't except more than that.'

But when Devaki comes to pick them up in the evening, Kalyani and Seema are the only two ready and waiting. Sumi comes out yawning, her face swollen with sleep.

'No, Devi, I'm not coming. What, dress up all over again and stand about talking to people I don't know? I admire your energy, I really do.'

'Oh, come on Sumi, if we don't go for these things, when will we wear our grand saris?'

'Saris! Aha, now I know what you really go out for.'

'Don't be silly. Tell this lazy thing to join us, Kalyani-mavshi.'

But Sumi won't be moved. And Devaki gets restless. 'Where are the girls? Seema, go and tell them ....'

Suddenly she stops. The two girls are walking towards them, Aru in a sari, a rich gold and red, parodying the model's slow, hip-swinging walk, her long plait snaking in fluid movements behind her. The girls, from their expressions, seem to be expecting laughter, mock applause perhaps, but there is only a dead silence.

Charu breaks in with an impatient 'Well?' standing beside Aru like the creator of this miracle. 'Say something, someone. Isn't this a surprise? We're ready to continue the family feud, we'll show them—eh, Aru?'

But the silence goes on, all of them still staring at Aru. Aru, who has been smiling, innocently charmed by her own changed image, becomes conscious of the silence, of their stares and asks, 'For Heaven's sake, what is the matter? Why is everyone staring at me?'

'Look,' Kalyani points to Manorama's picture on the wall. 'You look like her.'

Their eyes go to the picture on the wall. There is a marked difference between Manorama's strong-boned, rather sensual face, and Aru's delicate, ascetic one. But now, at this moment, Kalyani is right. Whatever resemblance there is, is emphasized, it springs out at them.

And then Hrishi rushes in exclaiming, 'Aren't we going?' He sees Aru, stops and says, 'Wow!' And then, 'That's the end of poor Rohit.'

'Don't be stupid.' Aru is red with anger, her hands move as if she would tear the sari off her.

'Let's go, we're wasting time.'

'Sure you won't join us, Sumi?'

'I say, Charu, why don't you wear a sari? Women should wear saris. And have long hair. It looks good.'

'Look at the arrogance of the man telling us how we should dress!'

'It's for your own good.'

'Oh, hurry up, everyone.'

And they are gone in a babble of sound, leaving Sumi alone with the image of her daughter's beauty and the picture of Manorama looking down at her.

It has been important for Sumi to contain her feelings about Gopal's desertion, not to let them spill over. Only in this way has it been possible for her to cope with the reality. It seems to have worked, for the picture she presents to the world is one of grace and courage, to be admired rather than pitied. Unchanged, except for a feeling—which only those who know her well are aware of—of something missing in her.

Now, since starting on her job, there are traces of her old vivacity in her. Aru is slightly ashamed of herself that this makes her uneasy. She rebukes herself for it, but her suspicions have begun to gather round Sumi's resumption of an old friendship. I shouldn't think this way, she tells herself, Sumi is only being friendly, she always was this way, why am I being suspicious now? And yet a third telephone call in a day makes her share her fears with Charu. She begins in an oddly devious way.

'Do you believe in stepfathers, Charu?'

Charu is taken aback, less by the question than by the way it is put.

'You talk as if they're fairies or ghosts or something.' And then, understanding comes in. 'Oh, oh, you mean Kumar.'

'He's called Sumi thrice today.'

'He's helping her with the play—her school play.'

'I know that, but still ... Have you seen him looking at her?'

'Oh, come on, Aru, it means nothing. She's a beautiful woman. And do you really believe Sumi has something like that in mind?'

'But the way he says "Sumi dear ..." ' Aru's tone is savagely mocking.

'That means nothing. He's harmless.'

'You mean ...?' Charu nods sagely. 'How do you know?'

'Oh, the way he talks—that prissy accent of his—and—oh, I don't know why, I just know.'

'You're only guessing. Wildly. You know nothing.'

'Okay, Aru, even if it's not true, you don't think Sumi would think of another man after what Papa's done to her.'

'Sometimes I wonder whether she minds that at all.'

'Now you're being mean.'

'I'm scared, Charu, I don't want anyone to take advantage of her.'

'Talk to her then.'

'I can't.' Aru is unusually humble. 'I know I'll only lose my temper and say something nasty. Can't you talk? You won't lose your temper, I know.'

'I? My God, no, I couldn't speak to her of such a thing.'

'All right, forget it, forget I said these things. I shouldn't have spoken to you.'

She doesn't tell Charu that she's decided to talk to her mother herself. But before she can do so, 'The Accident', as Charu names it, takes place.

You can never think of your own life as a series of happenings strung together. Even if it's not a seamless whole, it's still a whole, with the stitches absorbed and invisible. Yet this incident, the accident, will be a watershed in their lives, marking a division between their lives before and after it.

It begins oddly enough, considering Aru's words 'you won't lose your temper', with a burst of temper on Charu's part. Aru comes home in the evening to find Sumi pacing near the gate. The moment she sees Aru, she exclaims,

'Oh, thank God! I need the scooter.'

'Where's the moped?'

'Charu's taken it.'

'Didn't Hrishi come for her?'

'That's what I asked her. And she flew into a temper. I'll be back in half an hour, I just have to drop this book at Kumar's.'

'Kumar?' There's a small, almost unnoticeable pause. 'Come on, I'll take you.'

'I can manage.'

'No, come on.'

Sumi settles herself on the pillion, still speaking of Charu. 'I never expected Charu to throw a tantrum. When I asked her about Hrishi, she said, has he signed a contract to transport me every day? Aru, what's going on between them?'

'What?' Aru comes out of her absorption with a jerk.

'Between Hrishi and Charu—have they quarrelled?'

'Oh, they do that all the time. They had a nasty tiff yesterday. Hrishi bunked college, Charu says he'd gone out with a crowd, they were celebrating someone's birthday. They're a wild lot he went out with and Charu says Hrishi's breath was stinking of beer ... now, you won't go and tell Devi-mavshi all this, will you?'

'Don't be silly.'

'Hrishi said he didn't drink, not more than a sip, anyway, but Charu doesn't believe him. And she said something quite nasty about Hrishi not needing to study, about his rich father buying a seat for him and Hrishi was furious ....'

'Oh. You know what I felt sorry about, Aru? She said it's not fair for her not to have her own transport. Just because I don't make a fuss, because I don't complain, you ignore me, she said. Do you think that's true?'

'Charu with a vehicle! Don't be funny, Ma, she can't drive for toffee. She shuts her eyes when she sees anything, even a dog, approaching.'

'Oh my God!'

'Relax, Ma, I was just joking, she'll be back in one piece. Is this the right cross?'

Aru, waiting in the garden, sniffing in the flowery perfumes, trying to identify the flowers, is wondering—it's a beautiful house. Kumar is rich; will Sumi be able to turn this down if he asks her to marry him?

'That was quick,' she remarks when Sumi returns.

'Yes, Kumar wasn't at home.'

Which is no comfort to Aru at all.

'Damn,' Aru says when they turn off the main road. 'No lights.'

The road is wholly deserted and, overhung with trees on both sides, almost pitch dark. It is like entering a tunnel and Sumi suddenly shivers, her body feeling chilled to the bone. She moves closer to Aru's body for warmth and feels the sharp ridges of her spine through the thin fabric of her blouse. It fills her with tenderness.

'It's cold, Aru, you should have ....'

And then it happens. There is the sound of something rushing at them, an impact, the scooter seems to move away from under them. Sumi hears a scream—hers? or Aru's?—and feels herself being thrown off, her body hitting the ground with sickening, painful force. When she comes out of it, she finds herself sprawled on the ground, her ears filled with a whirring sound. The consciousness of being watched makes her look up and she sees two figures, dark silhouettes, looking down at her, blotting out everything else. Terror fills her, a panic that freezes her limbs and throttles her voice. The clattering sound has died away, leaving behind a total silence.

Suddenly the significance of the silence penetrates.

'Aru, oh my God, Aru.'

Energy comes back in a rush. She sits up, unaware of how painful it is, and notices Aru lying on the other side of the scooter, eyes closed, one arm flung out, another somewhere under her. Sumi moves to her and sees she is bleeding from a gash on her forehead. Stupidly, as if this is the most important thing to be done, Sumi pulls down

Aru's skirt that has climbed up to her thighs and only then tries to staunch the blood with her sari, calling out 'Aru' over and over again. She remembers the two figures, yes, they can help, but when she looks up there is no one; only the sound—distant now—of a motorcycle receding. She bends over Aru again. Thank God, she is breathing, but why doesn't she open her eyes, why doesn't she respond? Sumi is frantic.

A shaft of light pierces the darkness; it's the headlights of a car. Sumi gets up, waves, calls out and the car which has gone on ahead reverses and comes back.

'My daughter, oh please help me, my daughter ....'

In a few moments there is a crowd about them, standing around her and Aru. Later, Sumi can never remember getting into the car or telling the driver where to go, but she must have done it because she is in the car, Aru by her side, and in a few moments they are in the nursing home where Ramesh works. And there is Ramesh—she isn't surprised to see him, either, though it is not his usual time to be there. Later he tells her he was there to visit a critical patient; but now it is part of it, that he should be here, where she needs him. And it is the sight of Ramesh that brings Sumi out of the fog and things become real.

'Ramesh, it's Aru ....'

'You sit here, Sumi, we'll look after her.'

She is shivering uncontrollably. Someone gets her a cup of coffee—Ramesh must have asked them to do that—and she finds it hard to unclench her teeth; the cup makes a clattering sound against them. Ramesh, coming back, is aghast at her state. He has never seen her this way, she is hysterical.

'She's recovered consciousness, Sumi, she'll be all right, I promise you she's fine, Sumi, please ....'

It takes her a while to quieten down and even then she refuses to let them attend to her bruises until she has seen Aru. She is much more in control of herself by the time Charu and Shripati come there. But she won't go home, she's going to stay the night here, with Aru, Charu must go home. Nothing can move her, not even Charu's tears.

They have to give in, though Ramesh manages to persuade her to go home with him for a wash and a meal. 'I'll bring you back, the neurologist will be here by then, and Baba and Charu will be here until we return.'

Chitra has obviously been told of her coming, for there are three plates set at the table. The house seems unnaturally quiet without the noise and activity of the twins who have gone to bed. Chitra follows Ramesh's lead in leaving Sumi alone; they speak to each other in low tones, giving Sumi the freedom of being by herself, a mere spectator. She feels pleasantly remote from everything; the soothing, monotonous sound of the English news on TV, the clatter of spoons on plates and bowls, the low hum of conversation—everything comes to her from afar. And Ramesh and Chitra—she looks at them as if she has never seen them before. They look companionable—is it because the twins are not there with them, between them? And how different Chitra looks in her frilly nightdress, her hair loose; she seems gentler, her once-splendid athlete's body slightly thickened at the waist, plumper and softer.

'Shall we go, Sumi? Have you finished?'

Sumi comes out of the deadening cottonwool with a jerk. Yes, of course they must go. What if something has happened to Aru? She is frantic. But in the bathroom she is suddenly overcome by the desire for sleep. She rests her face against the mirror, feeling the cool pleasant smoothness of it against her warm face. And then it begins slipping away from her, like the scooter—the scooter ....

She jerks awake, splashes water on her face and goes out. Chitra is waiting for her with a plastic bag in her hands.

'Only a nightie and a shawl for you. I've put in a toothpaste and two brushes as well.'

It seems to Sumi this is the kindest thing anyone has done for her. Tears spill out of her eyes, she is overcome by remorse, certain that she has never been fair to Chitra, never done her justice; she has thought her cold, indifferent to everyone but her own sons, caring for no one, not even Ramesh ....

As if she has to make up for this, she talks to Ramesh about Chitra all the way back, about her devotion to Jai and Deep, about how successfully she has transformed herself from being an ambitious athlete to a devoted wife and mother, how wonderfully she is shaping the twins, doing so much for them, going jogging in the morning, tennis practice in the evening ....

Ramesh lets her talk, he listens silently, he smiles, a smile she cannot see in the darkness.

Aru is sleeping when they get back. 'Devi-mavshi was here,' Charu whispers. 'And Hrishi. They took Baba away, he seemed absolutely exhausted. I'll stay with you, Ma.'

But Sumi is so vehement about Charu going home— 'Amma and Seema shouldn't be alone'—that Ramesh silences Charu with a look and takes her away with him.

When they have all gone, the nurses too, as if they have been waiting for her to be alone, the pains begin. Her shoulder, her wrists, her hips—her whole body hurts unbearably. She knows that the painkillers they have given her will take effect after a while, but for now the pain is unendurable. The fear she had felt on the dark road, with the two faceless figures looking down at her, comes back. It seems to her that nothing in her life had equalled that moment of pure terror. She panics at the thought of being alone at night. Her hands and feet feel chilled and numb, she wants to ring the bell, to ask for help, to take Chitra's shawl and wrap it around herself, but she can't move. The chill is within her, her very bones are frozen. In a while she begins to shiver; it is like having convulsions, her body is shaken by spasms. This too passes, but her body is still cold. She moves now, slowly, stiffly, like an old woman, and goes to Aru's bed. She fits herself carefully into the little space left by the girl's body, careful not to touch her. Nevertheless, the warmth of the young body reaches her, she stops shivering and in a while she falls asleep.

She wakes up to a buzz of voices, to an instant realization

of where she is and why. She opens her eyes and sees Charu standing by the table pouring coffee out of a thermos, Aru in a chair, hands clasping a mug. Charu sees her and asks laughing, 'Well, who's the patient here?' And Aru begins to laugh too, the sound of their laughter filling the room like the aroma of Kalyani's coffee.

Aru is back home the next day. 'She's perfectly all right,' Ramesh assures them. And in fact there is nothing to show for the accident except a tiny scar, a pucker really, so high on the forehead that it is scarcely visible. Only a lover, tenderly pushing up her hair, will see it, only a lover will feel the roughness of it under his lips.

It is Sumi who bears the real scars of the accident. The moment of terror she had felt on the road in the darkness with the two figures looking menacingly down at her stays with her for long, it is never shorn of its nightmare qualities. It comes back to her, like nightmares do, suddenly, at odd moments, even during her waking hours. She tries to grapple with her fear, to understand it, she wonders whether there's a kind of message in it for her; but it remains what it was—a few moments of total fear. She tries to rationalize her fears: They were frightened, they wanted to see if we were all right, when they saw I was, they went away because they didn't want to get involved in a police case.

But it's no use, it never helps. And anger succeeds fear each time. My daughter could have been dead, she could have died for lack of help, and they walked away.

She calls to mind Nagi's philosophy, the sentence with which Nagi ends every story of cruelty, hardship and betrayal, even her own: 'Some people are like that.' Sumi now sees what the sentence that Nagi so mechanically repeats really means. It's a universal acceptance. All is excused, all is understood. There are no norms and therefore no deviations and aberrations either. It seems to remove all barriers and open up vast territories of human behaviour into one common ground.

'Some people are like that.'

For Nagi, perhaps, with an irresponsible husband, one son dead, the other uncaring, and a dependent daughter, this mantra is the only thing that makes life possible. What other way of survival is there?

But for Sumi, the feeling of being abandoned remains, the knowledge that came to her in Ramesh's house that night, though she had not recognised it then—'we are, all of us, always strangers to one another'—becomes part of her.

ॐ

THE RIVER

ॐ

Whatever desires are hard to attain in
this world of mortals, ask for all those
desires at thy will. O Nachiketas, (pray)
ask not about death.

—*Katha Upanishad* (I.1.25)

THERE IS A great deal to be said for a belief in many lives. To think that we have only one life given to us, to know that this is all there is, to understand the implications of this, is to be stricken by paralysis. What can we do, what do we fill our lives with, what will we eliminate, and above all, what will we find significant enough to fit into the enormity of this concept of just one chance?

Whatever we do, however, the presence of despair, even of desperation, seems inevitable. Hovering in the wings, if not centre-stage. Whispering to us: if this is all we have, we may as well sing and dance. Like the clown in the circus, keeping the darkness away with mirth and laughter.

There is also, of course, the other way—of selfishness, of recklessness. The voice in your ears whispering: Do what you want, take what you will, for this chance, these things, will not come your way again.

To reject both these alternatives is to let in despair.

'I can't go on,' Aru has confessed to her sister. 'If we can do nothing but go on muddling this way forever, I don't want to go on at all.'

The confession, coming as it did at the end of a harrowing day, nevertheless carried within it a grain of her true feelings; the despair was genuine.

Father, mother, son and daughter
go to the well to draw water

Gopal used to chant this couplet when Aru was a child and

she had loved it—perhaps because of the way Gopal had sung it, making a funny song of it to amuse her. Or, maybe even then, it had been the words, capturing an idea of a family, that had attracted her?

'Father, mother, son and daughter.' The complete family. They had been that; yes, in spite of the lack of a son (lack? it had never felt that way) they had been complete. Aru had seen this unit as something that was intact and forever. She had never imagined a time when it would no longer be in existence.

And now Gopal has gone. To Aru, it has not meant merely an empty space in the family, but the disintegration of it. There is no family left. We are five separate individuals, all of us going our different ways. Five units that don't add up to a whole.

Eighteen is not the age either to accept this or to understand it. Aru has a sense of having lost her footing in the world and she knows no way of getting it back. She sees that things are wrong, but has begun to realize that they can't be put right again. She wants to know that justice will prevail in this world, and it hurts to realize that it rarely does. To see her grandmother fills her with indignation, a sense of pity at the enormous waste. If this is all that life can offer you ....

It is a greater pity perhaps that Aru does not speak openly to her mother about this; because of her silence, she is denied a glimpse of Sumi's vision of Kalyani, so entirely different from Aru's.

To Sumi, her mother seems to have finally come out of the room she had inhabited in her childhood, hers and Premi's, a room that in her memory was always dark. There is one fearful memory of Kalyani standing in the centre of that room, striking herself on her face with both her hands, the muscles on her neck rigid like taut ropes, the veins on her temples standing out. And shrieking out to the child who stood in the doorway, as if hypnotised by this frightful sight, 'Go away, go, just go.'

Sumi, with her facility for forgetting, had put this

memory away in her chest of rejects, never letting it surface. And now, watching Kalyani moving through the house, it is impossible for Sumi, even if she wanted to, to resurrect the memory of that hysterical, self-punishing woman. In fact, noticing the complex net of relationships that Kalyani has with so many people, she is reminded of the spider she had seen one morning, scuttling from point to point, drawing silken threads out of itself, weaving in the process a web with a beautiful design.

But Sumi is forty to Aru's eighteen. Nevertheless, for the very reason that she is only eighteen, Aru will not wallow in despair for long. She will come out of it, she will go on with her life, though the hopelessness that she feels now will always be lying in wait for her. It is only later, nearly a decade after the time when these events are happening, that she will stumble on a secret that will take some of this weight off her. That time is waiting for her in the future and to hitch it to this narrative is not very difficult. A slight sleight of hand will be sufficient.

But to do this is to admit that Aru is the heroine of this story; only for the heroine can Time be bent backwards.

Is Aru the heroine? Why not? She has youth, one of the necessary requirements of a heroine. And the other— beauty? Well, possibly. The potential is there, anyway. (The *Natyashastra* lays down that the heroine should have nobility and steadfastness as well. But we can ignore this. We no longer make such demands on our heroines.) Perhaps there's this too, this above all, that Aru is trying to make sense of what is happening, her consciousness moving outside herself and reaching out to the others as well, embracing, in fact, the whole of what is happening. The moment of understanding is, however, denied to her now; it will come later, only when she hears the story of Yamunabai, when she sees her picture. A picture belonging to an age when taking a photograph was a serious business of recording an image for posterity.

And so there she is, Yamunabai, a rather stout woman, head covered by her sari, looking squarely, almost sternly at the camera. A fairly ordinary looking woman, Aru will think her to be, except for the eyes, which seem to reach across the century and more that separates them and hold Aru transfixed. Eyes that will remind her of the man in the picture Sumi had cut out some time from a photographic journal—Sumi herself couldn't remember why she had done it—and pushed under the glass top of the writing table. A cutting that became in course of time so familiar that they scarcely looked at it. The picture of an African storyteller, sitting in the centre of a group of women and children, caught by the photographer at a dramatic moment in his narration, arms raised high above his head, eyes wide open and compelling. The eyes of a dreamer.

And the audience, rapt, trapped in the web of the man's creation, their expressions mirroring his.

'When one goes to sleep, he takes along the material of this all-containing world, himself tears it apart, himself builds it up and dreams by his own brightness, by his own light. Then this person becomes self-illuminated ... For he is a creator.'

Yes, she who dreams is a creator. To dream is to cross the boundaries of the physical world, to enter the regions of pure light, to be illuminated, and to illuminate then, the world for others.

Yamunabai was a dreamer. How Aru will get to hear her story, the coincidences that will bring this about, can be a story in itself. It is enough to say that Aru, on a professional visit (she will be a lawyer—the novelist's crystal ball yields this revelation), finds herself by chance in Manorama's birthplace, the place in which Yamunabai lived and died. Her curiosity, on seeing a 'Yamunabai Pawar High School for Girls', leads her finally to an old lady, the first headmistress of the school, and, she is told, the one woman who is likely to know something about Yamunabai.

And so it is that Aru, sitting in a bare, low-roofed room, hears the story of Yamunabai from an old woman, almost blind as Aru discovers, for when the lights go off, she neither falters nor pauses, but goes on speaking with scarcely a change of inflection in her tone. In spite of this and her shabby surroundings, there is no sense of sadness about her; in fact, Aru thinks she has never seen a person so clearly herself, taking nothing from her surroundings, impressing herself, instead, on them. And as she listens to her story of Yamunabai and gets a glimpse of Yamunabai's dream, Aru has a thought, fanciful perhaps, that this old woman, the daughter of one of Yamunabai's students, and she, the great-granddaughter of Manorama, Yamunabai's prize student, are both part of that dream.

Yamunabai, the daughter of a well-to-do landlord, came back to live with her parents and brothers when she was left a widow at a young age. An only and well-loved daughter and sister, she could look forward to a reasonably comfortable and secure life. But Yamunabai had a vision, a vision in which girls and women would not have to live with nothing more in their lives than the slavery of endless drudgery and childbearing. In which, the minds of girls could be opened to the vastness and the beauty of the world around them, so that as women they would not be doomed to live in dark, airless rooms. In other words, education was the tool with which she would work for the realization of her dream.

And so she began, in a bit of open space next to the dung-smelling cattle shed, with just a handful of girls whose parents she had been able to persuade to send their daughters to her. One of these was Manorama.

'Yamunabai went on teaching until she died. Just a little before her death, she moved into a large room that her brothers built for her. For a long time our school was nothing more than that one room. We had to fight for everything, from a blackboard to a piece of chalk. Everything, we were made to feel, was a luxury we had no right to ask for. I sometimes think we moved forward crawling on our knees, begging for things.

'It was I who wanted to give the school her name. I don't think Yamunabai herself would have thought it important, I don't think she would have cared.

Nimittamatram bhava Savyasachi— that was her mantra, her article of faith. "We must never forget that we are only the instruments." My mother quoted Yamunabai's words to me when we were struggling with the school; I always remember them.'

Nimittamatram bhava Savyasachi— be thou only the instrument, Arjuna. The end is not us, it is outside us, it is quite separate from us. We are only the instruments.

This bit, the cat's tail that gives a hint that the jigsaw puzzle has a cat in the centre, will come into Aru's hand then, a gift from the past. But all this is, as has already been said, much later. Right now, Aru is fumbling, not knowing what she wants, not knowing what she has to do.

ॐ

SUMMER IS SUDDENLY upon them. The mango blossoms are already darkening and falling off, the pea-sized fruits beginning to be visible. And the cuckoo is with them. Kalyani is excited about it.

'There it is,' she says. 'Each year my father promised a gift to the one who heard it first. He was always the one who did.' And then she adds, 'It comes at exactly the same time every year.'

She speaks as if this is the same bird that sang in her childhood, in her father's lifetime. None of them can share her excitement, they are too involved in trying to get used to the sudden fierce heat. Kalyani is the only one who seems immune to it, as if her small body has a thermostat that keeps it at an even temperature.

'Stop complaining,' she chides them. 'Summer is the time of mangoes and jasmines, think of that. And look how much sweeter water tastes. And just think of ....'

'Spare us, Amma,' Charu groans. 'It's bad enough having to put up with this without your talking about mangoes and jasmines. What use are they to me now? I feel as if I'm on fire.'

It is a dry heat which the body seems to hoard jealously, not letting anything escape, so that the hair, the skin, seem to crackle with it. Charu, nearing her final examination, and, it seems to her anxious family, the limit of her endurance, feels it the most.

'What sadist thought of having exams in summer, only

God knows!'

'Would you like to move into my room? It's cooler there, you know.'

'No, thanks, Ma. It's all the same, really. And you know how I like to spread myself about.'

Sumi has moved out of the large room. 'It's impossibly hot in there,' she said. And it's true that in spite of the thick screen the trees provide against direct sunshine, the room is oppressive. The fan, hanging low in the centre of the room, does nothing to help. On the contrary, listening to the slow ponderous creaking of its blades at night, Sumi has had peculiar visions. She has seen the fan coming down on her body, crushing it, she has seen her body hanging from the fan, the ghastly shape slowly spinning and twirling.

She has not spoken of these things to anyone, but has asked herself: why, when I don't want to die, when I don't have the least desire to die, do I see these images? Suicide has never been on her agenda, not in adolescence, not even during those terrible days after Seema's birth. Post-natal depression, they had called it. To her, however, it had not been depression but fear, a sense of impending doom. It was this same fear that had overcome her after Aru's accident. This is it, she had thought that night, sitting by Aru's bed, her heart thudding and pounding in panic, this is it.

But Aru recovered and the feeling remained unspent. Now, Sumi feels she has left the darkness and the fears behind her in the big bedroom she has moved out of. There are no shadows in this, the 'corner room'. No ghosts either. Dispossessed of everything by her in-laws on her widowhood, perhaps Kalyani's aunt, whose room this had been, had had nothing to leave behind, not even sorrow or anger. And the room, in spite of being fanless, is cooler, the neem tree just outside the window bringing in, with a sursurating murmur, occasional whiffs of cool breeze.

'It's too small for you, Sumi,' Kalyani had warned her, but cleared of all the junk, the room proves to have enough room for a bed and a writing table, which is all that Sumi needs. Looking at the room after they have finished arranging it, Aru feels as if her mother has moved back to some earlier time of her life. It's a schoolgirl's room, she thinks, there is nothing here to show that Sumi is a woman, the mother of three grown daughters. The impression of being a student's room in a hostel is heightened by the untidiness that has crept in within a day. Aru, peeping in, is about to exclaim over the disorder, the crumpled bed, the books lying everywhere; but her mother's face, intensely absorbed, stops her and she goes away without speaking, wondering what it is her mother is doing that calls for such intense concentration.

Sumi is writing out, rewriting, rather, 'The Gardener's Son', incorporating into it some of the impromptu alterations made during the rehearsals. The success of the play on stage has given her the courage to take it seriously. And to her own surprise, there's another idea knocking at the door, slowly shaping itself into a second play.

'She's as ugly as Surpanakha,' she has heard Kalyani say. And she has been thinking since then of this demon sister of the demon king Ravana, who fell in love with the Aryan prince Rama. An unpleasant story, it's occured to her, with the two princes Rama and Lakshmana mocking and ridiculing her and finally mutilating her by cutting off her nose.

'Oh, I miss him so much,' Sumi's friend Vani had burst out when her husband was away for a year abroad. And then added, 'Specially at night. There! It's out. I can't say this to anyone.'

Female sexuality. We're ashamed of owning it, we can't speak of it, not even to our own selves. But Surpanakha was not, she spoke of her desires, she flaunted them. And therefore, were the men, unused to such women, frightened? Did they feel threatened by her? I think so. Surpanakha, neither ugly nor hideous, but a woman charged with sexuality, not frightened of displaying it—it is this Surpanakha I'm going to write about.

Sumi sighs, puts down her pen and goes in to make herself a cup of tea. The corner room, separated from the rest of the house by the staircase, is sheltered from sounds in the other wing. So that Sumi, coming out of her room, is surprised to find herself alone at home, except for Charu, who, head on her book, is fast asleep. Sumi picks up the pencil that has rolled away from Charu's fingers, looks down at the sleeping girl doubtfully, then softly says, 'Charu?'

Charu is wide awake in an instant. 'Sumi? My God, did I fall asleep? How long have I been sleeping? What's the time?'

'Past five.'

'Five. Damn damn damn, I should have finished this chapter by now.'

'Want some tea?'

'Yes, Ma. I'll just have a wash.'

But when Sumi returns with the tea, Charu is staring blankly at her book.

'What's the matter?'

'Nothing gets into my head. I can't do it, Ma, I just can't. There's only ten days left and I know nothing, I'm blank.'

'Come on, have your tea and then we're going for a walk.'

'A walk? Are you crazy? I don't have the time.'

'Yes, you do. You're coming with me. I'll give you five minutes to get ready.'

Charu suddenly smiles. 'Ten minutes, Ma, give me ten minutes.'

'Left right quick march?' she asks when they are on the road, reverting to the language of childhood.

'Okay.'

But in a while Sumi flags. 'It's no good, Charu, I can't do it.'

'Tired?'

'A little. I'm getting old, Charu.'

'Not you, Ma, not you.'

'Do I have to prove it to you like I did to Amma?'

Charu laughs, remembering Kalyani's horrified exclamation, 'Sumi! That's a grey hair!'

'One? Wear your specs, Amma and see how many more there are.'

At which Kalyani had seriously put on her glasses and Sumi had just as gravely offered her head for inspection.

'No, you don't! I know you're not old. You still have a long way to go.'

'The last year has been a long way. Let's sit down. I know a good place.'

She leads the way to a garden, a triangular bit of space really, between the two branches of a forking road. Nondescript, perhaps, at other times, with its few bushes and trees; but now with the tabubea flowering, it looks flamboyantly colourful. The grass under the jacaranda is a multicoloured carpet on which Sumi sinks down thankfully.

'I found this place by chance. I've stayed so many years in this area and I had never seen it before.'

She is silent, thinking of that day, of the despair she had brought here with her. And the man lying on the grass, eyes closed, as if sleeping, yet something about his body revealing that he was not. And how, in some way, when she got up to go, she had felt lighter, as if some of her despair had been absorbed by the sleeping man.

'Beautiful, isn't it?'

'Is it? Yeah, I guess it is. I'm sorry, Ma,' Charu seems a bit shamefaced, 'I can't see anything these days except the pages of my books, diagrams and questions and answers. I know it's crazy, but ....'

'That's how it is before any exam.'

'You know, Ma, just before I fell asleep, I couldn't read, I couldn't see any words on the pages, I just kept seeing us, as we were before. I remembered, God knows why, a day when we were playing cards. Seema kept sniffling, she had a cold, she couldn't help it, but I can remember I was irritated with her. Yet somehow, thinking of it, that day seemed so wonderful, all of it, even Seema's sniffles. I thought—if only we could go back there! My God, I must be mad to get sentimental about Seema's sniffles. But I want us to be like that again, the way we were. I keep thinking—surely Papa will want to be back with us, he'll come home and we'll be like before.' She turns to Sumi, a look of suspicion on her face. 'You will take him back, won't you, if he returns? You won't act all high and mighty, will you?'

'High and mighty? No, I can never be that. But taking him back—I don't know, Charu, that sounds odd to me. As if he's a pet dog who's strayed away or something. No, Charu, I'm not trying to be funny. The truth is, as I told Aru, I'm not a good hater. I can never keep it up for long. But even if he comes back, things can never be the way they were, you know that, don't you?'

'I want them to be, I don't like change.' Charu speaks like a mutinous child. 'What are you laughing at?'

'You silly girl, you're dying to finish your pre-university and get into medical college. Isn't that change?

'But that will be *my* doing. I don't want things to change because of what other people do.'

'It's never possible to avoid that. Come on, time to go back. And let's buy some ice-cream on the way.'

'What are we celebrating?'

'My last pay packet. No job from the first.'

Sumi's tone, even and light, gives no indication that she is worried by the prospect. Certainly the anxiety about money, like the by-now familiar incubus of loneliness, is almost a relief after the earlier inexplicable, haunting fears. But thoughts of money keep ticking in her mind almost all the time: Charu's exams, all the fees need to be paid, the scooter needs overhauling, the moped is on its last legs, Seema needs new clothes—and so it goes on and on. She knows the money that Ramesh has deposited in her name is there for her to use, she knows she can ask her father any time for money; nevertheless she longs intensely for some of her own. Not much, just enough to live on comfortably—to eat and drink, for fees, books, clothes and ... Suddenly, she laughs at herself, thinking of the bottomless pit of 'enough'.

And then she meets Nagaraj and her thoughts about money take a different, unexpected turn. Nagaraj greets her as if that evening, when she had walked out on him, has never happened. He is his normal surly self.

'You have not yet found a house, I think?' he asks.

Strange man, he seems almost pleased when she shakes her head.

'I've decided to stay on here with my parents.'

'That is a very good decision, madam, a very wise decision. Safer for you and your daughters to be with your parents. The world is not a good place for women to be on their own.'

Even as she is wondering how to respond to this statement, he goes on, 'And this is your parents' property, I think you said?'

'Yes.'

'Good property, madam, this is very valuable property.'

'I suppose so.'

'Have you people any idea of developing it?'

'Developing?'

'I mean demolishing this,' he seems quite unconscious of the irony, 'and building apartments.'

'No, I don't know, I don't think so ....'

'But if you ever think of it, please come to me, madam. I will put you in touch with a good party, I will see you are not cheated. Most people will cheat you.'

'But this is not mine, you know that. I have no say in the matter. It's my parents' property.'

'Now, yes, but some day it will be yours. And then ....'

Some day it will be yours.

For the first time she feels a sense of attachment to the house. Mine. No, ours. It will be Premi's and mine—or will it? Knowing Baba, it could well be Nikhil's. He's the only male in the family. Nikhil belongs to his father's family, he most clearly and emphatically does; yet, to Baba he may be the only possible heir.

Sumi is angry with herself for these thoughts but they don't leave her. Sitting in her room, she hears her father's footsteps go up the stairs. Slow, halting, tired. Yes, tired is the word. He's getting old, my father is getting old. He's nearly seventy, after all. A quiver of panic goes through her at the thought of his mortality. My father dying ....

Nevertheless, Nagaraj's words keep chiming in her mind.

'Some day it will be yours.'

'Good property, very valuable property.'

'And then ....'

Oh God, how can I think of such things? Sumi is ashamed of herself, she chastises herself for such thoughts, but once lodged inside her mind, the idea takes root, branches off to the present.

Whose is it now? Baba's, yes, I know that. But it was Amma's father's, it should have been hers. Why did they not give it to her? She finds herself looking into the conundrum of justice, a well so deep, dark and unfathomable, that she draws back.

❦

IF SUMI HAS turned away from the confusing maze of justice, her daughter Aru is moving into the heart of it, trying to reach it through the dusty lanes of the law. It is here that she meets Surekha.

Who is Surekha? (It seems wrong, unfair perhaps, to introduce a character at so late a stage. But no rules, if indeed there are any, can keep Surekha out.) Her name begins to punctuate Aru's conversation, making Sumi curious, for Aru has never, not even as a child, spoken much of her friends at home. That Surekha is not a friend, that she is a lawyer, is soon apparent; with Aru's current obsession, her association with a lawyer is to be expected. Nevertheless, Surekha will be a surprise to Sumi. She has pictured her as a young, smart professional; instead, she will see a woman closer to her age than to Aru's, overweight, sloppily dressed, talking too much. And both dogmatic and opinionated—qualities which, Sumi knows, Aru has never been able to put up with.

But Aru has changed: Sumi has to admit this. There is, for instance, her altered relationship with Kalyani. It has suddenly become evident to all of them that Aru and Kalyani have, at some time, without their having noticed it, forged a partnership. It becomes overt the day Aru comes home and finds Kalyani hobbling. She exclaims at the sight of her grandmother's tiny feet, swollen to a degree that makes it impossible for her to wear her slippers.

'It's nothing, only the heat, Aru.'

'Why didn't you tell us? We could have called Ramesh. I'll ring him up and ask him to come.'

'What! Ask that busy doctor to come home and examine my swollen feet? Poor boy. No, leave it alone, I'll be all right.'

Nevertheless she sinks down gratefully into the chair Aru leads her to. And when Aru gets her a basin of cold water to immerse her feet in, she lets them down into the water with an audible sigh.

'You shouldn't pamper an old woman like this, Aru,' she says when the girl gets her a cup of coffee.

'Why not?'

'What will I do when you go away?'

'I'm not going anywhere, Amma.'

'Of course you will. Daughters don't belong. All three of you birds will fly away to your own nests.'

Aru's response to Kalyani's playful, tender words is a serious, intent look. And when Kalyani speaks again, it is as if she is replying to all that the look conveyed.

'You can't stop living because someone else has got hurt.'

Coming from a woman who never speaks of 'life', the statement cannot be ignored; it has to be taken note of. Aru recognizes this.

'No, Amma, but I can take care that I don't get hurt the same way.'

Nothing more is said on the subject, but for that one brief moment Kalyani and Aru have met on common ground. Something has been stated in the silence that becomes a link between them. Kalyani no longer speaks of Rohit; there are no more references to 'what a good boy he is' and 'such a good thing that we know the family.'

She says nothing even when Rohit rings up Aru to invite her out. It is left to Hrishi and Charu, suddenly unemployed after finishing their exams, to make much of it.

'Where's he taking you, Aru?'

'What does it matter? As long as they're together ....'

'Give him a break, Aru, he's cute.'

'Cute! I knew this girl had no taste.'

'Oh you! You're just prejudiced—and all because he calls you Rishi. I wish you could have heard him, Aru! "I say, call me Hrishi." Hrishi! As if he's sneezing!'

'Will you stop it, both of you, and let me speak. First, I'm not the only one invited, it's his birthday and he's invited a lot of friends. And second, I think you're two of the silliest people I've ever met.'

To Charu's surprise, Aru is smiling. Yes, her tone is pedantic and chiding, but she's smiling. And, what's really astonishing, she's agreed to go for Rohit's party. She could easily have got out of it with the excuse of her exams—just a fortnight away now—but she's going.

'I don't know why I accepted,' she confesses to Charu. 'I know I'm going to be dead bored, I won't know anyone, except Rohit and his sister ....'

And yet she is neither isolated nor ignored; her reserve and air of composure attract a lot of attention, which she accepts with ease. To her surprise, Rohit makes no attempt to single her out, for which she is grateful. (Aru, for all her air of maturity, is naive in some matters. She has no idea that this is deliberate; she does not know how constantly she is impinging on Rohit's vision, how hard he tries to stay away from her, to seem cool and indifferent. She is yet to learn how infinitely patient Rohit can be, how cunning in the pursuit of what he wants.)

'I'm glad I went,' she says to Charu the next day and she has the air of someone who has proved a point. What point? She does not explain. Putting the evening behind her, she immerses herself in her exams, beginning the task of cramming a whole year's work in the last few days. Working so hard that she 'out-Charus Charu' as Gopal used to say. By the time the exams are done, her eyes are dark-ringed with fatigue and sleeplessness.

'Why don't Seema and you go to Premi's for a few days? Take a break,' Sumi suggests.

But Aru refuses. She has her own plans, a holiday is nowhere on her agenda. First, it's a computer class. And

then—this is something Aru has not spoken of to anyone—
it's a women activists' group. It's Devaki who sees her, one
of a number of silent demonstrators, standing in a public
place, attracting the curious stares of passers-by. Devaki is
startled and 'yes, frightened somehow, I don't know why.
Maybe it was the way they all looked, alike, almost
anonymous, you know. Or maybe it was the black gags they
had covered their mouths with.'

While Devaki goes on, Sumi's mind flies to a picture of
Kalyani, her tiny hand clamped tightly over their mouths,
Premi's and hers, silencing their cries.

'No, I didn't like it, I tell you, Sumi.'

'What were they demonstrating about?'

'You know, it's so stupid of me, I didn't try to find that
out. I guess I just wanted to get away, seeing Aru there. But
I imagine it was one of those women's causes.'

'In a way, I'm glad Aru is moving outwards, away from
herself and her family. Still, I agree with you, Devi, it makes
me uncomfortable. I don't know why, maybe because she's
too young. No, I don't like it.'

(None of them do actually, except, surprisingly, Kalyani,
the same Kalyani who had not let her daughters cry out
even at home.)

'Why don't you talk to her?'

'There's nothing I can do, Devi. It's too late for me to
exert my authority, I've never done it till now.'

'Would you like me to talk to her?'

'Hopeless. Gopal believed in democracy within the family
and I went along with him. I know now that I did it
because I was too lazy, I didn't like any unpleasantness. I've
started thinking Vasu and you are right and Gopal is
wrong. Much better to lay down the law.'

'Ha! Tell that to Hrishi. He's so resentful—he calls us
dictators.'

'But what else is there, Devi? Once you destroy the
hierarchial structure in a family, the whole thing goes to
pieces. I don't think affection can hold it up, it's too
delicate to be a prop.'

'Hrishi says we're hypocrites when we say he should at least keep up appearances of being dutiful and obedient.'

'Who knows? The pretence may become the real thing after some time.'

In the end, Sumi says nothing, so that Aru is unware of her mother's uneasiness. It would have made no difference to her even if she had. For the first time, Aru is finding a proper frame for her feelings about their situation. To be part of a group gives her a sense of getting somewhere. And it is because of her association with the group that she meets Surekha. Listening to Surekha speaking about 'Women and the law', she is filled with excitement. As soon as the lecture is over she approaches her and asks, 'Can I come and see you, ma'am?'

'Is it a legal matter? All right, come tomorrow. No, not tomorrow, the day after. Come after six.'

Aru is punctual to the minute, to the second almost, but Surekha seems surprised to see her, she doesn't immediately know who she is.

'I met you at your lecture, ma'am, I said I wanted to meet you and you asked me to come here.'

'I did, didn't I? All right, but you'll have to wait a while.'

'My office,' Surekha had called it. It's only a converted garage behind her house, a small, dark airless room. So dark that Surekha and her typist, working behind a wooden partition, need the lights on the whole day. The few potted plants look surprisingly healthy in such an atmosphere, but for the rest it is an untidy mess of papers and books.

'I started off here because it was convenient. My mother-in-law was a paralytic, I couldn't get away from the house. Even this was only wishful thinking, I had no real hopes of starting work seriously. But it was like a lighthouse for me; some day I would work here.'

This information comes to Aru later. Now, Surekha, having asked her to wait, seems to have forgotten about her. It is the typist who reminds her. Aru can hear her murmur and then Surekha's loud voice. 'My God, I forgot. Are you still there?' she shouts out.

'Yes, ma'am.'

'Okay, Nagma, we'll complete this tomorrow. Come on in here.'

The typist, having tidied her table, walks past Aru with a smile, then returns and touches Aru's plait.

'It's beautiful,' she says.

'What?' Surekha looks up, smiles at the two of them. The smile transforms her rather heavy face. 'Yes, it is, isn't it? Off you go, Nagma, or you'll miss your bus. And you, Rapunzel, come and sit down.'

Rapunzel? Aru is too confused to smile.

'Don't tell me you don't know the story? I can't believe your parents didn't send you to a convent school to learn all the fairy-tales!'

Aru does not immediately get the irony in her tone. It is some time before she learns to understand what Surekha is saying, not from the words, but from the way it is said.

'Well, let's get down to business. Tell me what it is.'

Aru has come prepared, but finds it hard to go on in the face of Surekha's obvious inattention. She keeps fiddling with the papers on her table, sips some water, stretches her legs, and when she does listen, or seems to, stares at some point behind Aru's right ear, her eyes unfocussed, the gaze turned inwards. Aru's words trail away. For a moment there is silence. Suddenly Surekha snaps to attention.

'Oh shoot!' Aru is fascinated by the expression. 'I wasn't listening. I'm sorry, I really am. I'm feeling quite stupid today. It's not a good day for me, the second day of my periods never is.'

Aru will soon get used to Surekha's total lack of inhibitions about her body. 'Growl, growl,' she will hear her muttering back to the rumbling sounds in her abdomen.

'It's not very urgent, is it? No? Then come back—next week? The courts close on Monday, I'll have more time then. Yes, come next week.'

What day, what time, Aru wants to know, but Surekha is vague. This, Aru soon realizes, is Surekha's style of functioning: she never commits herself to a day or a time. How do her clients cope, Aru wonders each time she comes and finds Surekha unprepared to see her. Like I do, I guess, she concludes.

The second time Aru goes to her, Surekha gives her all her attention. The staccato sounds of Nagma's typewriter form a steady background to their conversation. Conversation? It can't be called that; Surekha never seems to stop talking, she probes, she asks questions, scarcely listening, it seems, to the answers. How old are you? How many brothers and sisters? What do your parents do? And while she is eliciting answers to her questions, Aru has a feeling that this strange woman is doing something more, that she is peering into her—into her—Aru can't find the word and settles awkwardly for 'soul'.

Aru herself shows neither anger nor resentment at this inquisition. It's as if she thinks that this is something all lawyers put their clients through. There is something innocent about her obedience and her patience, which seems to touch Nagma, who keeps giving her sympathetic looks. But Surekha is unwavering.

'And your mother isn't interested in a divorce?'

'No, ma'am.'

'You live with your grandparents. No problem there?'

'No, ma'am.'

'They're willing to have you?'

'Yes, ma'am.'

'And your mother has a job now?'

'Yes, ma'am.'

Surekha closes the book in front of her with such a loud clap that Nagma looks at her in surprise.

'All right, then, Arundhati, what's your problem? What is it that you want?'

Justice. It's a word impossible to say aloud—Aru realizes that. You can stand in public holding up a placard asking for justice for someone else. But to say, 'I want justice' is not easy. Aru hesitates.

'You want your rights as a daughter, I guess.' Surekha helps her out. 'Is that it? Well, you do have rights as a daughter. It's your father's duty and responsibility to maintain you and your sisters until you are married. And your mother, too, of course.'

Aru is pleased. Surekha is on her side, after all, she's going to help her.

'You're lucky,' she tells Aru, 'to be living now. Do you know Manu doesn't mention any duty to maintain a daughter? The duty is only towards a wife, parents and sons.'

'So we can go to court against my father?'

'Yes, you can—under the Hindu Adoption and Maintenance Act. Under the Criminal Procedure Code too—but that's only to prevent vagrancy. And you and your mother are scarcely in danger of that, are you? Are you?'

Is she joking? Her face doesn't give that impression. Yet Aru is uncomfortable. She ignores it, however, and decides to go straight to the point.

'No. Will you help us, ma'am?'

'To sue your father for maintenance? That comes under the Family Courts—you don't need a lawyer. But I'll give you some advice. Free. Don't do it.'

'But ma'am ....'

'You say your mother has a job. Your father has given her all that they had. You have a home to live in. There are people prepared to help you with your education. So what more do you want, Arundhati? To punish him?'

'But all these other people helping us—that's charity. I don't want charity. It's not fair.'

'Don't speak to me of what's fair.'

Nagma's fingers stop again. Surekha's voice is crackling with anger. There is a sudden silence. Surekha looks at Aru's face and says, 'I'm sorry, I didn't mean to shout. Nothing is fair in this world, you have to learn to accept that.'

'So you won't help?'

'Well ... well,' she repeats and this time it's decisive. 'Let me think it over. Come again.'

Why am I going to her? She's hostile, she won't help me. But for some reason, Aru does. Again and yet again. She becomes less of a stranger, she even helps out when Nagma stays away because of the flu. And yet Surekha never slackens in her hostility to Aru's case.

'It's a pity,' she says once, 'that there's no property dispute in your case. The law takes property very seriously. Now, don't look so scornful. Property is an absolute fact. Unlike emotions. Just imagine how it would be if the law were to take those into account? Whose emotions would it give weight to? Your father's? Your mother's? Yours?'

'But, ma'am, you said in your lecture that we should always work through the law, not go outside it.'

'Quite right, so we should. I despised the law once. I thought then, it's only to protect the property of the rich. But I know now that even a beggar will put up a fight for his begging bowl. It's his.'

'But he can't go to the courts.'

'Ah, that's another matter. And in your case, I don't see that going to the law will help anyone. It would be just vendetta.'

And another time, Aru pleads, 'Isn't there anything at all we—I—can do? I heard ...' Aru says it hesitantly, 'that there is something called restitution of conjugal rights.'

'Aha! A wife asking for that! Yes, your mother could file such a suit, I guess. But she won't. I could scrape up something myself, but,' she looks at Aru like a stern teacher, 'I will not. The law is not a game, I never use it that way. You have to understand that, otherwise we have nothing to say to each other.'

Aru opens her mouth to say something, changes her mind and walks out.

She won't come back, Surekha thinks. But she does, the very next evening, just as Surekha is locking up.

'I'm sorry, ma'am, I'll come another time.'

'No, come on. I wound up early today, we're going out

for dinner.'

'I'll come tomorrow.'

'No, come in, I have half an hour.'

She opens the door, switches on the lights and fans. There's a strange smell in the room, not the usual muggy, closed-in odour but something stronger, more fruity, that makes Aru's nose twitch. In a while she connects it to her grandfather's room in the evening, when he has his usual single drink. Aru is not so naive as to imagine that women don't drink, but to think of Surekha sitting alone here with a drink fills her somehow with dismay. And pity. It makes her feel less intimidated by Surekha.

'Tell me, what is it?'

'I've been thinking of what you said. And maybe you're right. But it's not only that I'm trying to hurt my father, it's also ... I get so angry when I think of how stupid they are, they've just thrown it all away. And then I think, maybe it's my fault.'

It pours out of Aru. She tells Surekha about the article Gopal wrote, the students' attack on him, Gopal's retraction of the article ....

'I couldn't believe he could do that. If he didn't believe in it, why did he write it? And if he did, how could he say it was all wrong? I was furious, I said terrible things to him, I called him a coward and I said—oh, so many things I shouldn't have. And maybe that's why ...' Her face is anguished. 'It has to be because of that, there's nothing else, nothing went wrong between him and Sumi. And I feel so helpless. If I could go back and unsay all those things ....'

'No, Aru, you can never undo things you've done.'

Aru? Has she called her Aru? And her face ... it brings Aru out of her own distress.

'I'm sorry, have I said something wrong?' Aru asks timidly. There is no reply. 'Ma'am, can I ...?'

Surekha, face hidden, holds out a hand. With a heroic effort she recovers herself. The struggle to get out of whatever it is that has shaken her, leaves its mark on her face.

'Look, Arundhati, I'll do this much,' she says when she can speak. 'I'll meet your parents.'

'Why? Sorry, ma'am.'

Surekha disregards both the question and the apology.

'Separately. Will you arrange that? Right, let's go then.'

Coming out of the stuffy room into the soft fragrant night is like entering another world. They stand in silence for a while, savouring the freshness, a silence that is broken by Surekha's vigorous slap on her arm.

'Damn these mosquitoes, they make a beeline for me. Good night, Arundhati. Where's your scooter?'

'I don't have it. My mother needed it.'

'Come on then, we'll drop you. Come and wait while I get ready.'

Aru demurs, but Surekha is insistent. She takes her home, shows her the bathroom and leaving her with a glass of water, goes inside to get ready. Aru, overcome by the lassitude that follows extreme fatigue, is almost lulled into drowsiness by the soft murmurs from the bedroom. Surekha laughs once, it is a happy laugh. And yet her face when she spoke of never being able to undo things—what was it that had made her look that way?

'Right, Aru, let's go. You haven't met my husband, have you?'

Dressed in a bright silk sari, her hair piled high on her head, lipstick slashed across her mouth, Surekha is a transformed person. The fact that wisps of hair are already escaping from the knot, that her sari pleats hang unevenly and the lipstick is slightly smudged does not detract from her dignity. On the contrary, there is something about her unawareness of these things that adds to it. Aru unthinkingly moves to her, bends down to straighten the pleats, then stops, abashed by her own temerity.

'Oh, go on, do it, I'm used to it, this man is forever trying to smarten me up.'

'She never looks at herself in the mirror, that's her problem.'

But he is smiling at her and Aru, reassured, completes her job.

In the car, the couple converse in low voices. Aru can hear only murmurs, but there is no sense of being excluded; on the contrary, she finds it comforting. She is used to this kind of talk, two people exchanging the inconsequential trivia of their day. It makes her feel cocooned, safe. Like being a child again, listening to your parents converse companionably, knowing that all's well. She's suddenly overwhelmed by memories that rush out of some secret recess, of getting into her parents' bed, between them, the warmth of their bodies, the smell of the blankets which was them, which meant safety, happiness.

'Sleeping, Arundhati? Wake up, you have to direct us now.'

When she gets home, for a moment Aru is dazed by the bright lights, the sound of everyone talking at once. But she is soon part of it, listening to Charu's and Sumi's animated discussion, straightening the plates that Charu has set all askew, pouring water into the glasses ....

'Aru, hey, Aru,' Charu bangs a spoon on a plate to draw her attention. 'Get the curds from the fridge.'

'What a noisy girl this one is! Girls should be gentle and soft.'

'Ha! When I'm gone, you'll miss me, Amma, I bet you'll long for my voice.'

One day I will remember this, I will look back and see us and think how happy we were. Why can't I feel that happiness now? Why can't I get it at this moment when I want it so much?

'Anything wrong, Aru?' Charu asks later.

'No. Why?'

'You're very silent.'

'A little tired, nothing else.'

How can I say it, even to Charu, that today I saw the face of grief on a woman?

'I'LL LET YOU know when I can come,' Surekha has told Aru, but by now Aru knows enough of her ways to not be surprised when she turns up unannounced. Aru returns home to find her with Kalyani, the two of them chatting like old friends, Surekha relaxed and easy as Aru has not seen her until now. She cuts short Aru's apologies with 'why should you be sorry? I didn't warn you I was coming today. I found I had some work this side of town and took a chance.'

'Sumi's not at home, Amma?'

'She should be back soon.'

'Relax, Arundhati, I'll wait. So you call your mother by name, do you?'

'Listen to that, Aru. I always tell these girls they shouldn't do that. It's not right.'

'My mother would have agreed with you. I was just speaking to your grandmother about my mother, Aru. She reminds me a bit of her. My mother was a tiny person, too. I know,' Surekha laughs at their involuntary look. 'I'm like my father. He was huge, really huge. Only our horoscopes match, nothing else does, my mother used to grumble. But their tempers matched too. You should have heard their arguments! You should have been a lawyer instead of me, my father used to tell my mother.'

'Your father was a lawyer?'

'My father, my uncle, my brother—yes, we're a lawyers' family. But I never thought I'd join the gang, I never wanted to be a lawyer.'

'It's like Premi's family. They're all lawyers too. Her husband, his brother, his father, his grandfather—you must have heard of them, her father-in-law was a judge and his father a very famous lawyer.'

'Who?'

When Kalyani mentions the name, Surekha is suitably impressed and Kalyani is pleased.

'But tell me,' she pursues the thread Surekha has left dangling, 'why didn't you want to be a lawyer?'

'Because my father was one. Because he wanted me to be one. Because I thought the law was only for the rich.'

'Your father must have been very pleased when you changed your mind.'

'Oh, it was too late for that. He was dead by then.'

Kalyani clucks sympathetically. 'That's sad. It must have hurt you.'

'Yes, it did, I felt terrible. If only I had known he was going to die, I thought then, I'd have acted differently. But,' she gives a wry smile, 'we can't change our behaviour because someone will die some day. Mortality—that's a terminal disease all of us suffer from.' She says this sentence in English. 'But let that go. I'm talking too much—as usual. No more coffee for me. And what's your name? I don't want to call you Amma.'

'Kalyani.'

'What a beautiful name.'

Kalyani has the look of a pleased child. 'My father chose it. My grandfather thought of it actually. It seems that when he was told of my birth, he said—it's a good day for us then. And he recited: Shreyasam, Shivam, Bhadram, Kalyanam, Mangalam, Shubham.' Kalyani intones the words in a sing-song manner. 'And my father said—right, we'll name her Kalyani.'

'That's a lovely story.'

'She isn't just Kalyani, she's Kalyanibai Pandit.' Aru's tone is fond and teasing.

'Pandit—is that your surname? Of course, I saw the

board outside. Listen, is Shripati Pandit your husband?'

'He's my grandfather,' said Aru.

'Why, he's a lawyer too, isn't he? Why didn't you say so? He was my brother's teacher, my brother admired him, he used to speak a great deal about him.'

Surekha becomes aware of Kalyani's silence, a silence so dense and hard that Surekha's words bounce back at her. And Kalyani's face has the blank look of a retarded person. It's impossible not to recognize the fact that something has happened. Surekha's torrent of words abruptly ceases. She makes no effort to conceal the fact that this is deliberate. 'I must go,' she says. But as she gets to the door, Sumi enters.

The meeting, it is immediately clear, is not a success. Sumi does not want to talk to Surekha, the few replies that she gives are grudgingly given. Aru tries to apologise.

'You don't have to do that. Don't take the load of other people's actions on yourself.'

'Are you sure you'd like to meet my father, ma'am?'

'Yes, I'm not so easily frightened. Find out when he's free—either tomorrow or the day after. And let me know.'

It's Gopal's idea that they meet in Cubbon Park. 'Perfect,' Surekha says. 'It's ages since I went there. The gulmohar will have started blooming, gives me a chance to see them.'

Gopal is already waiting for them when they get there, sitting on the curb near the King's statue. The beds have been dug up in readiness for the monsoon planting and manure is piled up in heaps everywhere.

'Would you like me to go away?' Aru asks after introducing them.

'Yes, wait for me in the car.'

Surekha lets herself down gingerly beside Gopal, awkwardly balancing her bulk on the narrow edge of the curb. Then she says something to Gopal, about the strong odour of the manure perhaps, for she puts her sari to her nose and the two of them move to a bench. Aru keeps a watchful eye on them from a distance, like a parent watching her child fraternise with another. Will they be friends? Or will they quarrel?

When Surekha begins speaking and Gopal listens to her with his usual air of courteous attention, Aru relaxes. She buys a paper cone of peanuts from a vendor who's been waiting patiently for her to give in to his importuning, and sits munching, waiting for them to have done talking.

'Your wife doesn't approve of me. She thinks I'm encouraging Arundhati to go on with this.'

'You've met Sumi?'

'Yes. She's beautiful.'

'You should have seen her as a girl. Though I think she was at her best after Aru's birth. But there's more to Sumi than her looks. And she has no vanity at all about her appearance. She's proud of her quickness, her memory, but ....'

'You speak like a doting husband.'

'Do I?'

'Yes. And yet you left her.'

'My parents died when I was eight, they were crushed by a bus.'

Even as Gopal begins speaking, it flashes through his mind: why am I telling a strange woman this?

'They died together. You know all those Hindi film songs about living together and dying together? When I hear them, it is of my parents I think and of how their bodies were so fused together in death that they could not be separated. I heard someone say that and I've never forgotten it. Well, what I'm trying to say is—our journeys are always separate, that's how they're meant to be. If we travel together for a while, that's only a coincidence.'

'And therefore you left your wife?'

Gopal laughs. 'No, not for that. I suppose you want to know the real reason?'

'No, I don't. As a lawyer, it makes no difference to me whether you walked out for a bad reason or a noble one. Yes, certain things matter: were you cruel? Is there another woman? Otherwise the reason why you left her is of no significance whatsoever.'

'What does the law consider significant?'

'That you fulfil your legal responsibility of maintaining your wife and children.'

'We can't always live by the rules, can we? Even lawyers know that. There are things like human emotions.'

'Yes, and that's where the law comes in. If your emotions damage someone else, the law takes account of that. People speak of the law of the jungle, but that's some kind of a law too. It's lawlessness that's destructive and leads to chaos. But', suddenly she smiles, and it's like dropping a mask, 'why am I speaking of the law? I haven't come here as a lawyer.'

"Why are you here?'

'I'm trying to see if I can help Aru. Do you know Aru blames herself for your walking out?'

Gopal's look of astonishment is reply enough.

'Yes, she says she accused you of being a coward—something to do with an article you wrote and then retracted ....'

'But Aru is right. I was frightened.'

At this, Surekha sits up and takes notice of this man who so frankly admits to fear. To accuse a man of cowardice is to chip away at the base of the pedestal of his manhood. If, after this, a man is still standing, you have to respect him. Surekha understands Aru's feeling about her father, her desire to not let him go.

'You must have seen fight scenes in movies. They're so stylized, they're almost artistic and one begins to think it's really like that. So it was a shock when they attacked me. There was no "fight director" there to give it shape. They came at me all together, they hit me with their fists, their feet, anywhere, everywhere. Of course I was frightened. And much after it was over, when I saw the bruises—they healed so slowly, it was as if they'd injected some indelible dye under my skin—I was frightened all over again. I began to think that the marks were a map of my cowardice.'

'Is that why you withdrew your article?'

'No, not because of that. No, not *only* because of that.

There was something else.' He pauses for a moment, his decision not to elaborate shows on his face. 'But let that go. We were speaking of Aru, not of me. The problem is that Aru wants to put the world right.'

'When I was her age, I wanted to put the world right too. I was sure a revolution is the answer. Blow up all the baddies and all will be well. My father told me to read the story of Nahusha. I didn't know it then, I didn't even know it was in the *Mahabharata*. I read it much later, after my father's death, and now I know why he wanted me to read it. It tells us that every revolution carries within it the seed of its own destruction. One oppression only replaces another.'

'So you're not a—I mean, are you a ...?'

'Say it, say it, it's not a four-letter word.' Her smile reveals teeth of remarkable whiteness and evenness. 'I am a feminist, oh yes, I am. I am on the side of women. I know that we're all of us in this awesome game together, but the rules are almost always against women. I believe things have to change.'

'I don't understand how feminists can argue that a man is responsible for his family. If you reject patriarchy, you must reject all these things based on patriarchy too.'

'It should be that way, shouldn't it? But until patriarchy is thrown out as a whole, we still need to see that the rules are observed.'

'So you're here to get justice for a wronged woman.'

'No, I'm here to see Aru's father. I wanted to see the man who could walk out on such a daughter.'

Gopal's face clearly shows that he hadn't expected this. Until now, he has not taken the conversation seriously. He has enjoyed it, no more—Surekha is astute enough to have guessed this; but now he begins to take note of this woman, of what she is saying.

'For the desire for sons is the desire for wealth and the desire for wealth is the desire for the worlds. No, no, not my words, it's from the Upanishads,' he says in reply to her look of mute inquiry. 'I've always thought that the love for daughters is less tainted, more disinterested.'

'And yet you walked out on them.'

'They don't need me any more. There was a time when I used to wake up in a cold sweat thinking of dying, of leaving my children fatherless. I thought I had an obligation to stay alive because of them. But that's over.'

'They don't need you? You're fooling yourself. Is there any moment when our need for one another ceases? Well,' she gets up and dusts herself with large thwacks, 'I promised Aru I'd meet you and I've done that. And I know I'm right in telling her to get on with her life, to put all this behind her. But can I say one thing to you? I don't know why I'm asking you that question, I'm going to say it anyway. There are no second chances. Aru, your wife, your other daughters will survive this, it's amazing how we manage to survive the most terrible things. But you will have to live with this thought—there are no second chances.'

Aru, chewing her fingernails, looking now, for all the world, like the anxious chaperone of a romantic couple, sees them shaking hands formally as they part, something she has almost never seen Gopal do and she wonders what it means.

'No second chances'—what was she trying to tell me? I keep hearing the words and like words heard over and over again, they become just a collection of letters and sounds, devoid of any sense, any meaning.

No second chances ...?

And there's Premi's letter—she's never written to me, not once in all these years. That itself makes the letter significant. But is there something else in it, something that I'm missing? The letter puzzles me. There is nothing in it about Sumi and me, about what I have done. Yet as I read it, I have a sense of Premi continuing the conversation she had with me when she was here.

How can it be? Premi's letter is about her work, about

the Fertility Clinic which she says they may soon have to close down.

'It's a luxury, they say, in a public hospital, something we cannot afford. Do they realize what they're saying? It means that parenthood is for the rich. I wish these administrators, these budget-balancers would see the couples who come to us, the desperation of the women, the things they've done, the temples and dargas they've visited, the quacks they've gone to, the pills and powders they've swallowed, the amulets they've tied on, the trees they've circumambulated ....'

Yes, of course, that's it, now I understand. Premi is telling me about parenthood, she thinks I need to be told what it is. I don't blame her for thinking so, but Premi speaks from her experience as a mother, and what good is that to me? I heard Shankar speaking of his mother, almost apologising, it seemed, for his inability to protect his wife from his mother. 'She gave me birth, she brought me up, she looked after me ....'

That's a debt we can never repay, it's a burden we can never lay down. Women will never understand this, they don't need to, they are luckier: the day they become mothers themselves, they have repaid their debt, they are unburdened and free. What is fatherhood set against this weight, this certainty of motherhood?

I don't need Premi to remind me of my being a father, anyway. I knew what fatherhood was the day I felt the taut mound of Sumi's body that was Aru, I knew it when I looked at the frail bit of humanity in the cradle, I knew it when I held the tiny body in my arms. And it was then that the fear started. The baby seemed so vulnerable, her link to life so tenuous—how could she possibly survive? How could I make sure she did? I realized then that life is nothing but a battle against death, a battle that we ultimately lose.

Yama was wise when he refused to answer Nachiketas' questions about death. Wiser, in truth, than the wondrous boy who would not give up. The surprising thing is—how is it that Nachiketas didn't see through Yama when he fobbed him off finally with the idea of immortality? Immortality is only a placebo.

But P.K. believed in immortality. And to him immortality meant children; children, he said, are the means by which we can cheat death, they are our way of achieving immortality. As long as there are children, we will never be totally annihilated, the play will never end, the curtain will never come down.

P.K.—transparent as a windowpane washed clean by the rain. I grew up in his care, his face is to me the face of fatherhood, he showed me what fatherhood is. But Premi thinks me a thoughtless, callous man who needs to be reminded of fatherhood. In her eyes I have nullified all that I have done for my children by my one act of desertion. I cannot blame Premi; she has seen only the dark side of fatherhood. After marriage Premi moved away from here, she became defiantly a different person, but she has not escaped, she still carries within her the desolate land of her father's rejection. Camus is right. We carry our places of exile within us. It entered into me too, the day I learned the truth about my parents.

I think of Charu, a chubby four-year-old Charu, her little face wise and knowing, saying, when we spoke of a time before she was born: Then, I was in my mother's stomach. Laying her head, her ear, on Sumi's body, her face intent and grave, as if she could hear the trapped echoes of her unborn self within. Sitting up then and smiling at us, her face beatific, triumphant, fulfilled. Telling us: I know my beginnings.

Yes, we need to know our beginnings. Without that we are forever exiles, forever homeless. It was only after the Pandavas, all five of them, met their real fathers, that they were fully armed and ready for war. Armed with knowledge.

But we don't really have to go out in search of our beginnings; it lies in us, embedded in our beings, difficult to get rid of. Karna didn't need the armour Kunti had put by him when she abandoned him as a baby; the knowledge of his Kshatriyahood was part of him, it was through this knowledge that he reached an idea of himself.

'You bastard of a Brahmin'—I heard the abuse when they fell upon me and the words kept coming back to me later, they hurt me as much as the physical injuries. My father had disclaimed his identity as a Brahmin out of disgust when they reviled him for marrying his brother's widow, I had ignored it all my life; being a Brahmin meant nothing to me. And yet, they charged me with having written my article from the platform of Brahminism. Ultimately, I was nothing more than a 'bastard of a Brahmin'.

Perhaps they were right. Thus does your past come back to confront you, thus does it claim you. It's a fool's game trying to escape. But if I cannot escape my past, how will my children ever be free of me? I thought I had snapped the thread when I walked out, I thought there was nothing left to connect us, but ....

Yes, what about my children?

No second chances: I can hear the words still and they sound to me like a knell. You are right, lawyer woman, Aru's wise counsellor, there are no second chances.

The moment Sumi enters the room, she thinks it looks different. It's still as bare as it was when she saw it the last time, but there is a sense of movement, of activity about it. Is it because of the notebooks spread out on the table, all of them open, as if Gopal has been reading them at a stretch?

'Are you writing something?'

'Me? No. This is a novel Shankar is thinking of publishing. He wants my opinion.'

'Shankar? I didn't know he's a publisher.'

'He isn't. He wants to be one. That has been his dream for years.'

A slight shadow falls over his face, as if an unwelcome

thought is passing through his mind. He pushes the books away and turns to face her. Now that she can see his face, she notices a change there too. He seems—chastened? No, that's not it, she rejects the word. Subdued, perhaps; yes, subdued, but to a definite purpose.

'Do you know it's a year since you moved in here?'

It's strange. She could have said—it's a year since you left home. Or, since you left us. But she doesn't say that. Instead, she says, it's a year since you moved in here. As if this, his coming here, is a fact that has nothing to do with her life, with their life together, which he had brought to such an abrupt end.

'Yes, I've thought of that.'

'Living with Amma, I've begun to see it differently. A year, I mean. For her, it's not just a chunk that gets cut off and then it's over. No, it's all mixed up with the seasons and festivals and flowers and fruits. It's a cycle. Nothing is over, things keep coming back over and over again, they're all connected. Ganapati and the rains, Dussehara and marigolds, Diwali and the wintry feeling, Tulsi lagna and the tamarinds ....'

'I know. A resurgence for everything but us humans.'

'Oh, but that's not true!'

She is about to say this to him, to tell him about Seema's growing up and the sudden disturbance in the rhythm of her own cycle, presaging perhaps the end of it, coming at the same time. But she changes her mind, she does not speak of it. Not because she thinks he has forfeited the right to any information about her daughters, but because she knows that such facts are no longer relevant to his life.

And so she changes the subject and speaks of Surekha. Has she met Gopal? Did Aru bring her to him? Did she, the lawyer, give him any inkling of what she was advising Aru to do? And does he know Aru is now working with Surekha? Temporarily, she says, until college begins and only because Surekha's typist has taken leave; but still, she's there almost all day listening to her, 'as if she's a—she's an oracle.'

Gopal laughs, but Sumi goes on, her face serious and concerned. She tells Gopal that she wants him to know that she has no role in this scheme, this plan, to take Gopal to court. She disapproves of it entirely, she takes no part in any of it.

'Surekha told me she's advising Aru against doing anything. She's told Aru it's futile to go to court.'

'Then why was she here? Why did she want to meet you?'

'For Aru's sake. To placate her, perhaps. Maybe to satisfy herself about something. I don't know, but believe me, Sumi, Aru is in good hands. Believe me,' and Gopal's earnestness surprises even himself, 'Surekha is a good woman.'

'If you say so.' Sumi seems doubtful. 'It's not that I doubt her motives, I know she wouldn't egg Aru on just to have a case; after all, she knows Aru can't pay her, she knows we have no money. But I don't think she's good for Aru at this time. Making what has happened in our family part of the war between men and women—no, I don't like that. The truth is, Gopal, I want Aru to go on with her life. I'm selfish and lazy, I want life to be easy and comfortable. And I want my child's life to be that way too. I want her to enjoy the good things in life, I want her to taste life, I want her to relish it and not spit it out because she finds it bitter.'

'I think Surekha is good for Aru. Neither you nor I can do anything for her now, she won't take anything from us. But if Aru is influenced by this woman, it won't harm her. On the contrary, I think it will help her.'

'Baba is like you; he's pleased by her association with Surekha. He thinks Aru may take to the law, that she may become a lawyer, I mean.'

'She might.'

Sumi is too intent on her own purpose to realize that they are conversing like a couple, a husband and wife talking about their daughter. It is Gopal who thinks of it, and he also realizes that there's a difference. This is not how it was when we were together; this is how it would have been after a few years. It's as if, he thinks, we've lost a whole section of our lives, we've jumped over time and reached a much later stage of our life together.

Sumi's distress over Aru is only part of what has brought her here. She goes on now to say what she has really come here for. She is here to finish what Gopal began that night when he spoke to her as she watched the circus and the clown on TV.

'Do you remember, Gopal—I'm sure you do, though we have never spoken of it after that day—what you said to me the night I came to your room, the night we decided to get married? You said that at any time if either of us wanted to be free, the other would let go. We are not going to be tied together, you said. No handcuffs, you said. And I agreed. I was only eighteen then and you were twenty-six. Do you remember it, Gopal?'

His face tells her he does, though he says nothing.

'But it meant nothing to me then. How can you think of separating, of wanting to be apart, when you are eighteen and in love? If I thought about it at all, I thought we would always be together. I thought of separation for the first time before Seema's birth, when I was sure I was going to die. I never once thought of you dying and leaving me alone. Funny, isn't it, men most often die first, but I never thought of it.

'Then you began to move away from me. I knew exactly when it happened. And I knew I could not stop you, I could do nothing. When you left, I knew I would not question you, I would just let you go. None of them, not even our daughters, specially our daughters, could understand me. Sometimes I think if they had left me alone, if I had been by myself, with nothing expected of me, I could have coped with it better.

'But that did not happen. And I had to go back home with my daughters, I had to live with my parents, I had to see what had happened to my mother. I was frightened. It seemed like something being repeated—my mother then, me now. And my daughters? But now I know my life is not like my mother's. Our life, yours and mine, was complete.'

Our life was complete.

She's setting me free, she's giving it to me, what I wanted so much, the dream which I had locked into myself for so many years, the dream of being totally free.

And suddenly, the girl he had married comes into his mind: Sumi, sleeping in the bus, her head on his shoulder, oblivious to the crowd about them. It seems to him that he is sharing the memory of that girl, that night, with this woman who stands before him, that he is speaking aloud, though the words are only in his mind.

'When we reached our destination, I woke you up and you got off obediently and staggered after me like a sleepy child. We got to the guest house where we were to spend our honeymoon and there was no food for us—it was too late, they said, the cook had gone back home. So we ate what we had with us and then I bathed but you went off to sleep almost immediately. It was a deep and easy sleep; I watched you for a long time while you slept and thought about you and wondered. You were wearing a dark-coloured nightdress, I can remember that, and in the darkness I could see nothing but your face; there was no more to you than a disembodied face. When I woke up in the morning, you were not in bed, but I knew where you would be. I got out of the room, went down the steps and there was the river. You were in it as I had expected, floating, as if you were weightless. And so silent that a bird perched on a rock close by seemed serenely undisturbed by your presence. You saw me and smiled, a smile of radiant happiness, you raised your arm to greet me and as it flopped back into the water, the bird took fright at the sound and flew away. I can still remember the flap of its wings.

'I joined you in the river, you swam half-way to meet me. You were wearing your nightdress and it was clinging to you above the waist, but below, in the water, it billowed and ballooned about your body so that I could touch your bare flesh, I could feel it respond to my touch. I touched your face with my hands, with my lips and it was like touching a flower wet with dew. I put a finger to your face and tasted a drop and yes, it tasted like dew. We came out of the water then, we went to our room and it was there, with the sound of the river in our ears still, that we came together for the first time. And I knew then that it was for this, this losing yourself in another human being, that men give up their dreams of freedom. And women, too? Did you have your dreams of freedom as well? I never asked you, your body blocked out everything else about you for me ....'

Gopal comes out of his thoughts, he becomes aware that the space between them in the room is filled with desire, his desire, that his body, after all these many months, is awake. Why now, why here? He is angry with himself, his very struggle against it making it difficult for him to subdue his body. He gives up and begins listening to Sumi and slowly desire ebbs away from him. There has been something terminal about it, the last flare before the flame dies out. And it leaves him, when it is over, grey and spent.

Sumi notices it. 'What is it, Gopal? Are you all right?'

'Yes, I'm fine.'

Relieved, she goes on with what she's been saying.

'I'm getting a job, Gopal, I think I'm going to get it. I went for the interview and it seems I have a good chance. It's in Devgiri.'

There is a sparkle to Sumi, she is speaking with her old vivacity.

'The residential school?'

'Yes. And Seema can be with me, she can join the school, we can be together. I want the job so much, Gopal, I want it so much for Seema and me.'

'I'm glad for you. I'm very glad.'

His tone, in spite of the emphatic words, is flat and dull. Sumi can no longer ignore the fact that Gopal, in spite of his disclaimer, is not all right. She realizes, too, that there is nothing she can do for him, not now, anyway. Saying, 'I must go,' she gets up and prepares to leave.

'Must you?'

'Yes, it's late. Baba will be worrying ....'

Suddenly she stops. She remembers saying the same sentence when, as a girl, she had stealthily visited Gopal in his room. She can see from the look on Gopal's face that he is thinking of it too, that they are, after a very long while, sharing a memory. They stare at each other in silence for a moment. Gopal is the first to begin laughing and she joins in.

It is on this note of laughter that they part. They will not meet again.

♋

NOBODY KNOWS WITH whom the idea of celebrating Aru's eighteenth birthday began. It seems most likely that it was Charu who first thought of it, Charu, who is both restive and uneasy in the idle period between her examinations and the announcement of her results. Kalyani and Sumi, for their own differing reasons, welcome the thought which finally evolves into something that has not been done in the family for years: a 'proper happy birthday' as Charu calls it, 'with balloons, cake, streamers and all.' The awareness that they are on the brink of change, very imminent for both Sumi and Charu, adds a poignance to the occasion, but there is no sense of melancholy. When Aru thinks of the day later, it will come back to her as an insubstantial cloud of happiness, disembodied voices and laughter. It is only her conversation with Kalyani, in the morning, that she will remember with crystal clarity. Thinking of it, even years later, she will feel again the pricking in her palm where Kalyani pressed the earrings; when she looks into her palm, she will almost expect to see the tiny, angry red marks after all the years.

'This is for you,' Kalyani says, holding out a red box, the kind jewellers use to put pieces of jewellery in. She opens the box and Aru sees a pair of diamond earrings, their brilliance flashing out at her as if trying to escape after years of confinement.

'They were my mother's. They're for you now.'

'For me, Amma? Why?'

'It's your birthday, silly girl, that's why.'

'I know, but these—they're diamonds.'

'And what did you think I was giving you? Glass pieces? You're the eldest grandchild, aren't you?'

'But I'm not the only one!'

'Charu will have mine. And Seema ....'

'That's not what I meant. What will I do with them, anyway?'

'Wear them. Put them away. Keep them for your children. Sell them. Make something else out of them. Do what you want. They're yours now.'

'I couldn't—sell them or break them up, I mean. And just imagine me wearing them!'

'My mother wore them every day. My grandfather got them made for her when she got married, but she was too young, they were too large for her. She started wearing them later, when she was—yes, even then she must have been younger than what you are.'

Aru, who has been listening intently, asks the question again.

'But why me, Amma?'

This time Kalyani understands her. 'I think—I hope—my mother would have been proud of you. I was a great disappointment to her. Not only because I was a girl, but because—because—oh, maybe because I was none of those things she would have liked her daughter to be. I was not beautiful, not smart ....'

'Was that so important to her?'

'Why not? She was that way herself. I feel very sad sometimes to think that I gave her no joy at all. But Aru, I'm not giving these to you only for her sake, it's for mine too. For so many years I thought I had nothing, I was so unfortunate that I could get no pleasure even from my own children. My mother didn't care for my children, either. Daughters again, she said. And when you were born, a daughter, I wondered how she could have been so blind. Now when I look at you, my three granddaughters, especially at you, I think—I'm luckier than my mother. She's the unlucky one who didn't know how to enjoy her children and grandchildren. And so ...' She plucks the earrings from their velvet bed with a kind of frantic haste, as if afraid Aru will escape her, and presses them into Aru's palm. 'Take them,' she says and closes her hand so tightly on Aru's fist that the sharp edges of the earrings cut into her palms. 'Take them, child.'

Kalyani has now reverted to Marathi, for her the language of tenderness, calling her 'child' as she had done when they were babies.

'All right, Amma.' Aru's grave acceptance carries an understanding of what Kalyani is doing. 'But you've got to take them back right now.'

'Wear them, Aru.'

'Not today. And I can't keep them in my table drawer, can I? Keep them for me.'

Aru seems to have put away her prickliness for the time being. They are all surprised by the good humour with which she endures, not just Kalyani's and Goda's fussing, but all the greetings and gifts, even Hrishi's jokes. It seems to Sumi that Aru is no longer holding a moral scale against which she had appeared to be measuring everyone, including herself.

Nevertheless, her composure fails her when she enters the room she has been barred from since morning. Charu and Hrishi have roped in Shyam and Shweta and between them they have transformed the dining room.

'Balloons! I'm not a five-year-old, Charu.'

'Come on, Aru, I'd love someone to do this on my birthday, and I'm not five.'

'Sure, Hrishi?'

'Got you there. Good for you, Aru.'

'How old are you, Hrishi uncle? When is your happy birthday?'

'Don't call me un-kal, man.'

'And not "happy birthday", Shyam. It's just birthday.'

'Sumi, why didn't we have all this fuss for our birthdays at home? I'd like to have my birthdays celebrated this way from now on. Take note, everyone.'

'Noted.'

'Thank you, Charu, Seema, Hrishi. And yes, Shyam and Shweta. Thank you for this show. I'm touched.'

'There's only one thing missing, sorry, I mean one person who will be missing.'

'Who's that?'

'Rohit. What's the use of balloons, candles and presents without him, eh, Aru?'

'How funny!'

'I'm serious. We'd invited him, but he's out of town. He was heartbroken that he would miss your birthday.'

Ramesh is the last to arrive. Gopal is right, Ramesh *is* his father's son; he has taken on himself the responsibilities of this family. He will never forget an occasion, he will be with them at every crisis, for every celebration. Now, setting aside his usual gravity, he enters into the spirit of a birthday party and takes on the role of entertainer, surprising and enchanting his sons who have never seen him perform these tricks.

'If ever your patients desert you, Ramesh, you can earn a living with these cards and coins acts.'

'We doctors don't let our patients get away from us so easily. Remember that, Charu.'

'Oh, please! Don't, don't say things like that! I feel—I don't know, so superstitious and I've got butterflies in my tummy and I'm sure I've done badly and won't get admission anywhere. And what will I do then?'

'I told you, Charu, I've always said it's no use just burying your head in books. You become good for nothing else. Look at me now ....'

'Yes, Hrishi, we're looking. Go on.'

'I have an alternative.'

'Ah! Your restaurant.'

'You can be a waitress there, Charu, I'll let you keep all the tips. If you get any, that is.'

'Me become a waitress! Me not get admission! What do you mean? I can get a seat in any college I want. I'm a clever girl, yes, I am.' And then Charu covers her face in mock modesty. 'Did I really say that?'

It's that kind of an evening. 'Sssh,' Goda says fearfully when the voices and the laughter become loud. But when Aru goes up to her grandfather a little later, she finds him in an easy mood. 'What's that you've got for me? You know I don't eat much in the evenings.'

'That's why I've brought you just a slice of cake. It's home-made. Devi-mavshi made it.'

'All right, I'll have that.' Then he adds, 'I haven't given you anything for your birthday.'

'You don't have to. You're paying for my computer classes.'

'But an eighteenth birthday is an important event. Legally, you're a person now. What can I give you that can measure up to the significance of that? Let me think of something.'

She notices that he has brought in his washed clothes but, unusually for him, left them unfolded.

'Shall I fold them, Baba?'

He lets her fold them and put them away, again such an unusual occurence that she asks him, 'Are you all right, Baba?'

'Of course, I am. Why shouldn't I be? You go down and enjoy yourself. Take that plate away. And I don't want anything tonight, just a glass of milk.'

On her way down, she hesitates. There is something so melancholy in the thought of him sitting alone there that she has a strong impulse to go back and join him. But the certainty that he will reject her company, that he will send her away, makes her dismiss the thought.

After everyone has gone and the room and the table have been cleared, Sumi, who has been waiting for the right moment, tells them about her job. 'I have a job,' she says and her tone makes it seem as if she's crying out 'Hallelujah'. And then, calming down, she tells them what it is and where.

Charu is the first to react, suddenly and to her own

surprise, bursting into tears. It's the loud and unabashed grief of a child.

'I can't believe it, you're leaving us and going away, how can you do that?'

When she hears that Seema is going with her mother, that Seema knows about the job already, that she was the first to be told, her grief becomes louder, more uncontrollable.

'It's not fair,' she says between her sobs, 'it's not fair.'

Aru, watching silently, envies her sister the ease and openness with which she can display her jealousy. So flamboyantly exhibited, it sheds its dark hue and becomes a simple, childlike emotion.

'Let her go, child, let her go. You're going away, too, aren't you?' Kalyani comforts Charu, making an effort to staunch her tears with her sari.

'That's different.'

'And I'll be coming home often, Charu. Devgiri is less than an overnight journey. You can come, too, whenever you have holidays.'

When Aru leaves them, Charu, a little shamefaced, is wiping her tears, but is still unconsoled.

'You didn't say anything, Aru.' Sumi comes to her a little later.

'Charu didn't give me a chance.'

'Say it now.'

'It's over.'

'What's over?'

'Our family life. When Papa went I thought, I hoped, we would get it back some day, it was still possible, I could dream of it, but now—I don't know ....'

'That kind of a family life would have been over anyway, if not now, if not this year, the next year or the year after. The only difference is that Gopal and I would have been together. Now we'll be on our own.' Impulsively she adds, 'Be happy for me, Aru. This is the first thing in my life I think that I've got for myself. I was sure I wouldn't get it, there's my age, it's against me, and I have no experience at all. But one of the members of the Board saw my play ....'

'Your play?'

'The one I wrote for the school. 'The Gardener's Son'. They want someone for their Dramatics course. And so ....'

'I haven't read your play. May I?'

'Do you want to? Don't expect too much, it's only for children. It's gone for typing, when it comes back, I'll give it to you. And do you know, Aru, I'm already thinking of another one. It feels so good, you can't imagine! I've been so lazy all my life. And now suddenly I want to do so many things.'

Aru, looking at Sumi's face, remembers the diamonds flashing out at her from the box, sparkling in the sudden light.

'It's only a year since—since we came here and everything has changed.'

'Charu said the same thing the other day. But it goes on all the time, doesn't it? Change, I mean. One day is never exactly like another, each moment is different. When you think of it, we are always on the brink of uncertainty.'

'I'll be left alone here.'

'No, you won't. There's Amma and Baba. I feel good to think that you'll be with them.' Suddenly anxious, she asks, 'You'll be all right, won't you?'

It's verging on a plea. Aru recognises this, says, 'Yes,' and bursts into tears.

'More waterworks.'

Sumi's voice is resigned, but she holds her daughter close and tries to soothe her. 'You'll come to me often, I'm getting my own place, just a room and a kitchen, but we can be together ....'

It has rained during the night. They wake up to a freshness and a coolness. The oppressive heat has lifted, at least for now, though the early morning sun holds within itself the threat of an eventual punishing heat. Sumi, standing out in the yard, savours the smell of wet earth, the best smell there is, she thinks. There's something primitive in us that rushes out to meet this fragrance of water and earth mingling, there's the promise of rebirth in it.

'Do you need the scooter, Aru?'

'Only in the evening. You can have it now. Where are you going?'

'Bank, Post Office, market—lots of little things. I'll be back in an hour.'

Sumi finds her father at the gate, looking unusually undecided and hesitant. How old he looks—the thought strikes her again. Even his back is not as straight as it used to be, he seems so bent ....

'Where are you going, Baba?'

'The bank.'

'Come on, I'll take you, I'm going there myself.'

'I can walk, you know I always walk.'

'Give me a chance to take you for a ride, Baba.' She is smiling as she says it, speaking in English. 'You can walk back, can't you? That should satisfy you.'

He looks at her suspiciously, as if wary of such good humour.

'All right. You're an obstinate girl, Sumitra.'

'Girl?' And, after a moment, 'Sumitra?'

'That's your name, isn't it? I gave it to you.'

'I didn't know that.'

'Premlata—that was my sister's choice, I didn't like it, but she wanted it. Madhav, now, was mine.'

'Madhav?'

He has settled himself on the pillion behind her and she can't see his face. Negotiating her way carefully over the bumpy stones at the gate, she puzzles over it. Madhav? She has moved out on to the main road when it comes to her that he is speaking of the boy who was lost, the child who was the cause of it all. Why is he speaking of him now, the first time maybe, after all the years? And to her? She turns round and sees a kind of brooding tenderness on his face. At the sight, for a moment, a very brief moment, it's as if a veil of darkness has lifted, revealing a world beyond, bathed in a mellow luminous light. A picture in which everything is sharp and clear, in which there are no shadows at all.

She is about to speak, to say something, when his hoarse, strangled cry recalls her to the present. She looks ahead and sees the bus hurtling towards them. 'This is it'— the words spring into her mind. She tries to swerve, there is a moment of pure terror as she realizes it is too late, there is a tremendous sound and then darkness and silence.

Prasad brings the news home, Prasad, who, on his way to work, finds the road blocked and, moving through the crowd, sees and recognises the two mangled bodies. Shripati, flung off the scooter some distance away to land under the wheels of another vehicle, is dead. Sumi, barely alive, has been taken to hospital.

They get the news of her death in the afternoon. Aru has just come home, sent back by Premi who has driven straight to the hospital from the airport, when the phone rings. She picks it up, listens and without saying a word puts it down. She looks at Kalyani and Goda, her lips move but no words emerge. They are not needed; the two women know. Kalyani immediately turns to Goda, crying out in a terrible voice, a voice Aru will never forget, 'Look at me, Goda, look at me.' And even as Goda tries to put her arms around her, she slumps to the floor in a slow motion sequence, leaving Goda standing, her arms still shaped to Kalyani's body.

Aru, breaking out of her paralysis, rushes to Kalyani and kneeling by the huddled body says, 'Amma, I'm here, I'm your daughter, Amma, I'm your son, I'm here with you, Amma, I'm here ....'

Over and over again the same words, until her voice trails away and for a moment there is a hush, a deathly hush, which is broken by the sound of Goda's soft keening.

Nobody ever makes plans for coping with the aftermath of death. Yet, as if some ancient knowledge has been stored in each person, in every family, things are immediately set in motion. And, like something that has been rehearsed earlier until it is flawless and word-perfect, the macabre drama of a funeral is enacted without stumbling.

'Aru won't trust any of us, she'll organize her own wedding,' Sumi had said, half in exasperation, half in admiration. Now, while Gopal and Ramesh struggle with the formalities of two accidental deaths, it is Aru who takes charge at home, doing all the things that have to be done. As for the others, all of them, even Devaki, so proud of her competence and efficiency, seem to have been stunned into immobility. Rohit, watching Aru from a distance, thinks she has the concentration of a rope-walker, holding the weight of her grief in her two hands, not as if it is a burden, but to balance herself.

'I like it here. Hundreds of people.'

'Hundreds, Nikki?'

'No, thousands.'

Nikhil is not with them as yet, he is to come the next day with his father, but his words return like a prophecy of this day.

There are hundreds of people—family, friends, colleagues—most of them for Sumi, people who have been caught, if only for a while, in the enchantment of her being. Nagaraj is there, his face solemn, his cap and dark glasses, for some reason put away; nobody recognizes him, nor does he try to speak to anyone. He looks at Sumi and goes away, carrying with him the image of a woman who brought something he could not understand into his life. Manju comes with Shankar and sits silently among the women, thinking of the touch of Sumi's hand on her arm that evening, of the smile on her face.

It is a strangely silent concourse. Nobody speaks, nor is there any loud display of sorrow, not even from the family. Charu is the only exception. Standing against the wall from where she watches the two white-shrouded figures with almost unblinking concentration, she suddenly breaks into a sob, a sob that seems to come out of her without her volition, almost without her knowledge.

And then it comes, the most terrible moment of all, when Sumi and her father are to be taken away. Even now there is no breaking down, no sounds but the slithering of bare feet on the floor and soft murmurs from the men who are to carry the bodies out. Premi, who has been sitting stoically by her father, stands up when the pallbearers approach; shuffling like an old woman, she moves backwards until her groping hands can feel the wall. She leans against it and closes her eyes, but she can still hear the grunts as they lift the bodies, there's an involuntary sound, like a gasp, from someone.

Suddenly unable to bear it, she goes inside where Charu is standing, her face, like a punished child, to the wall. Premi turns her gently around. The girl's eyes are wide open and tearless, but filled with a fear that finds an echo in Premi's erratic heartbeats. They stand as if frozen into that attitude until a medley of sounds from outside, of cars and scooters starting simultaneously, arouses them. Realizing what it means, Charu runs out. Aru is there and the two sisters watch their mother and grandfather leave the house for the last time. They stand in an utter silence, as if their breaths, their very heartbeats have stopped, until the last car, the last scooter has disappeared. Only then do they move, only then do they start breathing again; and the pain begins. They come back inside to find everyone converging on Kalyani, Kalyani who has not moved, not even when they took away the bodies, from the place where she was sitting by her daughter. Suddenly the isolation breaks and they are together, holding one another, sobbing

in harsh wordless sounds, all of them, except Aru, who
stands looking down at the blank spaces where the bodies
had been, a puzzled look on her face.

Late at night, when some of them have fallen into an
exhausted sleep, the house is woken up by a cry. It is a cry
of pain, like that of a woman in labour. Premi wakes up,
wonders what or who it was and when it is not repeated,
thinking it was a dream, she tries to get back to sleep. Only
Goda knows that it was Kalyani, suddenly sitting up and
crying out the name by which she had called the man who
was later to become her husband, crying at last for him, as
if only by going back to her childhood, to her earlier
relationship with him, can she mourn him. Goda holds her
close, wipes her tears and in a while Kalyani quitens down.
While the two women lie awake in the dark, there is a
strange sound, as if the house has exhaled its breath and
shaken itself before settling down into a different rhythm
of breathing.

It is raining heavily, the rain falling with a monotonous
steadiness, drops of exactly the same size falling in exactly
the same place. The skies, the river and the rain seem to
come together in an angry, noisy accord. The menacing
rumble of thunder finds an echo in the depths of the river,
a resonance that comes back and joins the skies once
again.

Gopal, sitting under a tree that had promised shelter
when the rain began, is watching the river, the swiftness of
its flow impeded, it seems, by its turbulence, as if it is
tripping over itself in its haste. Gopal is doing his mourning
for his dead here, now, in private. Until now, he has held
himself in with an iron self-control, he has stayed aloof,
remained in the background, so that it has seemed that
Sumi has been mourned as a daughter, a mother, a sister
and friend—but not as a wife.

Gopal, staring at the river, is remembering with a sense

of wonder, the placid river of the morning into which they had mingled the ashes of both father and daughter. He is thinking of the word the priest had said at the end of the small ceremony.

'Runamukta'. They are free now, free of all human debts. Gopal had made a sudden exclamation at that and the priest, hearing him, had turned to him and said, 'What is it? What is the matter?' And then added, 'You must not grieve for them.' Words which he must have repeated mechanically, hundreds of times, to so many different mourners. And yet Gopal, looking at the old man standing in the knee-deep water, his mud-coloured dhoti flowing about him, his craggy face softened by the white stubble of his beard, had felt that his sharp worldly-wise eyes held the essence of wisdom.

He knows it all. Letting the ashes of the dead float away with the river, he has seen it all, he knows how ephemeral it is, not just human lives, but the grief and the mourning of the living. Everything passes, nothing remains.

Runamukta. Yes, Sumi is free, but at the cost of her body, of life itself. Is this freedom?

'You must not grieve for the dead.'

Yes, don't grieve, because they have not gone, they are still with us, they will always be with us: this is what they tell us, this is what we want to believe. But Sumi's body has gone, there is nothing left of it. Even the few bones and ashes, which was all that the flames left of her, have been dissolved in the river. We live through our bodies, we relate to the world, to others, through our bodies. Without the body there is nothing left; how can we evade this truth?

If I could believe that Sumi has gone to a region of everlasting peace and happiness, if I could think—maudlin thought—that we will meet again sometime ....

No, I can't; there is only this nothingness, this blankness.

But there's P.K.'s theory, that death only means that your role is over and you go backstage into the darkness while the play goes on. I had laughed at him, at his idea, then. I can no longer laugh, I want to believe in it. And yet, this monstrously large black shadow of death, reducing everything to insignificance, makes me wonder: does this play matter?

This is the philosophy of the burning ground. P.K. would have called it that. I know that once I move away from this time, things will go back to their normal size. I will learn to live with the knowledge that Sumi is dead, accepting the fact, putting it in its place.

And yet, if Sumi has truly gone, if there is nothing left of her, why do I, sitting by this river, see her clearly? I can see her floating in it, her body weightless, her face serene, smiling at me. I see her sitting on the river bank, her child in her arms, her face gleaming and beautiful in the twilight. I see her painted clown's face turning to me as we walked in the dappled moonlight under the trees.

Gopal, denied that glimpse of duality which Sumi was granted the moment before her death, the duality that ends all fragmentation and knits the world together, despairingly gives up his struggle to understand. And now, when he ceases to think, suddenly there comes to him a moment as when the body is fighting fever, all sensation heightened, sharpened to a fine point of acuity. He has a feeling of stepping out of his body, out of this plane of existence, of seeing time, past, present and future, existing simultaneously within him. It is like seeing a pageant, a pageant that both frightens and dazzles him, a pageant, the meaning of which eludes him.

And then he is back into himself, left with the thought: nothing is over. Whether our lives are long or short, we leave our marks on the world. Like the wall memorial to the Vietnam dead, our names are inscribed on it, visible to those who look for them. Nothing is lost, each moment remains, encapsulated in time.

Gopal sees a solitary figure in the distance moving towards him. It is Charu, holding an umbrella, carefully picking her way through the slush. He knows she is coming for him and getting up, mindless of the rain, he moves towards her. He takes the umbrella from her and holds it, futile shelter, over their drenched bodies. They walk back together to the room where the others are waiting for him so that they can return home.

THE HOUSE IS crying out 'biko, biko', Nagi says, weeping, and the words she uses for emptiness seem to carry traces of the cavernous echoes the house gives back to them. Sometimes they feel that it is not the dead who have become insubstantial, but they, the living, whose lives lack substance and solidity. Their voices sound thin and tinny, and their actions as illusory as the shadow play of someone's fingers on the wall.

Aru, sitting in her mother's room, thinks she can hear her grandfather's steps (as her mother did though she does not know that), slow, tired steps climbing up the stairs. She hears (or are they echoes of the past stored in her mind?) Sumi's quick footsteps, her voice calling out to them, speaking on the phone, saying 'Yes? Tell me.'

Aru is reading 'The Gardener's Son', the typescript that was brought back the day after Sumi's death. It's only for children, she said to me, but it's not, I know it's so much more. Sumi is saying something here which I must know. But I can't get it, not now, it's impossible, I can't think of anything but Sumi dead. Her figure keeps coming between me and her words, it won't let anything come through. I wish I'd read it earlier, I wish I had spoken to her about it. I thought she didn't care about what Papa did, I thought she was uncaring, indifferent, I said angry words to her, but I know now that was not true. It's too late now, I can never speak to her, it's too late.

She can't cry, that relief is still not possible for her; she can only stoically endure the pain-spiked guilt that lies heavy and sharp within her. In fact, they are all of them carrying their own burdens of guilt, though the luxury of tears seems reserved for Charu alone, whose bouts of sobbing frighten them.

'I was selfish, I should have spent more time with her, I kept saying "my exams, my studies," I never sat down with her, if only I had known.'

Gopal, who is present during one of these self-flaying bouts of Charu's, remembers her as an infant, crying, wanting her mother, so inconsolable that he could do nothing with her. Sumi had come rushing out of her bath then, her sari draped carelessly about her wet body, she had taken the child from Gopal and rocked her until Charu had hiccuped herself into an exhausted sleep.

Gopal has the same feeling of helplessness now as he had then. He is angry that he can do nothing to assuage his daughter's grief. His own grief, of course, he cannot share with anyone, that is impossible. He is still living with Shankar, though he visits the Big House every day. The day he comes to tell them he is leaving Bangalore, he has to walk through empty, silent streets. Life has come to a standstill, people driven into their homes by the terrible shock of another assassination. There is none of the violence that followed the mother's death, only this stunned silence, this wholly voluntary cessation of normal life.

Gopal finds them huddled together in front of the TV. Shocked and grieved as they are, there is for the time being, some respite from their own personal sorrow, they can lose themselves for a while in a larger calamity. But the relief does not last. They cannot ignore the gruesome pictures of violence the TV brings them, they cannot avoid a despair at being part of such a world.

'We've progressed, Gopal,' Kalyani says. 'They killed the Mahatma with a pistol, Indira with a machine gun and now they've used a bomb on Rajiv.' Looking at the young people about her, she cries out in despair, 'Such a young man—how could anyone have hated him so much! Can people hate so much?'

The answer is 'yes', but it is not the answer Kalyani can take now and so they are all silent.

'How will our children live in this world, Gopala? Where did we go wrong? What have we done to them?'

Gopal, appealed to directly, tries to speak and gives up, his hands falling helplessly by his sides. And Aru, coming out of her preoccupation for the first time, gives him a curious look.

Aru has stayed out of it so far; she has watched the TV silently, saying nothing, not even exclaming in pity, as the others have done, over the pictures of the family, the young wife and children, in their grief. If only she could cry like Charu, Gopal thinks, if only she had Seema's armour of self-centredness. No, Seema is not self-centred, she is different, she is this way because we treated her differently, we set her apart from her sisters.

Suddenly Gopal catches himself up and thinks: We? Did I say we? There's no more we, there is only 'I' now. My daughters have only me.

And so he goes to Seema and sits by her, talking to her of his plans. For some reason, he thinks of the birds pecking on the roads, which fly away, miraculously it seems, the instant a vehicle gets close. Escaping death in that needlepoint of a moment. Always, somehow, unharmed. Seema is like that. And then he sees she is crying—large tears that plummet down with their weight. He moves forward instinctively to hold her, but Kalyani is there before him, Kalyani who comforts the girl with words and caresses. This is how it is now, this is right, he thinks, I have forfeited my place in their lives.

There have been no visitors since morning, it is the first day since the deaths that they have been by themselves. The condolence visits have been a kind of punishment to be endured, making demands on them that have been difficult to meet. Yet now, without any visitors, they find themselves at a loss. Their own sorrow seeps back into them at the sight of Seema's tears and, without strangers to remain composed for, they feel themselves in danger of losing control. Kalyani gets up and brings them coffee. Looking at the midget-sized stainless steel glasses, Gopal remembers Sumi's habit of drinking minute amounts of strong milky coffee during the day, quaffing it in one gulp, then shuddering, a shudder not of distaste, but of intense pleasure; almost, Gopal had said to her once, laughing at her, like an orgasm.

The mood has changed, they are no longer able to be involved in watching television, that tragedy seems remote and irrelevant to their lives. Premi goes away silently to her father's room where she has been spending a great deal of her time. She is cleaning it up, she says, she wants to do as much as possible before she has to go back to Bombay, she says. And it is true that she began with great energy (the first thing that she did was to get rid of the bell, even the wires have gone, there is no reminder, except the marks on the wall, of its existence), opening the doors and the windows so that the staircase is flooded with light, light that seems to bridge the room to the rest of the house. But the frenzied activity soon faltered. It has become a kind of search now, though what Premi is searching for is not here, in her father's room. It is her father's mind that Premi is trying to probe into and that became impossible the moment his skull cracked open, spilling the grey slithery mass onto the road.

Now Premi sits in the room, silent and still, staring into the dark abyss that the deaths of her father and sister—the two people against whom she has always measured herself—has confronted her with. It is here, in this room, that Premi can so clearly see the face of death, it is here that she is beginning to realize what it means: an emptiness, a monumental disruption of the universe.

None of them can reach her; only Nikhil, they know, can bring her out of it. For the first time Kalyani is anxious for Premi to go back to Bombay, to her home and family. But Premi is adamant, she will not go until Charu's results are out. She is leaning heavily on the hope that Charu will get admission in Bombay, that she will live there, with her, in her house.

'Go to her,' Kalyani tells the girls, and though Charu obeys, she knows it is no use, Premi does not want anyone. It is a relief when Devaki, struggling to get back to her competent self, comes to take them to her home. Just to get away for a while, she says, it will do us all good. She succeeds in persuading all of them except Kalyani, who refuses to be tempted even by the bait of Goda's being there. And Aru, who stays back with her.

'I'm your daughter, Amma, I'm your son.'

Aru has taken the promise she had made to her grandmother very seriously, she is almost always by her side. Since she heard Kalyani's story from Premi, her imagination has oscillated between pictures of extreme cruelty, even of violence, in her grandparents' life, but they refuse to take shape, to gel and she is finally left with just two pictures: a woman, her two daughters by her side, frozen into an image of endurance and desperation. And a man, moving all over a city, tirelessly searching for his lost son.

All this has now ended. It ended for her the day Kalyani cried out, 'I lost my child, Goda.' Even at that moment Aru could not help wondering—is it *that* lost child she means? Is this a declaration of her innocence, now, when it is too late, when it no longer matters? Or, is she crying out for Sumi?

And then Aru saw Goda put her arms around Kalyani, she saw her envelop Kalyani in the folds of her love and compassion. And Aru gave up guessing. It no longer seemed important, it changed nothing about Kalyani. Forgiving, she realizes, has no place in this relationship; acceptance is all.

Now the others have gone with Devaki and only the three of them are left. It suits Gopal, because it is to these two that he wants to speak of his plans first. He had thought it would be hard, he had wondered how he would explain to them; except for the fact that he has to go, he can tell them very little.

It has to be done, though, and he tells them that he is taking some of Sumi's ashes for immersion in the Alaknanda, a river Sumi and he had seen together long ago. But there are things he cannot say; he cannot tell them that the river, flowing down the hills with a youthful exuberance, had seemed then to be, in its unsullied purity, like Sumi herself. He does not tell them, either, that there is more to this journey than this immersion. How can he and what can he say when he is not clear about it himself? Can he confess to them his hope—such a frail hope—that this ritual may help to exorcise his past of some ghosts?

Surprisingly, they ask him no questions. It spares him the explanations he had dreaded having to give. Kalyani, looking at his face, seems to understand he is being driven by a need he does not know himself, she seems to realize that he has to go to make peace with himself.

'Yes, go, Gopala,' she says. She holds his hand and strokes it tenderly, compassionately, and it is as if she is seeing again that strange young man who had been her tenant, the young man for whom she had felt such sympathy and affection. I know it has been very hard on you.'

'I'll be back, Amma, I'll be back as soon as I can.'

'Don't I know that? We'll be here, Aru, Seema and I. I'll always be here in this house.'

The house is now Kalyani's. They have found Shripati's will which left it to 'Kalyani, daughter of Vithalrao and Manoramabai'. Goda had looked anxiously at Kalyani when Anil read the will, but for Kalyani, clearly, there was no sting in the words that took away her marital status. On the contrary, it is as if the words have given her something more than the house, restored something she had lost; they seem, in fact, to have strengthened her.

'Aru?' Gopal turns to her.

She has said nothing until now. Suddenly, and to their consternation, Aru breaks down. It is the first time she has given way since her mother's death, except once, when she had burst into angry, stormy tears, crying out to Surekha,

'Look at us, ma'am, look at us. Charu adored her and Sumi was so happy, she was happy after such a long time.'

Now she cries bitterly, the tears of an adult. 'Sumi, Sumi,' she says the name over and over again. This time Kalyani does not move; it is left to Gopal to comfort her. Holding the thin quivering body, listening to the piteous heart-rending cries, Gopal is invaded by a piercing pain. This is what I wanted to avoid, this is what I had hoped to escape.

Aru, with an enormous effort, controls herself and moves away from her father's arms. They look at each other, father and daughter and then Aru says, echoing her grandmother, 'Yes, Papa, you go. We'll be all right, we'll be quite all right, don't worry about us.'

No words of farewell are said. They are not necessary. As he is leaving, Gopal looks back once and sees them standing side by side, two women, the two faces, one old and the other so young, linked by a curious resemblance. It is the steady watchful look on their faces, the smile of encouragement they have for him that makes them look alike.

'If it is indeed true that we are bound to our destinies, that there is no point struggling against them, even then this remains—that we do not submit passively or cravenly, but with dignity and strength. Surely, this, to some extent, frees us from our bonds?'

It is this thought that Gopal will carry with him on his wanderings, it is this picture of the two women that will be with him wherever he goes.

We leave them there.

Afterword

No Longer Silent

> One of the problems I've had to face as a writer is the isolation one works in when one writes in English in India—an isolation that is emphasized when one is a woman . . . For me the problems amounted to this: there was nothing, nobody I could model myself on . . . I could only tell myself, I don't want to write like this, not like this, not like this . . .
>
> —Shashi Deshpande, "The Dilemma of the Writer"[1]

I

By 1996, when *A Matter of Time* was published in India, Shashi Deshpande had seven novels, four books for children, more than eighty short stories, and a screenplay to her credit, making her one of the most published women writers in English in contemporary India. Her books are available in much of the Western world, either in English or in translation, and she is the recipient of a string of literary awards, including the prestigious national Sahitya Akademi Award in 1990 for her novel *That Long Silence.*

Yet she remains curiously "invisible" in her own perception, as well as that of the general public. At a time when a writer's stature seems to be determined by the number of column inches she gets in newspapers and periodicals and the amount of media attention her new work attracts, Deshpande's presence is low-key. Although her work has been published in English in India and the United Kingdom and has been translated into German, Russian, Finnish, Dutch, and Danish, she still doesn't attract the critical or popular attention that writers like Anita Desai, Bharati Mukherjee, or even Ruth Prawer Jhabvala do. This is only partly explained by her location—distant from the media capitals of Bombay and Delhi—and her own modest, almost reclusive, lifestyle. Much more likely an explanation is the fact that she is almost completely "home-grown," a writer so rooted in her reality and her social and cultural milieu as to feel "alienated" from what she refers to as the Westernized literary landscape of English writing in India. "I am different from other Indians who write in English," she said in an interview with translator and editor Lakshmi Holmström in 1993. "My background is very firmly here. I was never educated abroad, my novels don't have any westerners, for example. They are just about Indian people and the complexities of our lives . . . My English is as we use it. I don't make it easier for anyone, really."[2] Elaborating on this five years later, she said to me that "all those writers writing in English then—R. K. Narayan, Raja Rao, Nayantara Sahgal, Kamala Markandeya—were totally alien to my feelings as an Indian writer . . . I had no desire to feel any literary kinship with them." Explaining what she meant by "alienated," she went on to say that their world was "not my world," that what they created was seen from a certain "angle" that didn't allow a sense of intimacy either with the place or with the people. "Now when I think of it I realize that [this writing] was intended for a Western readership, so when I started writing I certainly wasn't using them as my role models. I had *no* role models. My path was totally unliterary, in one sense, because I was not a student of literature, so writing was never a literary exercise, it was just a means of self-expression."[3]

Shashi Deshpande came to writing quite late in her life, and she came to it by accident. Thirty years old and in England, where she had accompanied her husband for a year, she was encouraged by him to write about all they had seen and done so that she would not forget it. She began putting her experiences down on paper and sent her articles to her father, who in turn sent them on to the *Deccan Herald,* a southern Indian newspaper. Much to her surprise, they published her pieces and almost without her knowing it, her writing career had begun. "It was only much later that it struck me how discontented I had been with my life," she told me. "Not unhappy, just discontented. Everything changed after I started writing."

Three factors in her early life shaped Deshpande as a writer: her father, Adya Rangacharya, was one of the most well-known Kannada writers of his time; she was educated exclusively in

English; and she was a woman.[4] Born in 1938 in Dharwar, a small town in the southern Indian state of Karnataka, she grew up surrounded by books and literary personalities. Their house was redolent with an atmosphere of discussions, of teatime conversations on books and ideas, a place where play readings and rehearsals took place all the time. "I was happily submerged in it," she recalls.[5] Although the family could be defined as a typical middle-class professional and scholarly one, in actuality it was rather unconventional for the times. Her parents did not belong to the same region or community—her mother came from an affluent family in Maharashtra in western India—and their marriage was most unusual. In a country where marrying outside your class and community is still frowned upon, the fact that her parents had an arranged marriage that transgressed these norms was most remarkable. They didn't even speak the same language.

Like many educated Indians Deshpande is fluent in at least three languages and comfortable in four or five. Her parents' "mixed marriage" meant she spoke both their languages, Kannada and Marathi; she learned Sanskrit because it was her father's specialization; and her English-language education ensured that she was exposed to the best that English had to offer. This trilingualism worked in a most complicated way. As children, Shashi and her sister spoke to their mother and each other in what was literally their mother tongue, Marathi, and to their father and brother in Kannada. It was when they were much older that all three children adopted English as their language, and it is only now, years later, that Deshpande herself has been able to reconcile her Kannada and Marathi heritage.

Despite the unconventional decision to send their daughters to a missionary school rather than a local school, Deshpande's parents' household was by no means a Westernized one. Sanskrit classics and the Kannada greats were as much an influence as Ibsen and Shaw, and, she recalls, "if in school we did Wordsworth and Tennyson, at home we had to learn the *Amarkosa* by heart."[6] Nevertheless, English prevailed, and it is in English that she thinks and writes. Because she never studied in any of the other languages she speaks, she never used them as "working tools"; to try to write creatively in them, then, would be to presume too much.

The question of the language in which a writer *chooses* to write in a multilingual culture like India is fraught with contradiction, and it would be impossible to address it in all its complexity within the scope of this afterword. But it lies at the heart of every debate on indigenous versus alien, authentic versus fake, Westernized versus "Indian," even traditional versus modern. The much greater visibility of writers writing in English, now a world language with worldwide readership, lends an even sharper edge to the discussion. At the same time, it places the writers themselves in a bittersweet relationship with other writers in their own country.

Consider the ironies: India has twenty-two officially recognized languages—each of which has an old and venerable literary and critical tradition, and a history of sophisticated scholarship and publishing. Colonial rule implemented English-language education in the nineteenth century, a fact which has made for an unalterable—albeit poignant—reality: although it is equally foreign to every single Indian, English nevertheless functions as a link-language for all. It is the language of higher education, science and technology, and commerce. Increasingly, it has also become a literary language in its own right, elbowing its way into the literary pantheon in India.

Only 2 percent of Indians read and write English, but its importance in the cultural life of the country has grown steadily. Its much greater international access and exposure places it in an asymmetrical relationship with all other Indian languages, so that the decision to use it creatively is a much more overtly political act than choosing a regional language would be. Writers contend with issues of representation, of using the colonizer's language, of cultural baggage, of the translatability of the local and native, and, lastly, with the question of voice.

Especially over the last ten or fifteen years, young Indians writing in English have flashed across the world literary horizon and, in a way, have intensified the spotlight on these questions. Salman Rushdie, Arundhati Roy, Bharati Mukherjee, Githa Hariharan, Upamanyu Chatterjee, Amitav Ghosh,

Rohinton Mistry, Manjula Padmanabhan, Vikram Seth, Anjana Appachana, Allan Sealy, and Shashi Deshpande, among others, have forced literary and commercial establishments to reckon with what is sometimes called Indo-Anglican writing. The fact that these writers have won literary acclaim and have been commercially successful has, in turn, resulted in a somewhat unfortunate and unhappy comparison with writing in other Indian languages. The old question of who represents whom—and what and how—has become both acrimonious and troubled. None of the writers mentioned (and none of the many others not listed here) has ever admitted to being seriously disadvantaged because he or she writes in English—although Deshpande has said that she "regrets enormously that I was cut off from my own languages and literature."[7] And most of these writers would concur with Deshpande's statement that "English writing in this country is part of our literatures." The fact that an unmistakable cachet is attached to it goes without saying. The international notice and exposure writers gain by publishing in English adds enormously to their visibility and marketability. Being published in literary magazines like *Granta* or *The New Yorker,* or by literary presses like Faber & Faber, Cape, Bloomsbury, Farrar, Straus and Giroux, or Random House immediately guarantees a readership that runs into tens of thousands, and often has literary agents knocking at their doors. All this is in addition to the obvious financial gains. What also follows, however, is that choice of language to some extent determines the subject matter to some extent: most contemporary Indian writing in English is preoccupied with the life and times of the urban middle class and, willy-nilly, the label "Westernized" manages to stick.

Deshpande is quite clear that, for her, finding her own voice meant not just a woman's voice but a literary voice of her own: no magic realism, no concessions to "marketability," no themes or situations that pander to a so-called Western audience, no adapting her style to what a target readership might prefer. One will not find in her novels any element of the "exotic," a *National Geographic*-land-and-its-people kind of treatment of the unfamiliar. Rather than serve up a dish that experiments with the spices of the Orient, Deshpande assumes her readers' familiarity with the everyday ingredients of her offerings, relying upon their fresh, home-cooked flavor to have readers asking for more. Her writing style is marked by an absence of flamboyance or literary flourish. Nor does she beguile us with a Merchant Ivory–like gloss on "Indian culture." So, she has never, for example, felt any disjunction between her social self and her literary self, of the kind that critics have noted in other Indian women writers writing in English.[8] Part of the reason for this, she thinks, is her small-town origins. Growing up in Dharwar, where she lived until she was fourteen years old, made the difference. "A city shapes you differently," she maintains. "A small town never leaves you." Thus, locale has a very definite function and meaning in all her novels, and although no specific place may be named, its evocation can quite clearly be traced back to her childhood homes. So Saptagiri and the flat in Dadar (Bombay) in *That Long Silence,* Bangalore in *A Matter of Time,* and the ancestral villages that figure so prominently in *The Dark Holds No Terrors* and *A Matter of Time* are not just any geographical locations. They are the matrix from which her characters, particularly her female characters, spring, and they form an essential part of "the kind of people they are." And, indeed, the kind of people they are is the kind one would easily find in any medium-sized town in India: "ordinary people," Deshpande says, "people like you and me going about their daily business." Teachers, lawyers, doctors, an occasional accountant or banker, they are modest and unassuming—far removed from the flash of MTV and designer shoes. In a sense, they are the heart of middle India.

Another reason for Deshpande's distance from the glittering metropolis, so to speak, is the fact that she is such a solitary writer. Speaking of her early forays into writing, she recalls how she wrote in almost total isolation. A young mother cloistered at home with two small children, she had no one she could share her writing with or get feedback from, and she suffered terribly from low self-esteem. Like many women writers before and since, she never found the time to write "at a stretch. It was always in bits and pieces, in between chores, when the children were asleep or at school. And even these tiny bits were subject to constant interruption."⁹ No longer preoccupied with household responsibilities, she is still a most private person and almost never discusses work-in-progress with anyone. The intense interiority of her early novels—*The Dark Holds No Terrors* and *That Long Silence*—and her use of the first person for her female protagonists weave a web of intimacy around the reader, an effect that is enhanced by her near total focus on the domestic—the almost mundane. "I was born," says Jaya in *That Long Silence*. "My father died when I was fifteen. I got married to Mohan. I have two children and I did not let a third live. Maybe this is enough to start off with" (2). This is an almost eerie echo of her creator's sentiments, and indeed Jaya is the character who Deshpande feels corresponds most closely to herself. "A lifetime of introspection went into this novel," Deshpande writes, "the most autobiographical of all my writing, not in the personal details, but in the thinking and ideas."¹⁰ Later in the novel, Jaya comments directly on the writing process:

> Perhaps it is wrong to write from the inside. Perhaps what I have to do is see myself, us, from a distance. This has happened to me before; there have been times when I've had this queer sensation of being detached and distant from my own self. Times when I've been able to separate two distinct strands, my experience and my awareness of that experience. (2)

This twinning of "myself" with "us," of being "inside" with "being detached and distant from my own self," this alternating of the first person with the third, simultaneously allows Deshpande never to leave the homeground on which she is most comfortable, and creates the double perspective that is a characteristic of all her novels.

II

Each of Shashi Deshpande's novels—*The Dark Holds No Terrors*, *That Long Silence*, *The Binding Vine*, and *A Matter of*

Time—may be read individually and also as part of an oeuvre that deals with different aspects of women's lives. One can see a development of perspective and purpose, a deeper exploration, a finer characterization from her earliest to her most recent novel; one might even say that her female characters are just different facets of the same person.

The Dark Holds No Terrors was one of the earliest novels in English to deal with wife battering, a bold subject for a first novel by any reckoning. Saru, its heroine, is a successful doctor—more successful than her husband, a teacher. Slowly and terribly, his insecurity begins to manifest as physical violence—an old story. Saru is neither able to come to terms with it, nor speak of it to anyone. She flees the false normality of their waking lives as well as the blissful ignorance of her children, but her lips remain sealed.

Jaya in *That Long Silence* is the antithesis of Saru. She is a homemaker, homebound and, as far as one can tell, likely to live her life according to prescribed norms. But then, an unexpected calamity befalls her husband, Mohan, and they are forced to leave their home and flee to her apartment in a remote suburb of Bombay. Equally unexpectedly, Jaya finds release in this enforced confinement, and begins to write the script of her life for herself. By the end of the novel, she has sloughed off her old skin and made a quiet but decisive break with the past.

That Long Silence is almost eerily calm after the tumult of *The Dark Holds No Terrors,* and between it and Deshpande's next novel, *The Binding Vine,* there was a long lapse of time. "*Silence* condensed everything I wanted to say," she told me, "and after that I moved away from the personal, the internal, to the outward." In *The Binding Vine,* Urmila, the protagonist, is in the shadow, as it were, and it is the other women and their problems that are in focus—Urmila's mother-in-law and one of her friends, both victims of violence, silenced by their experiences. Very much a woman-centered writer, Deshpande presents us with ever more complex relationships between the women in her novels—sisters, mothers and daughters, mothers-in-law and daughters-in-law, women friends, and women in communities of women, bridging time and class—between women and society, and between women and the men with whom they live. The space the women occupy is primarily domestic (as is the case with most women writers);[11] it is in the elaboration of the changing equations within the private domain, *consequent upon a change in the women's consciousness,* that Shashi Deshpande is most adept. In their slow awakening to realization—and action—lies the transformation of the domestic space and all relationships contained therein.

Both Jaya in *That Long Silence* and Mira in *The Binding Vine* write their destinies in secret, breaking the silence imposed on them by societal norms. Although Mira's poems and diaries are discovered by her daughter-in-law Urmila after her death, these writings "speak" of the injustice Mira had to suffer and become the inspiration for Urmila in her fight against similar injustices. Having stumbled upon self-knowledge, neither Jaya nor Urmila will be the same again. Implicitly we know it is the men in their lives who will have to accommodate the changed reality because the women have now crossed what Malashri Lal calls the "threshold,"[12] metaphorically speaking. They need never leave the home or make a dramatic transition from private to public, but they have forever changed the space they inhabit.

Technically, Deshpande uses an alternating first person/third person voice to present what she calls a "double perspective": the past and present in continuous interplay and overlap. This device recurs in all her novels, a striking illustration of the Kierkegaardian axiom: 'Life must be lived forwards, but it can only be understood backwards' (paraphrased in *A Matter of Time,* 98). This juxtaposition, these backward glances, this excavation of the past is the key to the women's realization of self, and Deshpande's use of it in fiction is the clearest example of the feminist project of recovery at its most enabling—and sobering. Of all her novels, it is *A Matter of Time* that most fully explores the simultaneity of past and present, thematically and structurally. Four generations of women—the heroine, Sumi, her mother, Kalyani, grandmother Manorama, and Sumi's daughter Aru—are the axis around which the author spins her story. Once Sumi returns with her daughters to her mother's house following the desertion of her husband, Gopal, these four generations of women are more or less jointly present all the time, now physically brought together under one roof, and under Manorama's gaze as she looks down at them from her portrait. Despite the fact that the novel's span is a hundred years, a quality of timelessness lingers around it, a feeling of time standing still as the characters' stories unfold. Sumi remembers telling Gopal in the early days of their togetherness about her mother's and her aunt Goda's marriages, and laughing at his remark that it was never possible to disclaim the past. In her mother's house again now, face to face with what she had only hazily understood as a young girl, she thinks, "Gopal was right. Kalyani's past, which she has contained within herself, careful never to let it spill out, has nevertheless entered into us . . . it has stained our bones" (75).

As their past is unravelled through a series of events and rememberances—Goda and Kalyani recounting their early lives to Aru, quarrelling about relationships, holding up an incident here, an anecdote there, to the light—its imprint on the present becomes agonizingly clear. Kalyani, abandoned by her husband, Shripati, cries out in disbelief when, years later, Sumi is more or less abandoned by Gopal. Although it is clear that Gopal's desertion is of a quite different order from Shripati's, a woman abandoned is a woman abandoned. For Kalyani and Sumi, it can mean social stigma and avoidance at worst; barely concealed pity and condescension at best. Mother and daughter return to Vithalrao and Manorama's "Big House"—Kalyani with her two daughters, Sumi with her three—and prepare to inhabit their natal home almost as if they had never left it. Just as Shripati removes himself from the scene, so too does Gopal; both are present yet absent, and neither Sumi nor Kalyani question their withdrawal. Time, it seems, has come full circle. With Sumi's untimely death there appears to be a break in the cycle, but it is only temporary, and the torch passes to Aru—who bears an uncanny resemblance to Manorama. As with Kalyani and Sumi, is it only a matter of time before Aru succumbs to its inexorable passage? Was it only a matter of time before Gopal saw, with blinding clarity, the utter futility, the fleeting quality of the happiness he had known with Sumi? And is it only a matter of time before they all, like Kalyani, learn to embrace their destinies?

In Deshpande's scheme, it is Kalyani and Aru who are at the core of the family's fortunes; they are the fixed points around whom the fluidity of Sumi and Gopal's relationship finally resolves itself. Grandmother and granddaughter embody the past and future; the present, represented by Gopal and Sumi, has already splintered. With Sumi's death, Aru becomes both mother and daughter to Kalyani, desperately reassuring her, "'Amma, I'm here, I'm your daughter, Amma, I'm your son, I'm here with you'" (233). In the end, as Gopal leaves the ambit of the Big House with Sumi's ashes, Kalyani and Aru see him off, and "it is this picture of the two women that will be with him wherever he goes" (246). Even Gopal, with his foreknowledge of sorrow, could not have anticipated this cessation; and it is only Aru who will know the profound and terrible meaning of life lived forwards but understood backwards.

A linear unfolding of lives, in Shashi Deshpande's view, is an impossibility. People don't live that way, and she would be foolhardy as a writer to tell their stories as if there were a straight progression from start to finish. Nor can there be only one voice. In each of her novels, the past is presented in the first person (usually by the heroine), the present in the third. This alternating voice not only makes for the double perspective mentioned earlier, it enables the author to tell her story in *hindsight,* as it were. The effectiveness of this device is best demonstrated in *A Matter of Time,* where, in a decisive break, the first person voice is not the woman's, but a man's. It is Gopal who speaks of past and present, his and Sumi's (separate and together), in a way that renders these experiences far more complex than simple flashback could. Understanding life backwards demands hindsight, the perspective of distance and experience, even perhaps moving out of the frame of the narrative, as Gopal does, temporarily, and Sumi, permanently, on her death. Making the switch in voice took her a long time, says Deshpande, and for a while, she tried to do away with the first person voice altogether: "I wanted to try another way," she said, but it didn't work, and it was then that she hit upon the idea of Gopal speaking in this mode. This entailed a reconsideration of her technique, "something I have to worry a lot and think about."

> It is like setting a tanpura, you know, before a concert begins. The orchestra goes on strumming, tuning up, while you wonder what it's all about—to you all sounds are the same. And ultimately they nod their heads, and you know they've got it, the correct note . . . it's like that. Suddenly you know that this is exactly right for your needs.[13]

In addition to having the speaking voice, Gopal is unusual in other respects, too. In a significant departure from her earlier novels, Deshpande invests him with the qualities usually reserved for her female protagonists: reflection and introspection. Jaya in *That Long Silence,* Deshpande says, is the most autobiographical of her characters; Mira, the poet in *The Binding Vine,* is the one she's closest to; but Gopal has all her sympathy. It is he who feels the pain of living most acutely, who puzzles over the possible meaning of all those stories and aphorisms from ancient Hindu texts. His gentleness and humility cannot fail to register. "I wanted to see if I could use a male voice again," Deshpande told me, "but not as I used to earlier [in her short stories]. It was really something of a challenge." It is true that Gopal is the most fully realized of all her men. Mohan in *That Long Silence,* Urmila's husband, Kishore, in *Binding Vine,* and Manu in *The Dark Holds No Terrors,* as well as Shripati in *A Matter of Time* are insubstantial creatures, a foil for the women who propel the story. But Gopal sets the story in motion, and literally speaking, it begins and ends with him. His absent presence in the book is like a magnet for his daughters, especially Aru, and he is drawn back into the story in a movement almost parallel to Sumi's moving out of it. In the end, it is she who exits the frame. This is most unexpected. Moreover, with Sumi's death, it is entirely possible that Gopal will once again take up residence in the Big House—another cyclic return.

The novel begins with the Big House, opening with an epi-

graph drawn from the *Brhad-aranyaka Upanishad:* "'Maitreyi,'
said Yajnavalkya, 'verily I am about to go forth from this state
(of householder)'"(1). The reference is to the third stage of a man's
life according to the Ancients (the first two being that of child
and student), a householder, who in the course of the third
quarter of his life leaves his household and enters the fourth and
final stage of his life: that of renouncer. Here it refers obviously
to Gopal's decision to withdraw from the responsibilities of householding, but it also alerts us to what we will soon discover—that
Shripati, too, relinquished his role as a householder many, many
years ago, thus contributing to the strange history of the Big House.
Although such a departure is enjoined by the Ancients, both Gopal
and his father-in-law renounced householding much before the
prescribed time, and what's more, before they had fulfilled
their duties. And so the household reverts to the women.

The ancestral house, even more than the town or city, is cen-
tral to Deshpande's novels, because it is to this that the women
return. Saru in *The Dark Holds No Terrors,* Jaya in *That Long
Silence,* and Sumi in *A Matter of Time* make a womblike
retreat to the natal home, and it is always here that past and present meet and some kind of reckoning takes place.

> For me it's essential—almost as essential as it is for a movie direc-
> tor—to have the shape of the house clear. I know all the hous-
> es in my novels . . . as an architect does, all the rooms, even if
> I may not use them. If I have that clear then the rest of it can hap-
> pen, because it is there that it is going to happen.[14]

The house is most powerfully evoked in *A Matter of Time,* almost
as if it were another character. Deshpande describes in detail who
built it, and how, who lived in it, and how—and what it is today.

> Inside, the house seems to echo the schizophrenic character of its
> exterior. A long passage running along the length of the house bisects
> it with an almost mathematical accuracy, marking out clearly the
> two parts of its divided personality. The rooms on the left, unin-
> habited for years, are dark, brooding and cavernous. The rooms
> on the right where the family lives . . . have a lived-in look, with

> the constant disorder of living. . . . The small hall into which the
> front door opens is no man's land, belonging to neither zone. . . .
> There is, to the fanciful at least, a sense of expectancy about the
> house, as if it were holding its breath, waiting for something. (5)

The major events of all Deshpande's novels (with the exception of *The Binding Vine*) actually take place after the heroine
returns to her natal home. In *The Dark Holds No Terrors,*
Saru's own home is the abode of marital violence, but we know
little of it except the nightly enactment of abuse in the bedroom.
Her father's home, on the other hand, comes alive with details
of family use, memories of childhood, estrangement, tragedy.
It is a home she inhabits once again, just as Jaya in *That
Long Silence* comfortably settles into her own apartment in Dadar,
refusing even to let her husband unlock the front door. She lov-
ingly notes the familiar trail of garbage on the soiled cement
stairs, cigarette butts, squirts of betel-stained spit on the wall,
bits of vegetable peel. Mohan, revolted by the sight, sees
only dirt and ugliness; to him it is a place he has been forced
to turn to, a temporary refuge. For Jaya, it is a safe haven, the
place where she learns to write and break the long silence of
her married life, where she finally comes into her own.
Similarly, the Big House in *A Matter of Time,* waiting for
something to happen, does not wait in vain. Its air of decrepi-
tude and abandonment—"cobwebs, hanging in a canopy over
the huge front door," "a star-shaped sunken pond . . . now only
a pit harbouring all the trash blown in by the wind"(3)—is disturbed when Sumi and her girls arrive in a flurry of bags and
bedding rolls. And it is not long before the drama of their lives
is added to the rich history of family misfortune that the
house has seen for four generations.

The essentially familial scope of Deshpande's novels imbues
the domestic space with a greater charge than may otherwise
be the case. The playing out of family tensions, rivalries and
hostilities, and even happiness, takes place against a backdrop
of earlier joy and sorrow, so that nothing that the houses witness now is without its echo from the past. In *A Matter of Time*
this echo stretches as far back as three generations, and none

of its occupants has been immune to its reverberations. But the Big House exerts its power in other ways, too. Sumi, searching for a suitable place to live with her daughters, finds herself sketching the Big House over and over again for the estate agent. It is as if her very imagination has been colonized, as if there was a "tracing of this house already on the paper, on any paper . . . and the lines she draws have no choice but to follow that unseen tracing" (78). In its turn the Big House rearranges itself around the presence or absence of its inhabitants. On the night of Sumi and Shripati's death, Kalyani, in tearing grief, calls out the name of the man who was her husband:

> crying at last for him, as if only by going back to her childhood, to her earlier relationship with him, can she mourn him. Goda holds her close . . . While the two women lie awake in the dark, there is a strange sound, as if the house has exhaled its breath and shaken itself before settling down into a different rhythm of breathing. (236)

III

> What have I achieved by this writing? The thought occurs to me again as I look at the neat pile of papers. Well, I've achieved this. I'm not afraid anymore . . . If I have to plug that "hole in the heart" I will have to speak, to listen, I will have to erase the silence between us. (*That Long Silence*, 191–92)

The metaphor of silence is the single most powerfully recurring feature in Deshpande's novels. It is most shockingly realized in the story of Mohan's mother in *That Long Silence,* a woman whose mute resignation is trumpeted as courage by her totally obtuse son, Jaya's husband. Jaya, recounting a story he told her, says:

> He saw strength in the woman sitting silently in front of the fire, but I saw despair. I saw despair so great that it would not voice itself. I saw a struggle so bitter that silence was the only weapon. Silence and surrender. (36)

The silence that Jaya herself harbors for much of her married life is partially broken in *That Long Silence,* but it is a very private break. She writes, she conducts an intense interior monologue, and as her conversation with herself gathers momentum, her communication with her husband practically ceases. When, at the end of the novel, Mohan (who had been living under suspicion of financial misdemeanor) cables her to say "All's well," and they can come out of hiding, Jaya wonders, "Does he mean that we will go back to being 'as we were'? to our original positions?" And answers, "It is no longer possible for me" (192).

The silence in Deshpande's next novel, *The Binding Vine,* is of two kinds, both located outside its heroine, Urmila, but encompassing her as well: the comatose silence of Kalpana, brutally raped by her stepfather and lying like a living corpse in the hospital; and the silence of Urmila's mother-in-law, Mira, who died in childbirth and sublimated her unhappiness in elliptical poetry, which Urmila chances upon by accident. Urmila almost simultaneously finds herself pursuing Kalpana's story *and* Mira's poetry—two rapes separated by time and social class, two lives that intersect with Urmila's, binding the three women together, *as if they were one.*

It is in *A Matter of Time* that the silence of women is finally and conclusively broken but with a dreadful corollary: the death of Sumi; and a cruel irony: the willful silence of Shripati, as punishment for his wife. How then is it broken? The Big House, after Sumi and her daughters return to it, is a more or less cheerful community of women, affected by the vagaries of their men but not unhinged by them. Kalyani is quite reconciled to Shripati's rejection of her, and finds a happy, sparring companionship in Goda. Sumi is calm in the face of Gopal's sudden desertion, refusing to let it disturb her equilibrium. The speed with which she dismantles their home is almost ruthless, and in no time it has been stripped bare—a swift dismemberment. After an initial period of strangeness and adjustment in the Big House, Sumi actually begins to spread her wings, and her slow wonderment at her own prowess is exquisitely presented. The girls find their voices, too: Aru through her encounter with Surekha and women's legal rights, Charu through medicine. Emotionally and otherwise, they form a self-sufficient three-generational family with one major difference: it is a family of *women* living in their *natal* home. There's no one to silence them.

So why does Sumi die? There are several possible explanations, though none is entirely satisfying. If, however, one places Gopal at the center of the novel—and one might in another reading of the story—then Sumi's dying is inevitable, the cataclysmic end of happiness that Gopal has anticipated all along, the death wish fulfilled. *Runamukta,* he thinks, "free of all human debts." And yet, and yet, such piercing regret.

> Yes, Sumi is free, but at the cost of her body, of life itself. Is this freedom? . . . If I could believe that Sumi has gone to a region of everlasting peace and happiness, if I could think—maudlin thought—that we will meet again sometime. . . . No, I can't; there is only this nothingness, this blankness. (237)

Is this the moral of the story, then, that the wages of speech is death? One can't be sure because the novel is ambivalent on this score. Sumi's death comes just as she begins to develop her own career, embrace her independence, find her own voice. Deshpande would not be the first woman writer to suggest that for women, the wages of consciousness—and of speech—is sometimes death. (Think of the protagonists of Western feminist classics like Kate Chopin's *The Awakening,* driven to suicide, or Charlotte Perkins Gilman's *The Yellow Wall-Paper,* driven to madness.) But it is important to remember that the accident that kills Sumi also destroys Shripati. And it would be impossible to miss the significance of exactly when and how the accident takes place: remembering Madhav, the lost son, the missing piece of the puzzle of Sumi's parents' lives. It is the only time in the novel that father and daughter utter his name, and both die with it on their lips. A chapter closed. We should remember, too, that the future lies with Aru and that the novel ends not with Sumi's death but with Aru's life. "'Yes, Papa, you go,'" she says to her father as he leaves, "'we'll be quite all right, don't worry about us'" (246).

IV

> Most of my writing comes out of my own intense and long sup-
> pressed feelings about what it is to be a woman in our society;
> it comes out of the experience of the difficulty of playing the dif-
> ferent roles enjoined upon me by society, out of the knowledge
> that I am something more and something different from the sum
> total of these roles. My writing comes out of my consciousness
> of the conflict between my idea of myself as a human being and
> the idea that society has of me as a woman.[15]

Of all the women writers writing in English in India today,
Deshpande has been the most consistent in her exploration of
women's condition. She has dealt with practically every issue
raised by the women's movement in India regarding the sub-
ordination of women: rape, child abuse, single motherhood,
son-preference, denial of self-expression, deep inequality
and deep-seated prejudice, violence, resourcelessness, low self-
esteem, and the binds (and bonds) of domesticity. In a way this
exploration has corresponded to her own development as a writer
and, in her own words, helped her to find her "true voice." The
turning point, she says, came with a story entitled "The
Intrusion," written as early as 1970 or 1971, which was published in the collection *The Intrusion and Other Stories.*

> The consciousness of one's own voice is a very important devel-
> opment for a writer; until then most writers are groping, feeling
> their way, imitating other writers. After "The Intrusion" this
> would not happen to me. The stories I wrote then and the novels
> that followed, were all centered round women and had a distinctive
> woman's voice. It marked me out very definitely as a "woman
> writer". . . a woman who wrote about women.[16]

"The Intrusion" is a story about a honeymooning couple,
"not friends, not acquaintances even, only a husband and
wife," and the unwelcome consummation of their marriage. "The
cry I gave," says its unnamed protagonist when her husband
forces himself on her, "was not for the physical pain but for the

intrusion into my privacy, the violation of my right to myself" (41). This story laid the groundwork for Deshpande's first novel, *The Dark Holds No Terrors,* one of the most lacerating novels ever written on marital rape. Although Deshpande has said that of all her novels, *The Dark Holds No Terrors* most successfully realizes its potential, it was *That Long Silence* that finally "put the seal" on her style and subject matter.

> More than anything else I had written till then [it] was about the world of women, almost claustrophobically so . . . Through the articulation of a lifetime's experiences, thoughts and introspection, through the lives of the women I had created, I had done something so that I could never see myself or my writing in the same way again.[17]

The circumstances of women's lives and the choicelessness that characterizes their situation are highlighted through a microscopic—but not unsympathetic—examination of the familial and domestic, the so-called natural domain of women. Reacting sharply to the charge that her canvas is limited because she focuses on these aspects, Deshpande declares that nothing could be more universal than the family unit and no relationships more fundamental than those between the members of a family. Person to person and "person to society relationships," as she calls them, are all prefigured in the domestic arena "where everything begins."[18] Human relationships are the most mystifying, hence the most exciting for a novelist; within these relationships it is a woman's place that is of greatest concern to Deshpande because of the "abysmal difference" that women experience in relation to men. Her novels and her later short stories dwell on the daily slights and humiliations that women suffer, mostly in silence. By the simple device of describing the reality of many middle-class women in India, Deshpande lays bare the social discrimination and hypocrisy that underlie society's treatment of them; by the same token, she is also able to acknowledge the power that women manage to wield despite their disadvantaged status, especially within the family. Manorama in *A Matter of Time* is a shining example.

Yet Deshpande cannot in any way be said to have a propagandist or sexist perspective—to present her readers with "bad bad

men and good good women."[19] Nor does she acknowledge either
a deliberate or unconscious connection with the women's
movement or with feminist writers. Writing at more or less the
same time as Kate Millet, Susan Brownmiller, Germaine
Greer, and others, she says she came to these writers much later
in her writing, too late to be influenced by them directly.[20] As
if in support of this, she admits readily to her early fear of being
called sentimental, soft, insubstantial—a woman whose stories were destined to be read only by other women. Speaking
about her use of the male voice in most of her short stories,
she asks:

> Why did I have the male "I"? Did I do it to distance myself from
> the subject? Or . . . because I, too, felt there was something triv-
> ial about women's concerns, something very limited about their
> interests and experiences? Had I, without my knowledge, been
> so brainwashed that I had begun regarding women's experi-
> ences as second-rate? Did having a male narrator help me to pare
> down the emotions, intellectualize [my writing]? But the fact was
> that both the intellect and the emotions were mine . . . Yet the fact
> remains that I was trying to use an equivalent of the male pseu-
> donym which so many women employed to conceal their iden-
> tities. In other words, the writer in me was rejecting her femininity.
> Perhaps I felt that to be taken seriously as a writer I had to get out
> of my woman's skin.[21]

And so she struggled with the separation of emotion and
intellect, masculine and feminine, until she understood that both
were "hers" and she was able to write "The Intrusion," in which
she found her "true voice." Henceforth, and until the appearance of Gopal in *A Matter of Time,* the "I" was reserved for her
female protagonists, and she never again wrote a short story.
Her women had come out of the wings and now occupied center stage; her own confidence in representing their lives and giving them a speaking voice grew with each novel and, in a curious
way, she grew with them, too, as a writer.

"My feminism has come to me very gradually," she told
Holmström, "and for me it isn't a matter of theory . . . For me

feminism is translating what is used up in endurance into something positive: a real strength."[22] Although her writing preceded her awareness, she has no doubt at all that once awareness came to her, it was "like drinking Asterix's magic potion. You feel full of power. No more feeling that my gender made my work inferior."[23] And yet, the problem of women's writing being marginalized remains. Next to the isolation of writing in English in general, what Deshpande has come up against, time and again, is the marginalization she feels in her career as a woman writer.

The dilemma of being a woman writer in India—or should one say, a politically aware woman writer—is not unique to Deshpande. Few today would say that they have not felt marginalized to some extent by the mainstream—generally also male-stream—literary establishment. Notwithstanding the marginalization, Shashi Deshpande has demonstrated a remarkable integrity of purpose. Her presentation of the urban middle-class woman's reality is perceptive and insightful; and her exploration of it across time and space, through two or more generations, in small towns and big cities, allows her to see it in all its complexity. In this sense, she is indeed a women's writer, with all the expansiveness that this appellation affords, suffused with understanding and delicate observation.

"I believe in good and evil," she says of the moral vision that informs her writing, "and literature seeks always to find a balance between them. We struggle all our lives to attain moral heights but we also fail and fall from them. This is at the core of the human condition." By refusing to be deflected from her chosen subject matter with charges of "domesticity" she has rejected the "marginal" spaces reserved for women, declaring instead, "Where I stand is always the center to me; it's the others who are in the margins."[24] So, too, with the women in her novels.

Ritu Menon
New Delhi, India
November 1998

Notes

1. Shashi Deshpande, "The Dilemma of the Woman Writer," in *The Fiction of Shashi Deshpande,* edited by R. S. Pathak (Delhi: Creative Books, 1998), 229.

2. Deshpande, interview with Lakshmi Holmström, *Wasafiri* (Publication of the Association for New Teaching of Caribbean, African, Asian and Associated Literature, U.K.) 17 (Spring 1993): 26.

3. Deshpande, interview with Ritu Menon, Bangalore, India, June 1998. Except where otherwise noted, all subsequent quotations from Deshpande come from this interview.

4. Deshpande, "Of Concerns, of Anxieties," *Indian Literature* (September-October 1996): 104.

5. Ibid.

6. Ibid., 105.

7. Ibid.

8. Malashri Lal, *The Law of the Threshold: Women Writers in Indian English* (Shimla: Indian Institute of Advanced Study, 1995), 4.

9. Deshpande, "Of Concerns, of Anxieties," 106.

10. Ibid., 108.

11. Lal, *The Law of the Threshold,* 14–24.

12. Ibid.

13. Deshpande, interview with Holmström, 25.

14. Ibid., 23.

15. Deshpande, "Writing from the Margin," *The Book Review* 22, no. 3 (March 1998): 9.

16. Deshpande, "Writing from the Margin," 9.

17. Deshpande, interview with Holmström, 25.

18. Deshpande, "Denying the Otherness," interview with Geetha Gangadharan, in *The Fiction of Shashi Deshpande,* 252.

19. Deshpande, interview with Holmström, 25.

20. Deshpande, "Of Concerns, of Anxieties," 108; and interview with Holmström, 25.

21. Deshpande, "The Dilemma of the Woman Writer," 230.

22. Deshpande, interview with Holmström, 26.

23. Deshpande, "Of Concerns, of Anxieties," 108.

24. Deshpande, "Writing from the Margin," 10.

BOOKS BY SHASHI DESHPANDE

Collections of Short Stories

The Legacy. Calcutta: Writers Workshop, 1978.

It Was the Nightingale. Calcutta: Writers Workshop, 1986.

The Miracle. Calcutta: Writers Workshop, 1986.

It Was Dark. Calcutta: Writers Workshop, 1986.

The Intrusion and Other Stories. New Delhi: Penguin Books India, 1994.

Novels

The Dark Holds No Terrors. New Delhi: Vikas Publishing House, 1980; Delhi: Penguin India, 1990.

If I Die Today. New Delhi: Vikas Publishing House, 1982.

Come Up and Be Dead. New Delhi: Vikas Publishing House, 1982.

Roots and Shadows. Hyderabad: Orient Longman Ltd., 1983.

That Long Silence. London: Virago Press, 1988; New Delhi: Penguin Books India, 1989.

The Binding Vine. London: Virago Press, 1993; New Delhi: Penguin Books India, 1994.

Children's Books

A Summer Adventure. Bombay: India Book House, 1978.

The Hidden Treasure. Bombay: India Book House, 1980.

The Only Witness. Bombay: India Book House, 1980.

The Naryanpur Incident. Bombay: India Book House, 1982; New Delhi: Puffin Books, Penguin Books India, 1995.

CONTEMPORARY WOMEN'S FICTION
FROM AROUND THE WORLD
from The Feminist Press
at The City University of New York

A Matter of Time, a novel by Shashi Deshpande. $21.95 jacketed hard-cover.

Allegra Maud Goldman, a novel by Edith Konecky. $9.95 paper.

And They Didn't Die, a novel by Lauretta Ngcobo. $42.00 cloth. $13.95 paper.

An Estate of Memory, a novel by Ilona Karmel. $11.95 paper.

Apples from the Desert: Selected Stories, by Savyon Liebrecht. $19.95 jacketed hardcover.

Bamboo Shoots After the Rain: Contemporary Stories by Women Writers of Taiwan. $35.00 cloth. $14.95 paper.

Cast Me Out If You Will, stories and memoir by Lalithambika Antherjanam. $28.00 cloth. $11.95 paper.

Changes: A Love Story, a novel by Ama Ata Aidoo. $12.95 paper.

The Chinese Garden, a novel by Rosemary Manning. $29.00 cloth. $12.95 paper.

Confessions of Madame Psyche, a novel by Dorothy Bryant. $18.95 paper.

The House of Memory: Stories by Jewish Women Writers of Latin America. $37.00 cloth. $15.95 paper.

Mulberry and Peach: Two Women of China, a novel by Hualing Nieh. $12.95 paper.

No Sweetness Here and Other Stories, by Ama Ata Aidoo. $29.00 cloth. $10.95 paper.

Paper Fish, a novel by Tina De Rosa. $20.00 cloth. $9.95 paper.

Reena and Other Stories, by Paule Marshall. $11.95 paper.

The Silent Duchess, a novel by Dacia Maraini. $19.95 jacketed hardcover. $14.95 paper.

The Slate of Life: More Contemporary Stories by Women Writers of India. $35.00 cloth. $12.95 paper.

Songs My Mother Taught Me: Stories, Plays, and Memoir, by Wakako Yamauchi. $35.00 cloth. $14.95 paper.

Sultana's Dream: A Feminist Utopia, by Rokeya Sakhawat Hossain. $19.95 cloth. $9.95 paper.

The Tree and the Vine, a novel by Dola de Jong. $27.95 cloth. $9.95 paper.

Truth Tales: Contemporary Stories by Women Writers of India. $35.00 cloth. $12.95 paper.

Two Dreams: New and Selected Stories, by Shirley Geok-lin Lim. $10.95 paper.

What Did Miss Darrington See? An Anthology of Feminist Supernatural Fiction. $14.95 paper.

With Wings: An Anthology of Literature by and About Women with Disabilities. $14.95 paper.

Women Working: An Anthology of Stories and Poems. $13.95 paper.

Women Writing in India: 600 B.C. to the Present. Volume I: 600 B.C. to the Early Twentieth Century. $29.95 paper. Volume II: The Twentieth Century. $32.00 paper.

You Can't Get Lost in Cape Town, a novel by Zoë Wicomb. $13.95 paper.

To receive a free catalog of the Feminist Press's 170 titles, contact: The Feminist Press at The City University of New York, Wingate Hall, City College/CUNY, Convent Avenue at 138th Street, New York, NY 10031; phone: (212) 650-8966. Feminist Press books are available at bookstores, or can be ordered directly. Send check or money order (in U.S. dollars drawn on a U.S. bank) payable to The Feminist Press. Please add $4.00 shipping and handling for the first book and $1.00 for each additional book. VISA, Mastercard, and American Express are accepted for telephone orders. Prices subject to change. Visit The Feminist Press Web site at www.feministpress.org.